Obsessions

Janet Lane Walters

Hard Shell Word Factory

To my dad, Norman Lane.
When he pushed me into a career in Nursing,
he never knew how I'd use the experience.

To the Tuesday night critique group for loving my
villain as much as I did.
Thanks to Karen, Kathy, Renee, Mildred, Claire, Terri, Eileen,
Jennifer, Nan, Sunny, Maureen, Jeannie and Jenny.

ISBN: 0-7599-0091-4
Trade Paperback
Published November 2001

Ebook ISBN: 1-58200-523-0
Published November 1999

Hard Shell Word Factory
PO Box 161
Amherst Jct. WI 54407
books@hardshell.com
http://www.hardshell.com

Chapter 1

HE CROUCHED in the cemetery that embraced three sides of the hillside parking lot across from Bradley Memorial Hospital. A massive family marker shielded him from view, yet allowed him a clear view of the steps, the street and the door of the Emergency Room. Dark clouds slid across the surface of the moon. Lights, set high on poles around the perimeter of the lot sent finger shadows groping among the cars.

The watcher straightened and edged from behind the granite marker. White puffs of vapor from the shallow, rapid breaths he took coalesced around his face. He held his body as rigid as a tombstone. As he waited for the evening nurses to end their tour of duty and hurry across the street to their cars, his narrowed eyes focused on the brightly-lit hospital entrance. Every night for a week, he had watched while excitement and anticipation had circled like a swarm of hornets. Would she come tonight?

"I'll never leave you." When he was eight, Mommy had said the words that had become his litany. That broken promise had brought him here.

He stared at the steps. When would Susan come?

When Mommy was a patient, Susan had been her favorite nurse. He had liked Susan, too, but she hadn't stopped those other people from hurting Mommy. His shoulders tensed.

"I'll never leave you. They'll have to kill me first."

The night Mommy had died was etched into his memories. On that dreadful night, he had begun his plan to make them pay.

Mommy would be unhappy about what he meant to do. To her, nurses were special and Susan more wonderful than the rest.

He rocked from his heels to his toes. The last time he had disobeyed, Mommy had threatened to tell everyone how bad he was. He had promised her he would be good. His hands curled into fists. Sometimes he wanted to feel the heat of accomplishment so much he felt sick.

He gulped a breath. Tonight the heat would blossom and he would feel powerful again.

Susan was like Mommy. She would tell. He chewed on his lower lip. Her death would free him to still the people who had hurt Mommy on that dreadful night.

His smile became a grimace.

He had trusted Susan but she had failed to keep Mommy safe. Though he wished to see the others dead, Susan had to be first. He had laid his plans carefully, and while he had considered all the things that could go wrong, days had become weeks and then months.

The bright lights across the street caught his attention and stirred his hopes. She had to come tonight. He wanted to be free.

His hand brushed Mommy's tombstone. He pressed his fingers against the engraved letters of her name. He cocked his head and listened to the whisper of the wind.

"Nurses give so much to others. Someone should take care of them."

Mommy's husky voice thrummed in a corner of his mind. Her face appeared. Tears spilled from her eyes. He shook his head. Why should he listen to her when she had left him?

Sometimes at night when he slept in her bed, he caught a glimmer of her presence. For fleeting moments, the scent of her perfume brought her to him.

He squared his shoulders. Since he was eight and Daddy died, Mommy had watched him carefully. One day, her vigilance had wavered. The neighborhood bully had fallen from a tree and broken his neck. That awful boy shouldn't have torn up Mommy's flower garden.

Mommy had liked the candy and the other presents he had given her every time he disobeyed. He groaned. Who would like his presents now?

Where was Susan? Waiting made him anxious. She had to come so she would be just like Mommy.

He saw her. Hazel eyes, sad eyes, Susan's eyes, Mommy's eyes. Brown hair swirled to hide her siren smile. He reached for her, but she vanished into the darkness of the night.

The chill November wind flowed across his nape. He jammed his hands into the pockets of his black leather jacket and touched the weapon he had brought.

The sound of leather scuffling against asphalt caused him to turn and scan the parking lot. When he saw no one, his gaze returned to the hospital entrance.

Someone dashed across the street. A flash of white showed

beneath the woman's dark coat. He held his breath. Susan had come. It had to be her. A rush of anticipation built to a peak. She was here. The nurse ran up the steps beside the cemetery.

A darting shadow startled him. With stealthy movements, a dark-clad figure edged between the cars. The nurse paused beside a battered tan sedan. A hand stretched to grasp the purse that dangled from her shoulder.

"Susan, watch out." A bellow proclaimed his rage. If she was attacked, he should be the attacker.

Mommy wouldn't like that. "A good boy never hurts a woman." She had never guessed what he had done, not even when he had given her the tri-colored bracelet she had always worn.

"No," he shouted.

The dark figure fled and nearly tripped over the single strand of chain that separated the parking lot from the cemetery.

The watcher smiled. Mommy would be proud of him. He couldn't wait to go home and tell her what he had done tonight.

A shrill scream rose. From her? From him? He bit his lower lip and clenched his hands. He stared at the woman he had thought was Susan. She wasn't, but she had been in Mommy's room the night she died.

Intent on completing what the mugger had begun, he stepped toward the chain. What was he thinking about? He couldn't, not tonight. Susan had to be the first. He returned to Mommy's grave. Her voice rode on the wind.

"What will become of you when I'm not here to look after you? I'll never leave you. They'll have to kill me first."

But she was dead and they had killed her.

"Mommy, don't leave me. You promised you would never go."

The nurse ran to the steps. She shouted and waved to the group of women who hurried across the street. He slid deeper into the shadows. Car doors slammed. Engines roared. He waited until most of the cars had left the parking lot before he went to his own. As he drove home, he wondered why Susan hadn't come.

HOME AT LAST. Susan Randall moved her shoulders in slow circles to ease the tension raised by the series of delays she had experienced during the morning's journey from Florida. An hour's delay in the departure of the flight. Traffic snarls due to construction. She had hoped to be home long before noon. She looked at her watch. Nearly one o'clock.

The limousine driver dropped her bags on the porch. After paying the man, she waited for him to leave. Then she fished the house key from the jumble in her purse and opened the front door. Why hadn't she stuck to her original plan and left last night? Instead, she had allowed her parents to persuade her to stay until this morning. Another failure in assertiveness, she thought.

The two weeks in Florida had exhausted her. With a sigh, she opened the front door and lifted the suitcases. Worry over the outcome of her father's abdominal surgery and coping with her mother's fears had drained her. Her father's uncomplicated recovery had given her parents time to offer advice on how she should live her life.

"It's been nearly a year and a half since Jim's death. How long are you going to grieve? You're thirty-five. Isn't it time to let him go and build a new life?"

Variations on the theme had been endless. The unsolicited advice and opinions had only increased her inner restlessness.

Susan dropped the suitcases beside the brown and white couch. How could she admit to her parents that fear of losing her identity again and not grief had governed her choices? Until the restraints had vanished, she hadn't realized she had been wrapped in a cocoon. If Jim hadn't died, her contentment with her life would have lasted. He would have continued to make decisions for every moment of their life and she wouldn't have protested. He had bound her so tightly, there had been little need for family, friends or children. During the past eighteen months, making decisions for the slightest change had been difficult, but she had learned. She had no intention of ceding her *newfound* independence.

Why would she want to find another man and plunge into the same kind of dependency? The odds of settling into a similar relationship were high. How many of her friends had she watched leave one man and find another with the same traits? She couldn't take the chance— not until she gained confidence in herself. Besides, her life would remain serene as long as her emotions remained in a coma.

The wall clock chimed. Startled, she looked up. One forty-five. How long had she drifted in thought? She'd better move before she arrived late for work, an act she hadn't committed in her thirteen years at Bradley Memorial Hospital.

When she took off her coat, she saw the basket of gold and rust-colored chrysanthemums on the coffee table. She reached for the card.

"Welcome home. Talk to you soon. Patrick."

Warmth infused her. She touched one of the feathery blooms. This wasn't the first time one of his unexpected presents had raised her spirits.

As she ran upstairs, she pushed aside questions about his intentions. Patrick was her friend and tenant. He had been Jim's friend, too. She refused to believe there was more, and yet, she remembered a night when there had been. She shook her head. She needed a friend, not a lover.

Moments later, she stood in the shower. Warm water washed away the sour smell of nervous perspiration. Though the tension caused by the multitude of delays eased, she sensed it lurking like the remnants of a nightmare. She stepped from the shower, dried and dressed in a white uniform. If traffic cooperated and the line at the deli was short, she would reach the hospital in time to step into her role as a nurse. That Susan was completely different from the shadow woman Jim had created. At the hospital, she was confident, decisive and in control.

AT TWENTY minutes to three, Susan entered the locker room on Five Orthopedics. She changed from boots to shoes, punched her time card and draped a Sprague-Rappaport stethoscope around her neck. Then she stepped into the hall.

As she approached the nurses' lounge, her pace slowed. She inhaled a deep breath. Why the sudden reluctance? For the past year and a half, being at the hospital five evenings a week had been her escape from loneliness. What had changed? While searching for an answer, she opened the lounge door.

"Do you really think I'll tell you?" Barbara Denton's strident voice rasped against Susan's nerve endings. "Believe me when I say it's dynamite. Someone isn't going to like what I've learned. And let me tell you, this time, I have all the facts."

The practical nurse's harsh laughter and the veiled threat in her voice added to Susan's uneasiness. Whom had Barbara targeted this time? Her stories always contained a dram of truth but little more. Susan halted in the doorway and waited to hear further hints of scandal. When the practical remained silent, Susan stepped into the room and closed the door.

The hospital's gossip queen sprawled on the bright green loveseat facing the door. She stabbed a cigarette toward the round table that was partly hidden by the jutting powder room wall. A gold bracelet glittered on her arm and slid up and down as she used the cigarette to emphasize the importance of the tidbit she dangled.

Susan shook her head. Had anyone reminded Barbara that smoking in the hospital was illegal? Would it matter? The practical had chosen to break the rule, but so did the unit's nurse manager.

"Don't tease," Susan said. "We know you're dying to tell all."

One of the two nurses seated at the round table jumped up. "Welcome back," Julie Gilbert said. "How was your trip? You look terrific."

"The trip was nice." Susan smiled. A year ago, during Julie's first three months on the unit, Susan had been the younger nurse's mentor. They had become friends.

Barbara flicked a long ash from her cigarette. "Would you look at the tan. Bet you didn't spend your entire two weeks playing private duty nurse. Sure wish I could afford two weeks in the sun."

"The rent was free." Susan crossed to the credenza and reached for the coffeepot.

"As if you have to worry." Barbara's words flowed on a stream of smoke. "Bet your husband left you tons of insurance money. All I ever got from mine was a stack of unpaid bills."

"Three times." When Julie turned to look at the practical, sunlight glinted on the silver clip that held her long hair at her nape. "You sure know how to pick them." Her grin was as saucy as her voice.

"About as good as you." Barbara's hand hovered over a Styrofoam cup. "If you think you're going anywhere with De Witt, think again."

Julie made a face. "You'll soon see how wrong you are."

"Sure I will," Barbara drawled. "Ask Trish about him. After all, she followed him here. Hey, Trish, was it love or another reason?"

What did Barbara mean? Susan glanced at Trish Fallon. Her bony shoulders hunched and her lower lip trembled. Trish and De Witt? The unlikely combination made Susan want to laugh. She stepped toward the table until a flash of anger in the thin nurse's pale eyes halted her in mid stride. Why the attempt to provoke a quarrel between Julie and Trish?

Julie walked around Susan. "It's really great to have you back. Like the new hairstyle. How much weight did you lose?" She grinned. "Is there something you're not telling us? Who is he?"

Susan added milk to the coffee she had poured. "I have no secrets."

"Ain't that the truth," Barbara said. "And believe me, I've searched." She stubbed her cigarette. "Let me tell you what happened to me while you were gone. You saved my life."

Trish rose. Julie groaned.

Though curious, Susan didn't want to be a captive audience for one of Barbara's tales. She edged toward the door. "Catch you later. I want to check meds before report."

"Hold on. This is something you need to know. I'll give you the abridged version." Barbara lit another cigarette.

Susan glared. "Put that out. You know the rules."

The practical took a deep drag. "Saturday night, I was nearly mugged in the parking lot. If some man hadn't shouted your name, who knows what would have happened. Any idea who your guardian is?"

"No. I'd say you were lucky someone yelled."

"Pity." Trish pushed past Susan and entered the powder room.

Susan shook her head. What had Barbara done to Trish?

Barbara blew smoke rings at Susan. "You'd better be careful. Most nights, you're the last one out of here."

The words sent a chill along Susan's spine. "Who would want to hurt me?"

"Susan's never careless. Susan has no secrets. She's perfect." Trish slammed the powder room door.

Susan shook her head. During the past two weeks, the atmosphere on the evening shift had deteriorated. When she had left for vacation, there had been no problems. Tonight, Barbara seemed determined to make trouble. One of these days, the practical would irritate the wrong person and she'd find herself out of a job.

"Don't you think someone should do something about the parking problem?" Barbara asked. "Why should days get to park beside the hospital and evenings get stuck across the street in the middle of a cemetery?" Her voice rose to a crescendo.

Susan stepped into the hall. "Don't ask me. Talk to someone from administration."

"I have and all they say is there's never been a problem before. How—" The door closed and cut of the woman's strident voice.

Welcome back to Five Orthopedics. Did every hospital have a Barbara? Susan groaned. This was rapidly becoming one of those evenings when she didn't want to be here.

She paused beside the doctor's desk and studied the census board. Would she be happier on another unit? Should she leave Bradley

Memorial? The urge to change, to explore, to do something different
arose, but she knew she wasn't ready to take such drastic action.

"That's the first time she's related her grand adventure in less than
thirty minutes and without dramatic embellishments," Julie said. "Why
don't they put her on probation or something?"

Susan shrugged. "Guess she knows where the bodies are buried. I
swear she knows how many times we breathe during a shift."

Julie laughed. "And if she doesn't, she'll invent a number."

"Are you having a problem with her?"

"Not exactly."

"Can I help?"

"No one can." Julie pushed a portable chart rack toward Susan.
"Good luck. Since Trish and I refuse to work with her, you have the
honor tonight. District Two."

"Some things never change." Resentment tightened Susan's
shoulder muscles. Since Barbara usually cooperated with her, the nurse
manager routinely paired them.

Unfair, Susan thought. Tomorrow, she planned to come in early
and confront Meg about the situation.

She pulled the chart rack to the section of the desk where she
usually sat. Several of the day nurses clustered in front of the counter.
One of them pulled Julie into the medication room for narcotic count.
Susan answered questions about her vacation and checked the
medication book against the doctors' orders.

Julie emerged from the med room. "How's your father? Barbara
had me so rattled I forgot to ask."

"As stubborn as ever. When I lectured him about the need for
fiber in his diet, he laughed. What does one do with a father who's a
junk food addict?"

"Love him."

Susan chuckled. "He handles the temporary colostomy like a pro."

"Then I was right. He has diverticulitis."

Susan nodded. "I owe you a dinner. Let me know when you're
ready to collect." She reached for the district care plan book and
motioned to one of the day nurses. As the woman began her report,
Barbara sauntered into the station and leaned against the counter.

The early hours of the shift were hectic. Susan felt as though she
chased the hours she'd lost on the airport runway and in crawling past
construction barriers. With eleven unfamiliar patients, she had no time
to dwell on the undercurrents she had sensed in the lounge or on her

own restlessness.

At six thirty, she finished second medication rounds and walked to the lounge for her dinner break. As she entered the room, Barbara lit another cigarette.

"Go out and watch for call lights," Susan said.

"Will you be finished by seven?" Barbara asked. "I want evening care to be done before you drop out for nine o'clock meds."

"My break begins when you're out of here."

"I'm going. I'm going." Barbara stubbed her cigarette and slipped the butt into a silver case she said one of the patients had given her. "Isn't it about time for Leila to make rounds? Wouldn't want the supervisor to think I was goofing off."

"Goodbye, Barbara." Susan carried a salad and a cup of coffee to the table. Fifteen minutes later, the lounge door opened and Leila walked in.

"You're late," Susan said.

Leila poured a cup of coffee. "It's been one of those evenings. ICU had a visitor who refused to leave. The OR needed four units of blood stat. A patient on Five Med/Surg fell." She sat across from Susan. "I like the hair. It's about time you colored the gray."

"That's what my mother said, plus a lot of other advice." Susan closed the salad container. "Why don't we get together for lunch tomorrow and I'll fill you in about the state of nursing practice in Florida?"

Leila lit a cigarette.

Susan raised an eyebrow. "I thought you quit."

"Stress."

"And the rules?"

"Will you turn me in?"

"I might. About lunch?"

"I can't. I have class. Just one more semester."

Susan cleaned the area of the table she had used. "Wednesday?"

Leila shook her head. "I'm picking up my new car. Do you have time to talk about one of your co-workers?"

"Here? I wouldn't want to chance being overheard. What about Friday?"

"I'll be away. It's a four-day weekend."

"Joe?" Susan asked.

A dreamy look misted Leila's dark eyes. "We're going to his hunting cabin."

"Don't you ever get tired of spending so little time with him?"

"Quality counts." Leila's smile brought an elegant charm to her pointed features. "It's a good relationship. We both know how much we're willing to give. I don't want him to leave his wife and marry me."

A fleeting shadow in her friend's eyes made Susan wonder why Leila lied to herself. On the surface, her friend acted like a realist, but Susan knew the hidden romantic. For twelve years, she had watched Leila hide that part of her nature.

Susan rose. "I'd better leave before Barbara comes looking for me. Wouldn't want her to think I was goofing off with the supervisor."

Leila made a face. "She's at the top of my problem list."

"Then we definitely couldn't talk here. I think she's bugged the lounge."

"I wouldn't put it past her." Leila raked her fingers through her short blonde curls in a nervous gesture Susan had seen Leila use since her divorce.

Susan stepped into the hall. "Let me know when we can get together."

"Probably next week." Leila waved and ducked into the storage room hall used by the nurses as a shortcut to the elevators.

As Susan neared the utility room, a cart shot from the doorway. Barbara caught the handle in time to prevent an accident. "Good," she said. "You're right on time."

"And you're efficient."

"Wasn't me." The practical's hands rested on her ample hips. "While you were loafing in the sun, the volunteer took over the job."

Susan smiled. "How nice of him. Let's go."

From seven until nearly nine, Susan and Barbara moved from room to room, straightening beds, rubbing backs and doing special treatments. Each time Susan stopped to explain a test of to do pre-op teaching, Barbara groaned and looked at her watch. Susan refused to be pushed and deliberately ignored the broad hints.

While they worked, Barbara's mouth remained in constant motion. "Kit has a new boy friend. He's a real loser... The other night De Witt and Mendoza nearly came to blows over a patient's treatment. Julie blew up at Trish and defended De Witt. That girl sure is uptight these days. You saw the way she reacted this afternoon when I tried to warn her about his intentions...I think Trish is anorexic or something... Boy, Leila's sure looking smug these days. Wonder who she plans to stomp. Better not be me... I know...."

By the midpoint of the district, Susan had tuned out the strident voice. She refused to request details or ask the questions Barbara's statements demanded. At nine, she left Barbara in the last room of the district and stepped into the hall.

Trish pushed a med cart past the door. "Aren't you caught up yet? You should learn to cut corners the way the rest of us do." The thin nurse spoke so fast her words ran together.

"Slow down," Susan said.

As though Trish hadn't heard the warning, she moved away with the speed of the final runner on a relay team. Susan shook her head. One of these days, in her haste to finish first, Trish would make a mistake.

Moments later, Susan entered the pentagon-shaped med room. Julie stood at the refrigerator. In both hands, she clutched plastic pouches of intravenous antibiotics. She closed the door with her foot. "Looks like you're almost caught up. Wish I could have helped you."

"There wasn't any way you could have." Susan put her med book on top of her district's cart. "If Barbara does her share of charting, I'll be out of here on time."

"Your idea of on time, no doubt. Have you ever clocked out at eleven thirty?"

"A time or two."

"What did you learn from Barbara? Any hints about her big story?"

"Before I tuned her out, she rattled on and I've jumbled all her tales together." Susan unlocked the narcotic cabinet and removed a box of Valium. "If you want to help me untangle them, we could stop at the diner after work."

"I can't. Larry's here to clear a patient for surgery tomorrow. We're meeting at the Oasis. Though Barbara doesn't believe me, I'm getting a ring for Christmas."

Susan returned the Valium to the cabinet. Would there really be an engagement ring for Julie? What the younger nurse saw in De Witt puzzled Susan. In the two and a half years since the leonine young doctor had joined his uncle's practice, De Witt had dated most of the hospital's available nurses and a few who weren't. Did Julie really believe he'd marry her? Julie was young enough to think she was different from the other victims of his charm.

Five minutes later, Susan pushed the med cart into the cull de sac off the main corridor. The patients in the private rooms along the short hall were being treated for bone infections and she had to hang the first round of IV medications.

The volunteer stepped out of the first private room. "Mrs. Randall, welcome back. How's your father?"

"Doing nicely." She smiled.

"I'm glad." A matching smile softened his chiseled features. "You've been busy this evening."

She nodded. "It's a matter of settling into the routine again. Tomorrow will be better." She entered the room he had just left.

After hanging the medicine, she left the room and halted in the doorway. The volunteer leaned against the wall across from the door with a hand pressed against his chest. His dark eyes held a glimmer of fear.

"Mr. Martin, are you all right?"

As she spoke, his stance relaxed. "Angina. Took a nitro."

"Is there anything I can do?"

He shook his head. "I'm fine now."

She watched him walk away. His short clipped hair suited his bearing and his gait. He seemed to have recovered from the brief attack, but she decided to check him when she finished the first round of antibiotics. She entered the room next to the patients' lounge.

Barbara stepped away from the bed. "She's on the bedpan. Take her off. I'm going on break and I'm late."

As the practical left the room, Susan saw a gold bracelet. Glimpses of the unusual piece had tantalized her all evening and she wanted a closer look. Was this another gift from a "grateful" patient?

HE STOOD in the shadows just beyond the brightly-lit Emergency Room entrance. She was here. A series of quickly inhaled breaths brought a feeling of euphoria. He caught his lower lip between his teeth and savored visions of what was to come.

He felt the softness of her skin and of his fists pummeling her body. Susan would be with Mommy and he would be free. There would be no one to scold him for doing the things that made him feel so powerful and so strong.

He slapped his jacket pocket and growled. No hard piece of metal pressed against his hip. Susan was here. What had he done? He had planned this event so carefully but somehow, he had forgotten a vital piece of the plan. He pulled off his gloves and shoved his hands into his pockets.

What would he do now? He rocked from his heels to his toes. It had to be tonight. He couldn't wait.

The glow of anticipation faded. He struggled to renew the fire.

Susan was like Mommy. Until he closed her eyes, he couldn't act. Before he had a chance to make those people pay for what they had done to Mommy she had to die. He knew she would tell on him.

"I'll never leave you. They'll have to kill me first."

"Mommy, don't leave me."

AT TEN FIFTEEN, Susan pushed the med cart into the nurses' station. "If anyone wants me, I'll be in the back." Her feet ached. She needed the lift a cup of coffee would bring.

When the unit secretary turned in her chair, her red hair swirled like a matador's cape. "Bad news," Kit Carbonari said. "When I got back from break, I found a note about an admission. Guess who has the empty bed? It's a seventy-year-old with a fractured hip."

"Murphy's Law," Susan mumbled. No break tonight. The next half-hour would be spent with the new patient. She abandoned the med cart in the middle of the nurses' lounge, strode to the lounge and opened the door.

"Barbara, let's go. We're getting an admission."

No strident voice answered. No acrid aroma of cigarette smoke tainted the air. Where was the practical?

As she retraced her steps to the nurses' station, her shoes slapped against the dark green carpet. She paused at the desk. "Has anyone seen Barbara?"

Kit shook her head. "She didn't take break with us. Acted like she had a hot date."

"Guess it's gossip rounds tonight." One of the practicals giggled. "Think of all the juicy stories she'll have when she gets back."

"And the ones about us she'll spread." Trish reached for another chart. "Someone should plug her mouth."

Julie turned in the chair at the doctors' desk where she sat beside De Witt. "Is there a problem?" she asked. "Can I help?"

"Just an admission and no Barbara." On her way to the clean utility room, Susan paused beside the younger nurse.

De Witt captured Julie's hand the way a lion grasps its prey. "Don't be late." As he rose, he smoothed his ash blond hair and slung a black leather jacket over his shoulder. He strode down the hall.

"Go get the equipment," Julie said. "As soon as I finish this chart,

I'll meet you in the patient's room."

Moments later, Susan entered the semi-private room and dropped an eggcrate mattress on the foot of the bed next to the door. Leaving the hospital at eleven thirty had become an impossible dream.

"I knew it was too good to last." The patient by the window raised the head of her bed. "Sure hope she doesn't snore."

"You'll soon know."

"What's wrong with her?"

"You know I can't tell you. After she arrives, you can share tales of your adventures."

"Maybe she'll be as jolly as my last roommate."

The traction apparatus from the former patient remained in place. Susan moved the weight bar from the right to the left. As she worked, she mentally listed the equipment she'd need. A foam Buck's boot, weights, ropes, elastic bandages, *Barbara's help*.

The clot of anger she had hidden from the other nurses loosened. The moment she saw the practical, Susan knew she would explode. Barbara had been away from the unit for more than an hour. Had she been the one to take the message about the admission? How typical of Barbara to leave without preparing the bed.

Susan pulled the sheets to the bottom of the bed. She lifted the foam mattress.

"I'll do that," Julie said. "Get the weights and stuff. Kit's calling around for Barbara."

"By the time she returns, the work will be done."

"Does that surprise you?" Julie asked. "You can always report her for being off the unit so long."

Susan sighed. She could, but would anything be done? The practical had been reported more times than the rest of the evening staff combined. She had never been warned let alone disciplined.

With quick steps, she headed for the storage room. To her surprise, the door was locked. "Why? Had Kit forgotten to open the door after the day shift left? Susan pulled the large ring of keys from her pocket. She unlocked the door and flipped on the lights.

The disorder made her groan. Why had the orthopedic cart been left in the middle of the room? The stench of urine assaulted her. Who had left a dirty bedpan behind?

The cart blocked the path to the shelves at the end of the room where most of the supplies she needed were stored. She pushed the cart toward the wall. The wheels caught on an obstacle. She tried a different angle with the same result. With a jerk, she yanked the cart toward the door and edged around it.

Her eyes widened. A harsh gasp escaped. "Barbara!" Guilt over her earlier anger warred with fear. She stepped closer. "Oh God!"

The streak of red on the practical's white uniform spoke of violence. Susan had seen death many times, but never like this. A soundless scream reverberated in her thoughts. Who had done this and why? She stared at Barbara's battered head and face and fought the need to flee.

Several minutes passed before the scattered hundred dollar bills registered. Susan blinked but the money remained. Who had given Barbara the money? Had it been her killer?

She inhaled. She had to do something. Like a robot programmed to perform a series of tasks, she knelt beside her co-worker. She pressed the bell of her stethoscope against Barbara's chest and stared at the sweep second hand on her watch. One minute passed. Then two. She heard nothing.

With a shudder, she rose. Questions fomented in her thoughts. The desire to bolt grew stronger. The clutter in the room impeded her escape. Step by step, she backed around the ortho cart. Three more steps took her into the hall. She held back the fear-generated sobs that threatened to burst free and hurried to the nurses' station.

There for stability, she grasped the counter of the U-shaped desk. She swallowed convulsively.

Kit held the phone to her ear. The two practicals sat at the long section of the desk. Trish lounged in the med room doorway. The mundane scene failed to erase the bizarre picture in the storage room.

"In...in..." The words emerged as a harsh whisper. She gulped a breath.

Julie stepped out of the semi-private room across from the desk. "What took you... Susan, what's wrong?"

"In...in..." Susan couldn't force her frozen tongue to form the words.

Trish strode across the green carpet. "You look like you've seen a ghost."

Susan cleared her throat. Her knees buckled. Only her grasp on the counter kept her erect. "In the storage room... Barbara..."

Chapter 2

TRISH PUSHED past Susan and trotted down the hall. Julie and the pair of practicals scurried after the thin nurse. Unable to move or think, Susan leaned against the counter.

A piercing scream pulled the unit secretary from her chair at the desk. The scream thawed Susan's frozen thoughts. If someone didn't take charge, the unit would dissolve into chaos.

"Kit, you can't go yet. Call Security and the house doctor. We need them stat. Then call the Nursing Office. I'll speak to any supervisor who answers."

"What's wrong with Barbara?" Kit asked.

"She's dead." Susan glanced up. Above nearly every door, a call light shone. A patient on crutches swung down the hall. Immediately behind him, a woman walked with crab-like movements. Susan left the desk to intercept the pair.

"What happened?" the man asked.

"Who screamed?" The woman stumbled and put her hand on the wall.

Susan paused and considered how to make them return to their rooms without frightening them. She couldn't tell them about Barbara's death, but she had to say something. "One of the nurses had an accident."

"Is there anything I can do?" the woman asked.

"Go back to your room and let your roommate know everything is being taken care of. A nurse will be in soon."

After the patients left, Susan strode to where her coworkers clustered around the storage room doorway. Trish blocked the doorway. A thin smile appeared on her face. The practicals jostled each other and peered into the room. Julie huddled against the wall with her hand pressed against her mouth.

"Close the door and start answering lights," Susan said. "It looks like Christmas at the desk."

"What should we tell the patients?" Julie asked.

"That one of the nurses had an accident," Susan said.

"What if one of them wants to know who she is?" one of the

practicals asked. "Shouldn't we tell them she's...well...you know?"

"Use your common sense. Say that one of the nurses had an accident and is being seen by the house doctor."

From the corner of her eye, Susan saw the stocky house doctor stride past the end of the hall. She hurried to catch up with him. "Dr. Mendoza, one of the nurses had an accident. She's in the storage room. You need to check her."

His dark eyes flashed irritation. "Why do you not take her to the Emergency Room? I am here to care for the patients, not the nurses."

"We can't move her until Security comes." Susan lowered her voice. "She's dead."

"What?"

Susan inhaled. Why was Dr. Mendoza the doctor in the house tonight? He always behaved as though unexpected incidents had been staged to annoy him. "She's—"

"Susan, Ms. Vernon's on the line," Kit said.

Trish grabbed Mendoza's arm. "Come on. I'll go with you."

Glad she didn't have to face the scene in the storage room again, Susan hurried away. She sat on the edge of the desk and took the receiver from Kit. "Leila, it's Susan. There's a problem here."

"What has Barbara done? I heard Kit was tracking her."

"She's dead. I found her in the storage room and I don't think it was an accident."

"I'll be right there," Leila said. "What kind of injuries?"

"She...her head..." A picture of Barbara's battered head and face flashed in Susan's thoughts. Acid burned her throat. She dropped the receiver and bolted for the utility room. There, she leaned over the sink. Even after her stomach was empty, she continued to heave.

Footsteps sounded on the tile floor. Susan looked up. Leila looked as though she had run the entire distance from the Nursing Office.

"Are you all right?" Leila asked.

Susan gulped deep breaths of air. "I don't know. She looked ghastly." She blotted her tearing eyes with a paper towel and rinsed her mouth.

Leila took Susan's arm and they walked to the nurses' station. "Come and sit down."

Susan shook her head. If she sat, she would fall apart. She had to remain calm and strong. Who would see to her patients if she gave in to the hysteria that threatened to erupt? Once again, flashes of the gruesome still-life in the storage room surfaced. She shivered and rubbed her upper arms. Activity would keep the memories at bay.

"Are you sure she's dead?" Leila asked.

The sharp toned question acted like a splash of cold water. "Yes." The word exploded from Susan's mouth. "I checked her. So did Mendoza. Talk to him. I have to answer lights."

"Are you sure you're up to facing patients?"

"If I don't, who will?"

Kit turned in her chair at the desk. "I sure wish I could have seen her instead of being stuck at the desk. Wonder who got her. Was she gross?"

"I don't want to talk about her," Susan said.

"You're going to have to." Kit pursed her lips. "Security called the police. I think you're in big trouble. The guard was upset because you and Mendoza messed with the body. He's afraid you tampered with the evidence."

"I had to see if I could help her."

"You did the right thing." Leila reached for the phone. "I'd better call Murry Johnson before someone else does. This could be a real problem for the hospital."

"I bet they'll be major upset," Kit said. "You know, the guard took my key for the storage room and he wants the one from the narcotic ring. He's checking the rooms for an intruder. A bit late, I'd say. The killer's probably long gone."

Or here among us. Susan's hand flew to her mouth. Had she said the words aloud?

"I wonder what we were doing when she died?" Kit asked. "She wasn't exactly the most popular person on the unit."

Susan walked away. Kit sounded like Barbara. Was the unit secretary planning to take the practical's place as gossip queen?

"Aren't you glad this didn't happen during visiting hours? Just think of the mess that would have been." Kit's comments followed Susan from the station.

She made a face and ducked into the first room of her district. Why was Kit making Barbara's death sound like an adventure? Finding the body had been a nightmare. Susan forced her lips into a smile and approached the first bed. "You rang?"

"Fifteen minutes ago. When I heard that scream." The gray-haired man shifted his leg. The canvas-supporting sling shifted. Weights attached to pins embedded in his tibia clanged against the frame of the bed. "Is everything all right? I rang six times."

"One of the nurses had an accident."

"Where's your buddy?" the second patient asked.

"She's the one who had the accident. What can I do for you?"

The older man winked. "A lot, but my leg aches. When you have time, I'd like an injection."

"And I'm due for my sleeping pull," the second patient said.

"Give me fifteen minutes."

Susan left the room and repeated the scene with slight variations in the other rooms of the district. She hated to lie, but there was no reason for the patients to know one of the nurses had been murdered. What could they do but worry?

When she returned to the nurses' station, she had a list of requests for pain medication and sleepers for eleven patients. She and Julie reached the desk at the same time.

"Will we ever get done?" Julie asked.

Susan looked at Trish and the two practicals who were seated at the desk charting. "You will. I'll be here for hours. I have all the charts to write." She remembered the expected admission and groaned. "Kit, what's happening with the new patient?"

"The ER thinks we're having a silent code. Ms. Vernon backed me up. They weren't pleased, but they agreed to hold the patient until nights arrive. The police are here. No one can leave until they've been questioned."

"You're kidding," Julie said. "I have a date."

"He'll have to wait." Kit smiled slyly. "We're all suspects."

Once again, Susan heard echoes of Barbara in Kit's voice. "The police will have to wait until my patients are settled. After all, this is a hospital." She nodded to Trish and opened the med room door.

SHE'S DEAD. Waves of relief suffused Trish's body. She beat the fingers of her left hand against the desk. The fingers of her right hand touched the pill in her pocket. Should she take it now or wait? She always carried an amphetamine for emergencies, and tonight certainly qualified as one. Since the police wanted to question everyone, timing was essential. She needed the rush, but taking the pill too soon would put her on the downside when she talked to them. Too soon and her eyes would give her away.

Trish's stomach knotted. What should she tell them about Barbara? Should she reveal her knowledge and tell them that the practical hadn't been just a harmless gossip? But if she did, they might learn she had been one of Barbara's victims.

Her body shook as she rose and walked into the med room. Had Barbara left records?

Trish waited for Susan and Julie to leave. Then she closed the door and stood at the sink. She couldn't worry about Barbara now. She had to believe she was safe. Her supplier had more to fear from discovery than she did.

Trish pulled the pill from her pocket. As she swallowed the medication, the med room door banged against one of the med carts. She jumped. Her heart raced in imitation of the rush the medication would bring.

The way Trish jumped when the door hit the cart made Susan gasp. Though usually hyperactive, the thin nurse's edginess was palpable. "Sorry. Are you all right?" Susan asked.

"Headache." Trish dropped a paper cup in the trash and reached for the door.

"We'll all have one before the night's over." Susan opened the controlled substance book and checked to see that she had signed for all the sedatives and narcotics she had just dispersed. An error in the count tonight would be more than she could handle.

Moments later, she entered the nurses' station and pulled the district's rack to the desk. Julie huddled in a chair at the doctors' desk. Leila stood at the desk with the hospital's assistant administrator. They talked to two men.

The police. Though she had done nothing wrong, her body tensed. She bent her head and began to chart.

Leila slipped into the chair beside Susan. "You'll be questioned first. Murry wants you to consider your answers carefully."

"What can I say but the truth?"

Leila raked her fingers through her hair. "About Barbara? Probably nothing someone else won't say but don't paint her too dark. Murry's concerned about adverse publicity."

With good reason, Susan thought. Outside of war, how often was a nurse killed while on duty? An icy lump settled in her chest. The killer probably worked here. Though she didn't want to believe that, a stranger's presence in the hospital after visiting hours would be noted.

"Good luck," Leila said. "Be careful."

Why? As Susan trudged to the lounge, exhaustion rounded her shoulders. Should she tell the police about the afternoon's tension-filled scene in the lounge? What about the secret Barbara had threatened to reveal? When she opened the door, she hadn't reached a decision.

Two men stood at the credenza. The broad-shouldered black man turned. "Mrs. Randall, I'm Greg Davies." He indicated the other man. "Ben Malone...would you like coffee?"

She cleared her throat. "Yes, please. Milk, no sugar."

"Take a seat at the table. We'll be taping your statement. Any problem with that?"

She shook her head and gripped the back of the chair. Fear and uncertainty filled her thoughts. Why did she feel this way when she had done nothing wrong? Her legs felt as unsteady as they had when she had discovered Barbara's body.

"I understand you found her." Greg Davies said. "We'd like to ask some questions about what you saw."

Susan eased into the chair. "What—" Her voice squealed and broke. She gulped a breath. "What would you like to know?" The storm of emotions she had experienced earlier arose again. For a moment, she felt dizzy and she feared she would faint.

Greg Davies pushed a Styrofoam cup across the table. "Take your time and tell us everything you noticed when you entered the storage room."

Her throat constricted. She saw the practical's crumpled body, the bloody wounds and the staring eyes. She gulped a swallow of coffee. Then with the impersonal voice she used when reporting a patient's condition to a doctor, she related the story.

Ben Malone held a pen between the index fingers and thumbs of both hands. "About the keys? How many sets are floating around?" As he spoke, he rolled the pen.

Susan wiped her sweaty palms on her uniform. "Kit has one. There's one on the narcotic key ring and the nurse manager has one. Security would know if there are any others." She lifted the cup. "The door is usually kept open on this shift."

"Is this general knowledge?"

"I guess so."

"Was it open tonight?"

"I passed the hall several times, but when you're expecting to see something, sometimes you see it when it isn't there."

"What about when you found the body?"

She swallowed. "I had to unlock the door."

Greg Davies nodded. "Where were the other nurses?"

"In the station...except Julie Gilbert. She was waiting for me in one of the rooms across the hall." She stared at the table. Why had he asked that? Did he suspect one of her coworkers?

"When was the last time you saw Mrs. Denton?"

Susan closed her eyes. "Around nine. Just after I started med rounds. She was leaving a patient's room and going on break."

"With some of the other nurses?"

"Kit said she didn't go with them. She often left the unit."

"Any idea where she might have gone?"

Susan shook her head. "Some evenings, she visited every unit in the hospital. Gossip rounds."

Greg Davies smiled. "Your supervisor told us Mrs. Denton was a gossip. Did she have any special story tonight?"

She dropped her hands to her lap so their shaking wouldn't be noticed. How could she answer and not compromise her friends?

"The stories?" Ben Malone asked.

"She had so many, but mostly generalities."

"What about the past two weeks?"

"I was on vacation."

Ben Malone leaned forward. "Surely she told you something this evening that you remember."

She rubbed her hands together. "We worked in the same district and she tried to fill me in on two weeks in one lump. I tuned her out like I always do. Oh, she said someone tried to mug her in the parking lot."

"When?"

"Saturday night, I think."

"Did you touch anything in the storage room?"

The sudden shift startled her. A few minutes passed before she collected her scattered thoughts. "The light switch, the door, the ortho cart. It blocked the way to the shelves. That's why I didn't see her at first. I touched her to look for a pulse." She gulped a breath. "To see if...if she was dead."

Greg Davies leaned back in the chair. "Notice anything else?"

"The money."

"Any idea how it got there? Could she have been blackmailing someone?"

"It's a possibility, but I can't imagine who. Maybe I don't want to believe she would."

"What about enemies?"

Once again, Susan paused to consider what she knew about Barbara's relationships with the others. Julie, Trish, Leila. None of them had liked the practical. Trish had even suggested someone plug Barbara's mouth. Had Trish been the one?

"A lot of people didn't like her. She wasn't a nice person but I can't imagine...imagine someone deciding to kill her."

After a series of questions that revealed how little she knew about Barbara's private life, Greg Davies walked her to the door. "If you think of anything, just call the station and ask for Ben or me." He looked at his notebook. "Send Kit Carbonari in."

Susan passed the message to Kit. Before returning to the charts, she tried to catch Julie's eye. The younger nurse presented a picture of misery.

Though she noticed Susan's attempt to gain her attention, Julie kept her head bent. What am I going to do? She feared Larry had given Barbara the money that had been scattered around her body. Julie loved him. For that reason, she had to keep her knowledge secret.

She pressed a bent finger against her teeth. Was he still in the hospital? She had to warn him but if she paged him, someone would remember he had been here for part of the evening. What could she do? Until she talked to him, she couldn't tell the police anything.

Why had Larry asked her to meet him at the Oasis instead of at his apartment? An announcement of Barbara's death wasn't a message she wanted to leave with his answering service. Her teeth clamped on her finger to stop the questions, the fears, the scream, but nothing could stop her from thinking about Barbara's accusations.

TWO OF THE night nurses pushed a stretcher past the desk. Susan picked up an admission form and left her pen in the chart. Julie and Trish joined the group in the semi-private room across from the nurses' station.

"On the count of three," Susan said.

After the patient had been transferred to the bed, Susan reached for the admission form. One of the night nurses plucked it from her hand. "I know we're bitchy about doing your work, but she arrived on our time."

Susan stepped into the hall. "She should have been here an hour ago, but there were problems."

"Things do seem a bit odd," Beth said. "What's this about a silent code and why are the police occupying the lounge?"

Susan inhaled. "Barbara was killed tonight."

"Good grief," said another of the night nurses. "What happened?"

"I don't know. I found her body in the storage room." Susan took a quick breath. Even that didn't help the queasy feeling in her gut.

Beth shook her head. "How horrible. What did you see?"

"I'm not sure how much I'm allowed to say. The police are still questioning people." She shivered. "I'd rather forget it happened."

"How ironic," Beth said. "Barbara's missing what could have been her finest story. Look at what she did with the parking lot incident. Do you think there's a connection?"

How, Susan wondered. She opened the care plan book. "Let me start report so I can finish charts and get out of here before the day shift arrives."

Around her, she heard whispered comments as the other three members of the night staff tried to gain information about the death. Her thoughts drifted to Beth's comment about the attempted mugging. Had someone really warned Barbara by shouting her name?

Beth touched Susan's shoulder. "Just don't try to solve this the way you do all the other problems around here."

Susan shuddered. "The police can have this one. Murder is a bigger problem than petty theft or laziness... Room 512, Mr. Bliss."

When Susan closed the care plan book, she reached for the stack of unfinished charts. As Kit and the practicals left, they waved.

Fifteen minutes later, Trish entered the station. "Julie, your turn." The thin nurse stopped in front of Susan and leaned against the counter. "Aren't you finished yet? I was hoping we could walk to the parking lot together. Place gives me the creeps."

Susan glanced up. "Don't wait. I'll be at least another hour."

Trish shrugged. "I'd offer to help, but—"

"You don't know the patients."

Finally, Susan signed her name to the eleventh chart. She looked around the deserted station. One thirty. She grabbed her purse and walked down the hall. Leila sat outside the lounge.

"Will you be finished soon?" Susan asked.

Leila shook her head. "After the police leave, there's an emergency meeting of administration."

"Right now, I wish Jim was home waiting for me."

"Do you really? Think of how he'd react. Do you want to return to the bad old days when you couldn't breathe without his permission?"

"Was it that bad?"

"Think about it." Leila nodded. "You've grown so much since his death. I wouldn't want to see you slide back."

"You're right. It's just...just..." She inhaled. "I hate the thought of being alone tonight. I don't think I'll be able to sleep."

"Me either." Leila's hand moved toward her hair. "Being alone is the toughest part of being single. I'd stop by, but who knows when I'll finish here."

"I told the police about the mugging."

"So did everyone else. Go home. We'll talk tomorrow."

"See you." Susan waved and walked away.

LEILA WATCHED until Susan vanished around the corner and wished they could have talked about Barbara earlier this evening. The practical's death had come too late to solve the problems she had created. Somehow, Barbara had learned about the investigation into patients' complaints about her and about Leila's affair with Joe.

The practical had threatened public exposure. Joe had asked Leila to put the investigation aside. How could she have done that without losing respect for herself and destroying her effectiveness as a supervisor?

She wished for the comfort of Joe's arms. Though they were spending the weekend at his cabin, she feared the trip signaled the end and she didn't want that to be. Damn her, she thought. Barbara's threats had destroyed a fragile part of the relationship. Why had the killer waited so long?

The lounge door opened. Julie Gilbert rushed past. Leila rose and waited for the officers. "That's the last of the nurses."

Greg Davies nodded. "Let's go see what we can glean from her records."

Leila walked ahead of them. And from the report hidden in her desk. Once again, she wished she and Susan had been able to discuss the situation.

AS SUSAN left the hospital, she remembered Barbara's warning about going to the parking lot alone. Tonight she was so exhausted even a hundred muggers couldn't make her run. She felt as if a week had passed since morning.

When she reached her car, she unlocked the door and slid behind the wheel. The radio came on with the engine. "...report the body of a nurse was found..." She pressed the off button. Tears stung her eyes. Why did she want to cry? She hadn't liked Barbara. Susan gripped the wheel. Who had hated the practical enough to kill her?

By the time she pulled into the driveway at home, her suspicions centered on De Witt. He had been the focus of Barbara's attempts to stir trouble between Trish and Julie. Why had he come to the hospital this evening when he could have waited until morning to clear the patient for surgery? She shook her head. Leave suspicions to the police. She turned off the headlights and stared at the house.

Patrick stood on the porch. The ceiling light glinted on his honey-blond hair. She left the car and walked to the porch.

"Welcome home. Long night." His deep voice promised security.

For an instant, she thought of finding forgetfulness in his arms the way she had the night Jim had died. But that encounter had nearly destroyed their friendship.

Tears spilled down her cheeks. Were they for Barbara, herself or some unknown reason? She fought to control feelings of helplessness. If Patrick saw her as weak, he would react the same way Jim had. She never wanted to be smothered again.

He reached for her hand. "Don't tell me you knew the nurse I heard about on the police band."

She nodded. "I found the body." She fumbled in her purse for the house key. Patrick put his arm around her shoulders. For a moment, she leaned against him. "I'll be all right."

"I know, but it must have been a brutal shock. If you need a shoulder, mine's broad." He plucked the keys from her hand and opened the door.

She dropped her coat on the arm of the couch. A splotch of dried blood stained the right knee of her uniform. She gasped. Why hadn't someone told her?

She felt unclean. Her skin itched. She wanted to tear off the uniform. As she hurried to the stairs, she unfastened the buttons of her white shirt. "I have to shower."

THE NOTE OF panic in Susan's voice drew Patrick to the stairs. When she turned, he saw the bloodstained knee of her uniform. He gripped the newel post. She must have found the body not long after the woman had been killed. His muscles tensed. Had the murderer seen her?

Long after she vanished, he remained at the foot of the steps. He wanted to follow her, to hold her, to protect her. She might be in danger. What if she had seen something that could identify the killer?

He released his held breath and walked to the kitchen. There, he measured coffee and turned on the machine. While the coffee brewed, he returned to the living room and took a bottle of brandy from the antique icebox Susan used as a bar.

Memories of the night Jim died arose. He had held Susan in his arms. A light kiss meant to offer comfort had ignited passion. He had forgotten her grief, forgotten his friend and had drowned in the heady sensations of making love with the woman he had wanted for years. The shock of hearing her call him Jim had iced his desire.

For months after the funeral, she had avoided him. Though he had understood and shared the guilt, he had feared they would never regain what had been lost. This past summer, they had become friends again, but he wanted more. Sometimes, he thought his desire for her had become an obsession.

Patrick leaned against the counter. He loved her, but she had to be more secure about her ability to deal with life before she would be ready for a relationship.

He reached for two mugs hanging from hooks above the kitchen table, poured coffee and laced Susan's with brandy. Just as she came down the stairs, he entered the living room. His body reacted to the gentle sway of her light brown caftan.

She sat on one end of the couch and tucked her feet under her. After taking the mug in her hands, she sipped and coughed. "You should have warned me."

"The perfect antidote for tonight's shock. Will help you sleep."

"Thanks, and thank you for the flowers." She leaned forward and stroked one of the chrysanthemums with a finger.

Patrick imagined her touching him in the same way. He lifted his mug. "Who was killed?"

"Barbara Denton."

"The infamous Barbara?"

"The very one."

"Any idea why?"

She cradled the coffee mug between her hands. "I think she was blackmailing someone."

The instincts Patrick had honed when he'd been a crime reporter rose to the surface. "Someone you work with?"

She looked up. "I don't know."

Who was she protecting? "What made you think of blackmail?"

"There was money scattered—" She leaned against the back of the couch. "Even talking about the murder makes me sick. I didn't like her, but I like the way she died even less." She put the mug on the end table.

"More?" he asked.

She shook her head. "I want to curl into a fetal position and stay that way for a month."

"What would that solve?" He put his hand on her shoulder.

"Nothing. I don't want to go to work tomorrow."

"Call in sick."

"They won't buy that. I'm just back from vacation."

"Ask for a different unit."

"Transfers take months."

He inched closer. "You don't have to stay at Bradley Memorial. What about home care?"

"Would you leave the newspaper for a magazine?"

Even when the erratic hours had destroyed his marriage, he hadn't considered changing jobs. "You win."

Susan stretched. "You've helped me answer a question I've been asking myself all evening. I don't want to leave the hospital."

"Have you considered a different shift?"

"I might." She spoke through a yawn.

"I'd better go. Will you be all right?" He reached for her hand. If she asked, he would gladly stay.

"Thanks for being here."

He tapped her chin with his fingers. "Remember, I'm just a wall away. Bang three times and I'll be over."

"You're a good man, Patrick Macleith."

Her reaction wasn't the one he wanted, but for now, her admiration was enough. He pushed aside the urge to take her into his arms. Moving too fast would scare her. He rose and reached for his black jacket. "Would you like to have Thanksgiving dinner at my place? The twins will be here."

"I'm working."

"Then we'll eat at noon. Will you come?"

"Only if I can bring something?"

"The pies. Your crusts are terrific. Come early and help."

"What time?"

"Nine thirty. We'll watch the parades."

She walked to the door with him. "Again, thanks."

He jammed his hands in his jacket pockets and crossed the porch to his side of the large house. How much longer could he be with her without betraying his feelings? If he let her know how he felt, he was sure she would back away again.

Chapter 3

WITH A FIRM click, Susan closed the front door and walked to her car. She wanted to be anywhere except at the hospital, but she had no choice. She backed out of the driveway and headed for the Thruway. Each revolution of the wheel increased her level of anxiety.

Fifteen minutes later, she pulled into the last open space on the second tier of the parking lot. After several rounds of relaxing breaths, she reached for the door. The rows of tombstones in the cemetery reminded her of Barbara's death. She grabbed her lunch and purse and before her courage vanished, dashed down the steps and into the street.

Abruptly, she halted. A crowd spilled into the street and blocked the sidewalk in front of the Emergency Room entrance. Had there been a major disaster? To avoid reminders of the previous evening, she hadn't turned on the radio or television.

She skirted the crowd and then wove her way toward the entrance. Too late to retreat to another door, she spotted the television crew from the local cable news service.

"We're here at Bradley Memorial Hospital where last evening, Barbara Denton, a practical nurse, was brutally slain. The nurses who work the same shift are just arriving for work." He thrust the microphone toward the crowd. "How does it feel to be coming to work at the scene of a murder?" As the reporter spoke, he moved into the crowd.

"Awful."

"I'm petrified."

"I'd rather be at home."

The shouted comments matched Susan's feelings. She craned her neck to see if anyone else from Five Orthopedics had been trapped by the mob.

Like an amoeba, the crowd shifted and engulfed her. When the reporter reached the woman on Susan's left, she flinched and edged away.

"Did you know the murdered woman?" he asked.

The woman giggled. "Everyone knew her. She had her nose in everything."

Susan wiggled between two women. "Excuse me."

Why had she stopped to gape with the same fascination as the rest of the women? She had to break free of the mob before she faced a microphone. Talking to a reporter wasn't on her list of want-to-do things. At last, she broke free of the milling crowd.

"Susan Randall, did you really find her body?"

Susan pretended not to hear and walked briskly down the sidewalk. The desire to run pushed her into a trot.

"What did she look like?" a voice shrill with excitement shouted.

"Was there really a hundred grand on the floor around her body?"

"Hold on." The reporter pushed his way through the mass of women. "I'd like a statement from you."

"I have nothing to say." The automatic doors opened. Susan evaded the hand that reached for her and dashed into the hospital.

"Damn!" the reporter cried.

The doors slid shut on his shouts and demands for information. Susan shook her head. No wonder the administrators were worried about bad publicity. The crowd outside had acted like they were attending a Roman circus.

Two nurses and a doctor stood in the hall outside the ER lounge. "Susan, what happened last night?" They leaned toward her.

Susan ignored the question. She reached the elevators and pressed the button with an urgency that spoke of her rising panic. An enormous lump settled in her stomach.

I should have stayed home. The thought wove a course through the knowledge that the bombardment of questions would continue when she reached the unit.

The elevator doors opened. She stepped inside and pressed five. Her anxiety rose with the indicator. Her thoughts raced. Had she seen something last night she hadn't told the police? Had the killer seen her enter the storage room?

The moment she had seen Barbara, her entire awareness had centered on the dead woman. The killer could have been in the room and she wouldn't have noticed. Had a stranger killed Barbara? Whom had the practical planned to meet? Who had given her the money? Though Susan wanted a stranger to be blamed, that was unlikely. But that left few choices. She didn't want the murderer to be someone she knew.

On the fifth floor, she gulped a breath and rushed past the entrance to the storage room hall. The ceiling light had burned out. Shadows reached for her. Her mouth felt dry. The pulse at her throat throbbed with staccato rhythm.

I should have called in sick. How can I give my patients the care and attention that deserve when my instinct is to cower?

In the locker room, she leaned against the wall and changed into white shoes. Then grasping the stethoscope like a weapon, she ran to the nurses' lounge.

At first, she thought the room was deserted, but before she reached the credenza, she saw Julie standing at the window. Trish sat in a corner behind the round table. Susan put her lunch in the refrigerator. What kind of scene had she interrupted? The atmosphere felt as charged as it had yesterday.

Julie turned. "I was sure you'd call in sick. I nearly did. Weren't you scared to come?" She pushed wisps of hair from her face.

Trish's bony shoulders shook. "Looks like she's ready to launch an attack."

Susan remembered the way she clutched the stethoscope. Self-conscious laughter erupted. "I've spent the last five minutes calling myself a fool for coming in today." She draped the tubing around her neck.

"Were you trapped by the reporter?" Julie asked.

"Almost. One of our colleagues identified me, but I escaped."

"Why are they allowed to block the entrance?" Julie asked.

"Technically, they're on the sidewalk and that's public property," Trish said. "It's not much better here. The vultures on the day shift badgered us for details."

Julie giggled. "Trish impolitely told them to get lost."

"I'm sure that didn't stop them." Susan reached for a cup. "Part of me can't believe she's dead. When I opened the door, I expected to hear her spouting some tale."

"And spewing cigarette smoke." Trish pushed her chair back. "Thank heavens we're spared that forever."

"How can you be so callous?" Julie asked.

"Come off it. Don't pretend you liked her."

"I wish it hadn't happened," Susan said.

Trish jumped to her feet and knocked her chair against the wall. "You're both hypocrites." She stabbed a finger at Julie and then at Susan. "At least neither of you have been one of her victims."

The violent overtones in Trish's voice shook Susan. "I know she pushed you last night, but I thought she was probing for something she could use."

"She already knew too much."

"Do you want to talk about it?"

Trish's thin body stiffened. "And give you some ammunition to use against me? Forget that."

"I don't gossip," Susan said.

Trish moved from behind the table. "I'm glad she's dead."

As Susan studied Trish's face, she remembered Barbara had named Trish as an anorexic. Had the practical said more? Instead of tuning Barbara out, Susan wished she had listened.

"She asked to be killed." Trish edged past Susan. "You're lucky she never learned your secrets. At least you don't have to worry if the police will find a written record of your mistakes."

"Do you really think Barbara kept records?" Julie asked. "She seldom noted our calls. If it wasn't gossip she could wrap her tongue around, forget it."

Susan nodded. "Remember how we had to nag so she'd do her share of charts."

"I tried to ignore what she said about you and Larry," Julie said.

"What kind of things?" Trish's voice rose to a shrill pitch.

"Like your reasons for being here," Julie said. "How Larry dumped you and how you planned to get revenge by telling lies about the things he's done."

Trish laughed. "You don't know what went down between Larry and me and I'm not going to tell you. If you're curious, ask him."

The edge of anger in Trish's voice stirred Susan's curiosity. Why hadn't she listened to the practical? Every one of Barbara's tales had contained a bit of truth. Susan didn't believe love for De Witt had brought Trish to Bradley Memorial. But what had?

She put the coffee carafe on the heating plate. "In a week or two, no one will remember anything she said."

Julie nodded. "Lord, half the people who work here have survived one of her attacks."

"This time it's different. She's dead...murdered. Everyone wants the police to look at someone else." Trish's thin body shook. "I've been accused of being the one."

"So have I," Julie said. "Rhonda asked me what I used as a weapon. The police didn't find one."

"Rhonda was teasing," Susan said.

"You're a fool if you believe that." Trish entered the powder room. "She has her reasons, too."

"Even dead, Barbara's causing problems," Julie said.

"She never accused you of being anything but a fool for believing De Witt will marry you. She was right. You don't have the money or the social position to interest him for the long haul." Trish slammed the powder room door.

"You'll see." Julie stepped into the hall. "I don't understand why everyone thinks the worst of Larry."

Because we've seen him in action, Susan thought. "I hope the police will solve this before we're all screaming at each other."

"I wonder what happens to the money. Five thousand is a lot of cash."

"How do you know how much money there was?"

"From the newspaper."

Susan glanced at Julie. Why had the police revealed the amount of money? Were they hoping to trick someone by giving a false number?

Dark circles made Julie's eyes appear larger. Her skin had a muddy hue. Did she think De Witt had given Barbara the money? He had been here last evening. When Julie stopped at the doctors' desk, Susan continued across the station.

One of the day nurses looked up. "Susan, how are you? What luck finding her and all. Last evening must have been ghastly. How could you force yourself to come to work today? But since you're here, why not tell me what happened."

Susan hated the whine of anticipation in the woman's voice. "Yes I'm worried, but I'm not talking about last night." She picked up the medication book for District Two. "Did I have a choice about coming? They don't give sick days for fear."

"I guess they don't. One good thing happened though." The day nurse waved a pen in the air. "They found a float to replace Barbara."

A second nurse leaned her elbows on the counter. "Now for the bad news. The storage room is sealed. Supplies are to be obtained from the ER and Central." She cracked her gum.

While the conversation swirled around her, Susan opened the med book. Before she finished checking the charts for new orders, most of the day shift had gathered at her desk.

"So tell us what she looked like?" one of the practical nurses said. "I heard her head was a real mess."

"I don't want to talk about last night or Barbara," Susan said.

"What's with you guys?" The whine had returned to the day

nurse's voice. "Trish cursed us out. Julie stared out the window and didn't even say hello. Come on, give."

"Where's your sense of loyalty?" The voice belonged to the unit's sole male nurse. "This is where it happened and everyone in the hospital will know the details before we do."

"Who was Barbara after?" The breathy voice was Rhonda's. "Was it you?"

Susan exhaled slowly. She refused to answer the snide remark.

"Wait 'til you hear the rumors. Even Barbara couldn't top them."

Susan gripped a chart. Vultures would be the right word to describe them. "Read the newspapers. Tune your radios and televisions to the local stations. They seem to know more than I do."

"Are you acting on orders from administration? I hear there's going to be a shake-up at the top."

Susan slammed a chart on the desk. "Stop it. I'm not giving out details and I don't want to hear any speculations." She rose. "Since I can't check orders, would someone like to count narcotics with me?"

AFTER ROUNDS, Susan returned to the station. Facing the patients' questions had been nearly as difficult as confronting the curiosity of her colleagues. She slumped on a chair at the desk.

"What's with Trish tonight?" Kit turned in her chair. Her red hair swirled like an opening fan. "You'd think she'd be glad Barbara's dead. You know she threatened Trish last week. I heard them arguing. What do you suppose it was about?"

Susan shrugged. "Ask Trish."

"I did. She said if I didn't stop prying, I'd end up like Barbara. Do you think that's a threat?"

"I was about to say the same thing." Irritation hardened Susan's voice. She took three charts from the order basked. "It would be wonderful to work where everyone was too busy to gossip." She handed one chart to Kit and returned the others to the chart rack.

By six thirty, Susan craved adult company. Every chance the practical nurses had, they clustered around Kit. Their giggles reminded Susan of geese. If she heard one more speculation about who had killed Barbara, she would scream. She hurried to the lounge for dinner and waited for Leila.

By five to seven, she realized her friend wasn't coming. Susan cleared the table and returned to the nurses' station. Kit asked her to decipher a doctor's handwriting. After reading the scrawl, Susan glanced at her section of the desk. A large brown paper bag sat on the care plan book. "Who left this?" she asked.

Kit looked up. "I haven't the slightest idea. I saw it when I returned from delivering the mail. You'd think the day secretary would do her job."

"She's new." Susan reached for the bag.

"Are you going to open it here? What if it's a bomb?"

"Kit, please."

"After last night, we should expect the worst."

As though infected by Kit's comment, Susan gingerly opened the top of the bag. "No bomb. Chocolates."

"Is the box sealed?"

"Wrapped in cellophane like it came straight from the store."

"Whom do we thank?"

Susan slid the box from the bag and opened the card. "When she was here, you were good to her. These were her favorite chocolates. I am sure they are yours, too. F."

"F," Kit said. "Who's F?"

"I haven't any idea."

Julie appeared in the med room doorway. "Peer's Chocolates. Who from?"

"F." Kit giggled.

Julie perched on a corner of the desk. "Are you sure there isn't something you want to tell us?"

"I have no secrets." Susan shivered as memories of the conversation in the lounge the previous evening surfaced. To keep the pair from seeing how her hands shook, she fumbled with the ribbon and slid the cellophane. "Enjoy."

Her offer sparked a gathering. The rest of the evening staff gathered at the desk and passed the box around. Susan pulled the single chart from the order basket. The red checks told her Kit had sent the requisitions for special tests.

"Susan has a secret admirer," Julie said. "Have a piece. We're trying to guess who F is."

Susan looked up. Leila leaned against the counter that separated the station from the hall.

"You mean you don't know who sent them?" Leila asked. She looked at the card. "He has good taste."

"At least it's a better surprise than last night's," Trish said.

"Have you heard anything about the investigation?" Though Susan wanted to ask about suspects, she hesitated to put Leila on the spot.

Leila shrugged. "The police haven't said much. There are a hundred rumors. That's why it took me so long to get here. Some people will believe anything." She looked at Susan. "Are you all right?"

Susan waited until the crowd dispersed before she answered. "I didn't want to come today and once I arrived, I kept expecting to see her."

"And hear her annoying voice," Leila said. "She definitely had a presence. Were you one of the people on her list?"

"She laughed because I have no secrets. What bothers me is why I'm so upset. She wasn't my favorite person."

"Or mine," Leila said. "It's the shock of finding her, the brutality of the attack and maybe a touch of guilt."

"You're right about the guilt. I was furious because she took such a long break and didn't tell me about the admission. I was going to tear into her. Then I found her body and had to short-circuit my anger."

"Do you have time for coffee?"

Faye pushed the cart past the desk. "I'm ready when you are."

"Does that answer your question? Maybe I can get away when you stop to pick up report."

HE CHECKED his watch. Twenty minutes of his vigil remained. Since ten-thirty, he had waited in his car on the lower tier of the parking lot across from the hospital. Last night, he had realized he knew very little about Susan. He had to discover more. In less than an hour, he would know where she lived. The knowledge would help him make new plans so she would be like Mommy.

A smile formed. Had Susan liked the chocolates he had left at the desk for her? Had she put a piece in her mouth and rolled her tongue over the candy to savor the flavor? Mommy liked chocolates. Had Susan guessed he had left them to show her he had been bad.

Ten minutes and counting. Would Susan be on time? Her sporty white sedan waited on the second tier.

Time crept. Waiting made him restless. He turned the key in the ignition. The gentle rumbling of the engine soothed his ragged emotions. Hurry. Hurry. He chewed the inside of his lower lip and stared at the digital clock.

Rather than the numbers, he saw Susan. She opened the door of a house just like the one where he lived with Mommy. A white satin nightgown clung to her slender body. Her smile made him shiver with delight. Would she touch him and send heat to the private parts of his body? Her face became Mommy's. He smiled.

At eleven thirty, the sound of slamming car doors and the roar of engines woke him from his reverie. Lights from Susan's car cut through the darkness. Blood pulsed in his veins.

Her car passed his parking space. He switched on the lights and pulled into line behind her. Then keeping enough distance to prevent recognition, he followed her.

On the highway, her speed remained at a steady fifty-five. When she exited, his hand hovered over the horn. Someone should warn her about the danger of not using turn signals. He could have lost her and that would have made him angry. Mommy always tried to keep him happy. Why had Susan forgotten the rule?

Her car made a series of turns along streets where Victorian houses mingled with those of more recent vintage. He inched closer. Five turns later, the white sedan pulled into the driveway of a large gray house tucked behind a high yew hedge. After circling the block, he parked across the street, stared down the dark driveway and noted the pattern of lights on one side of the house. A second car was parked near Susan's.

Did Susan live alone? Who owned the car? Some widows took in boarders. Mommy had. She had believed the presence of a man provided safety. He was a man. Mommy didn't need any man but him, so one day, the boarder vanished.

The presence of the other car troubled him. Mommy, why? Don't you remember the last time?

He left the car and stood at the head of the driveway. A lawn stretched on either side of the asphalt. The yew hedge separated the house from the neighboring one. At the corner of the wide porch, a clump of rhododendrons grew.

Perfect. Anticipation stirred the embers of desire. Tomorrow Susan would be like Mommy.

ON WEDNESDAY night, Susan left the unit ten minutes late. As she drove from the parking lot, she glanced in the rearview mirror. Was the dark car the same one she had seen last night?

Just as the light at the corner changed from green to yellow, she turned. A horn blared. She looked back. The dark car had sped through the red light. A splash of common sense dampened the flare of panic. Just because the car had run the light didn't mean she was being followed.

When she stopped to pay the toll, the dark car slid into the next lane. The booth blocked her view of the driver.

Ten minutes later, she left the high-speed road and began the circuitous route she used through town. Headlights remained centered in the mirror. She strained to see but dirt covered the license plate and the driver was a blur.

She gripped the wheel. With great effort, she held at bay the panic that made her mouth dry and urged her to speed down the street. What was wrong with her? Why would anyone follow her? Had she seen something in the storage room that put her life at risk?

The dark car loomed. Her heart rate accelerated. Coincidence. It had to be. Soon the car would turn into one of the side streets. She swore off reading mysteries at night. Barbara's death had turned her life into one.

Without warning, the scene in the storage room flashed into her thoughts. Susan frowned. Something about Barbara's body troubled her. What had she seen? The more she searched, the more elusive the thought became.

Her hand gripped the wheel with such force her arms ached. She made the final turn into the street where she lived. Her tension eased. If she needed him, Patrick would be there.

She stopped the car at the head of the driveway. His spot was empty. Where was he? Weeknights usually found him at home. As she parked in front of the porch, the dark car drove slowly past. She dashed to the porch.

Fear of being alone made her hands shake so badly she dropped the key. Where was Patrick? She gulped a breath. What was wrong with her tonight? The dark car had driven past.

Once inside the house, in hopes of chasing the shadows, she switched on all the lights.

INSTEAD OF circling the block, he parked just beyond the corner. Blood pulsed in an erratic rhythm through his veins. Until his breathing and his heart rate steadied, he remained in the car.

Anticipation blossomed. He patted his jacket and felt the weapon he had remembered to bring. Tonight, she would be with Mommy and he would be free.

With his hands in his jacket pockets and his senses alert, he strolled down the street. For a moment, he paused at the top of the driveway and peered both ways. Relieved to find the street deserted, he turned to study the house and noted the absence of the other car. Light oozed from the edges of the curtained windows on both floors.

Did she sense his presence? Would she welcome him?

The lights on the upper floor went out. With the stealth of a shadow, he crept down the driveway. Before climbing the steps to the porch, he turned and checked the street. His gloved hand fondled the gun.

A narrow gap between the drapes allowed him to see into the room. He rocked from his heels to his toes. At the foot of the staircase, Susan stood. Instead of the clinging nightgown of his fantasy, she wore a shapeless robe. He pursed his lips together. Why wasn't she dressed the way he knew she should be?

His fingers moved to the trigger. He willed her to approach. She walked to the center of the room and stared at the window.

She wasn't close enough. Her eyes appeared to narrow. He gasped and moved back. His heart bucked in his chest.

SUSAN PAUSED in the center of the living room and listened to the sounds of the house. After a hectic evening at the hospital, she usually welcomed the solitude she found at home. Tonight was different and she wasn't sure why she felt wary and unsettled. Had a dark car really followed her home and driven slowly past the driveway?

She gulped a breath. Barbara's death had spooked her. Something about the practical's body had been different, but she couldn't remember what. She reached for the coat draped over the arm of the couch.

A scuffling noise, subtle and out of place, caused her to tense and stare at the living room window. A shadow moved. Someone was on the porch. Who? Man or woman? Should she go to the door and look?

Not a good idea. The doors were locked and so were the windows. If anyone attempted to break in, she could slip down the cellar steps and into Patrick's side of the house.

Cautiously, she moved from the living room into the kitchen alcove. Her coat fell to the floor. With one hand on the doorknob, she listened for the sounds that didn't belong to the house and the night.

HE STOOD with his back pressed against the clapboard siding of the house. Ninety-nine. One hundred. He returned to the spot where the drapes parted and peered into the living room. Where was she? Had she seen him and called the police? He pressed his face against the glass, but he couldn't see her.

With care, he crept across the porch and down the side steps. He edged past the clump of rhododendrons and walked around the side of the house. The absence of windows low enough to provide a view of the interior of the house irritated him. He reached the back and peered through the glass pane of the kitchen door.

Why was she hiding? She couldn't be afraid of him. That wouldn't be right. Mommy was never afraid.

Cautiously, he continued the exploration. He stared through French doors into a deserted dining room. Where is she? He rattled the door.

Maybe he should return to the porch and knock. She would be surprised to see him. He frowned. Had she left the house? How? He would have heard the door. His breath fogged the glass.

Finally, he retraced his steps. When he reached the porch, he stood with his finger poised over the bell. Would she answer? He chewed the inside of his lower lip.

Headlights from a car halted at the top of the driveway and startled him. He scurried away from the door and moved into the shadows. The lights drew nearer. He jumped down the side steps and crouched in the thicket of rhododendrons. Afraid to breathe, he bit his lip.

The car stopped and the lights went out. When a man entered a door on the other side of the house, the watcher began to shake. The derringer fell from his hand. On hands and knees, he searched for the weapon but couldn't find it.

A surge of anger engulfed him. What was the man to Susan? She didn't need another man. She was a widow. Mommy was a widow, too, and he had been the only man she had needed. It wasn't fair. It wasn't right. Susan had to be like Mommy.

FROM THE moment she heard the rattle of the French doors, Susan froze. Her muscles tightened like cloth that had shrunk. She cowered in the pantry and willed herself to move, to run down the cellar steps.

A car door slammed. She recognized Patrick's footsteps on the porch. Relief flooded her. She shook her arms to release tense shoulder muscles.

For months after Jim's death, night noises had taken on similar overtones. She had thought she'd moved past those fears. For almost a year, until Barbara's death, she hadn't been afraid to be alone.

Slowly, her breathing resumed a normal rhythm and her heart regained a steady beat. She bent and picked up the coat she had dropped. Had she really seen the shadow of a person or had her imagination conjured the sight? She hung the coat on a hook and turned on the kitchen light.

She sank on a chair at the kitchen table and reached for the phone. Patrick might have seen something. She let her hand drop. If she told him about her scare, his protective instincts would go into overdrive. She couldn't run to him every time some nameless fear held her captive. That action would erode her carefully nurtured independence.

Unbidden memories of the night Jim died flooded her thoughts. The moments of forgetfulness found in Patrick's arms stirred anew. For months afterward, she had felt guilty, alone and afraid. Patrick's caresses had promised things Jim's touches never had.

She put her hand to her face. Jim and Patrick had formed their values in the same neighborhood and had grown up in families who had shared the same ideals. Jim had shielded her from life. How could she believe Patrick would be any different?

Susan pushed these thoughts aside. As she lifted the pies she had baked that morning and put them in the refrigerator, she inhaled the spicy aroma. Instead of coffee, she poured a glass of orange juice, rinsed the few dishes and wiped the counters.

Then she carried the juice to the living room. Noises from the other side of the house reminded her of Patrick's presence. As she walked upstairs, her hand slid along the banister. Thoughts of Patrick's smile and his touch seemed impossible to dislodge. Her body felt the way a tree must feel when the season changes from the dormancy of winter into the flowering of spring.

Upstairs, she sat on the bed. Patrick was just beyond the wall. This new awareness made her edgy. With a sigh, she lifted Jim's picture from the bedside stand.

"Patrick has his eye on you." Jim's voice filled her thoughts. He'd said those words after their friend's divorce.

"We're friends, the three of us," she had said.

"That's why he keeps his distance and only visits when I'm home. You know if anything happens to me, he'll let you know how he feels."

"Don't say such things." In that instant, her fears that Jim would leave her had been so strong, she hadn't heard him say how he would feel if his prediction came true.

She shook her head. Jim's eyes appeared to change. Almost, she heard a whispered, "I told you so."

Several tears rolled down her cheeks. She replaced the picture on the night stand. The queen-sized bed seemed too large, too cold and too empty. What if—

No fantasies, she thought. Since the night Patrick had held her in his arms, kissed and loved her, he had never done or said anything a friend wouldn't. She had allowed remnants of Monday night's traumatic discovery and tonight's imagined intruder to create the need to find security in Patrick's arms. There was no reason to be afraid...or was there?

:

Chapter 4

THE NEXT morning when Patrick opened the door on his side of the large house what Susan saw in his blue eyes confirmed what she had been denying. She didn't see the open welcome of friendship, but desire and need. Before she glanced away, she knew Jim had been right about Patrick's feelings for her.

"Good morning." His smile raised a delicious warmth. "Ready for the parades?"

"Hi." She forced the greeting across her lips. She moved past him into the family room and put the pie containers on the counter that divided the long room into two areas. Then unsure of what to do or say, she walked to the kitchen door and stared into the barren yard.

"Do the pies go in the refrigerator?" Patrick asked.

"The pumpkin should." The aroma of poultry seasoning and the other spices scented the air. "What do you want me to do?"

"I'll take your sweater."

He stood behind her, close enough that she felt the warmth of his body. The awareness increased her uneasiness.

"Good idea." She handed him the sweater and rolled up the sleeves of her aqua shirt. "Smells wonderful." She stopped at the counter and tasted the cranberry relish. "Is there anything left to do?"

He winked. "I saved the potatoes for you." He brushed her cheek with his knuckles.

For a moment, Susan thought he meant to kiss her. Did she want that? Her confusion must have shown. He stepped back and headed to the living room.

She wondered if he had sensed her need to be alone. His knowledge of her moods often bordered on the uncanny. She recalled a dozen instances of closeness during the past summer when they had shared chores in the yard. Was she ready for a change between them?

Susan carried a bowl and paring knife to the deacon's bench in the living room. The flames in the fireplace competed with the flickering colors on the television screen though neither held her attention. Her thoughts dwelled on the confusion caused by what she had learned about Patrick's feelings for her. What was she going to do?

Some time later, Patrick's deep voice startled her. "What?" she asked.

He chuckled. "You've been paring that spud for five minutes. What's wrong?"

She shook her head. "Nothing, really. Watching a fire can be hypnotic. I've always loved fireplaces."

"I never thought it fair for both to be on my side of the house."

"Jim's choice. He thought fires were messy so when the architect drew up the plans to convert the house, he insisted both be on the tenant's side. For once, I argued and lost."

She had difficulty deciphering the meaning of the look on Patrick's face. Surprise, and something more. No wonder. This was the first time she had criticized her husband's decisions with Patrick as an audience. She looked away. "When are the children due?"

"At nine thirty." He grinned. "I know, they're late, but when was Lisa ever on time?" Amusement tinged his voice.

"Don't I remember missing a couple of movies because she couldn't get organized? How long will the twins be here?"

"Until Sunday evening."

"That's a switch."

"Things are changing. Lisa and Rob are on their way to Vermont for business and skiing. He thought the kids would be in the way."

"Why? They're great kids. How could he think they'd be a problem?"

Patrick shrugged. "I don't ask those kind of questions. Rob is on the fast track these days. I'll have the twins for Christmas, too. Rob has a business meeting in Europe and Lisa wouldn't dream of being left behind."

Susan smiled. "You'll enjoy your time with them."

Patrick settled into the Victorian smoker that Susan had helped him refinish last summer. His long legs stretched in front of him. "Being a sometimes father was never my choice. I wish Lisa had been willing to try joint custody."

The yearning in his voice made Susan wish she could offer a solution. "They're older now. Why not ask again?"

"I have. She objects to my bachelor status. And of course, there's the child support. She and Rob would miss the extra money."

Susan stared at her hands. She couldn't point out his ex-wife's selfishness without adding to his pain. The bitter note in his voice made her realize he was very aware of the fact.

"How are things at Bradley Memorial?" he asked. "Anything new about the Denton woman's death?"

"Everyone has a theory about what the police are doing, but no one knows anything."

Patrick leaned forward. "I know the covering reporter. She says the police are working on a connection between the death and the alleged attack in the parking lot."

"Which may have been a dramatized version of a petty incident. Barbara had an inventive imagination."

"I don't think so," Patrick said. "When we had dinner last night, Laura said several of the nurses reported seeing a man run into the cemetery on the night of the attack."

At least no one told the reporter that a man shouted my name, Susan thought. She could imagine Patrick's reaction if he knew. Like Jim, he would want her to leave her job. She didn't want to quarrel with Patrick.

A shock that had nothing to do with Barbara's death jolted Susan. A friend? Dinner? She reached for the last potato. Did she think he had lived as a monk since his divorce? Why did his closeness to this female reporter trouble her?

"Another thing Laura said was that Barbara was adept at making enemies."

Susan concentrated on the knife. "They aren't really enemies, but people considered her an annoyance. I've only heard one person admit to wanting her dead."

"Who?"

She reached for the bowl. "One of the nurses on my unit, but it was just talk."

"Are you sure? Could she have been the one being blackmailed?"

"Five thousand on a nurse's salary? I don't think so." She carried the potatoes to the kitchen sink. "All this speculation and gossip are some of the reasons I'm not enjoying work these days."

"Have you remembered anything else?"

Susan turned on the water. "I thought I did, but whatever I thought I saw eludes me." For a moment, she wondered if she should tell him about the dark car and the sounds of a prowler last night. Did she want to trigger his protective instincts? Then he would want to take charge of her life.

"Maybe I can help. Was it something about the room?"

She shook her head. "Her body. That's where the memory stops."

She quartered the potatoes and put them in a pan. She turned. Patrick leaned against the end of the counter. His intent stare made her wary.

"When's your next weekend off?"

The abrupt change of subject confused her. She fumbled for an answer. "Next week."

"Great. I'm covering a concert for the paper. We'll go to dinner before and maybe dancing later."

She hesitated. Did she want to go? If she accepted, he might believe she wanted more than an evening with him. He stepped closer and left her with no retreat. She pressed against the sink. Did she want to run? Before she discovered the answer, he pulled her into an embrace. His lips touched hers. She felt a shiver of delight and fear slide along her nerves.

The doorbell rang. Patrick groaned and released her. "Lisa always had bad timing."

Or good, she thought. She wanted to surrender and also to fight the confusion he had stirred.

The moment he opened the door, the twins shot into the room. Patrick gathered them into his arms.

Susan listened to the enthusiastic greetings. She set the pan on the burner. Tears misted her vision and she fought a surge of envy. The room blurred. Had she wanted children? Since Jim hadn't, she had never considered motherhood. She walked to the deacon's bench and stared at the television.

"Aunt Susan." Robin's light soprano voice lilted the honorary title Susan had been given years before. "Dad didn't tell us you'd be here. I have a zillion things to tell you. There's this boy—" She tossed her coat to her brother. "Adam, where are your manners? Aren't you going to tell Aunt Susan hello?"

Adam grinned. "It's not polite to interrupt someone, even a motor mouth like you." His voice cracked. "Hi, Aunt Susan. He's a creep." He sprawled in front of the deacon's bench.

"Just because he's better at basketball than you are," Robin said.

Adam stuck out his tongue. Susan ruffled his honey blond hair. "You've grown a foot."

"That's because you haven't seen me since summer. You're never here when we come to see Dad. Did they give you the day off?"

"I have to be at the hospital by three."

"When are you off?" Robin asked.

"Tomorrow."

"Good." Robin kicked off her sneakers. "You can take us Christmas shopping like you did before —"

Divorce and death, Susan silently finished. She reached for the girl's hand. "Sounds like fun, but your dad might have plans."

Patrick shook his head. "The day is yours, but only if you promise to come back and eat leftovers with us. Put together a game plan while I finish dinner. Then we'll set the table together."

Susan's gaze met Patrick's. Her cheeks flushed and she glanced away. Had her eyes promised too much, she wondered. She wanted to spend the day with him, yet she feared the erosion of their friendship and the ceding of her independence.

The twins chattered with one often finishing a sentence for the other. Susan felt a sense of belonging that troubled her. He wasn't her husband. Still, for a moment, she allowed herself to pretend they were a family.

A short time later, they gathered in the dining room. Patrick handed Susan heavy plates made from pale cream-colored pottery that was streaked with rust tones. Robin and Adam put the silverware and glasses at each plate.

"Aunt Susan, did you know the nurse who was killed?" Adam asked.

The intrusion of reality startled Susan. Her smile faded.

"Aren't you scared to go to work?" Adam asked.

"Yes to both questions." Susan's voice broke.

Patrick touched her hand. Comfort mingled with awareness. "Cool it kids. Susan doesn't want to talk about the murder."

"Maybe tomorrow?" Adam asked.

The wistful tone of his voice made Susan smile. "Maybe, but don't bug me."

"Let me tell you about Jeff Midori," Robin said.

"That creep."

"He's better at baseball, too."

The moment of panic passed. Susan folded the linen napkins into fans and listened to Robin's enthusiastic chatter about the boy who had captured her attention.

THAT EVENING, Susan sat in the lounge and prodded a piece of celery with her fork. If Leila hadn't planned to join her for dinner this evening, she would have skipped the meal. With luck, the loss of appetite would last through the holiday season, or until the last five pounds she wanted to lose had been shed.

She stretched and remembered the plate of food, a reprise of Thanksgiving dinner, she had left on the counter at Patrick's. The twins, the feeling of belonging, her wishes to prolong the sense of family had nearly made her late for work. At the last minute, she had hurried home to change clothes.

For a moment, she closed her eyes and recaptured memories of the morning. Robin's chatter. Adam's questions. The interrupted kiss. Her fingers touched her lips. What had the kiss meant to Patrick?

When he had jumped in to protect her from his son's curiosity, she had felt warmth instead of resentment. Yet, as she drove to work, she had found herself wishing he had let her answer. She would have said the same thing, but he had taken her option away.

Jim would have answered for her, too. Was that the reason for her annoyance? Did her resentment stem from seeing another similarity between the men? She dropped the fork on the plate. Friendship was the key. She didn't want to fall in love again. Her fears of forming another dependent relationship were too strong. For that reason, she hadn't told Patrick about the dark car or about the prowler she had heard.

The lounge door closed with a bang. Susan gasped and immediately recovered. Leila held a tray. Susan raised an eyebrow. "Thought trays weren't to be taken from the cafeteria."

"They trust me to return it." Leila put her dinner on the table. "I knew you'd never join me there."

"And waste half my dinner break waiting for an elevator?" Susan speared a piece of cucumber. Leila looked drained. Shadows and lines that hadn't been there Monday night marked her face. "Have you heard anything more about Barbara?"

"The funeral's tomorrow." Leila reached for a fork. "Some of the supervisors are going. I'm glad I won't be in town. She caused me enough heartache."

"How?"

"One of these days, I'll tell you. Are you going?"

"No." Susan carried two cups of coffee to the table. "When will things get back to normal around here?"

Leila sighed. "I'm not sure they ever will."

"Don't say that."

"A death like Barbara's will take a long time to forget."

"We have to try." Susan sipped the coffee. "Any idea when we can use the storage room? Sending to Central and the ER every time we need equipment is a pain."

"The police have promised to finish by Monday afternoon. They're still searching for the murder weapon. Your shift will have first rights."

Susan shuddered. "I don't think I'll ever willingly go in there alone. What's the scoop on the killing? There has to be some news."

"More rumors than facts. Murry said they're looking at the men in her life."

"That could take forever. Three ex-husbands, plus the maintenance men and security guards from here whom she dated." Susan shook her head. "I didn't think she was attractive, but men sure did."

"She wasn't ugly, just her attitude." Leila cradled her coffee cup. "One of her husbands was recently released from jail. He served time for burglary. Used to work here. At the trial, he said she told him what houses to hit. I believe she might have. They were homes of patients on her former unit." Leila shook her head. "She charged one of her ex-husbands with abuse. How am I doing?"

"Tons better than Kit and about par with Patrick. He knows a reporter who says the police are trying to connect her death with the attack in the parking lot."

"Doesn't that trouble you?"

"Why?"

"She said someone called your name in warning."

Susan inhaled a breath. "And how often did she tell the truth? I think she was trying for shock value."

Leila winked. "How is that good-looking neighbor of yours?"

Susan shifted in her chair. "I had Thanksgiving dinner with him."

"And?"

"His children were there. They're great. I enjoyed listening to Robin talk about her latest crush and Adam tease her about the boy."

"You're evading the question."

"I think he's in love with me."

"Grab that man and run."

Susan laughed. "It's not as simple as that. There are many things I have to consider before I leap into his arms. What I feel toward him, my job, my independence."

"What does independence have to do with love?" Leila shook her head.

"Friendship is all I can handle right now. If we were dating, that would change."

"Why?" Leila lit a cigarette.

"Leila, no." Susan pointed to the cigarette.

Leila walked to the powder room. "Once more, why?"

"How often does a dating couple remain friends?"

"Must have happened a time or two. You could start a new trend. You can't be alone forever."

"A lot of women are."

"You're not one of them. Instead of spending your energies on the patients, you need someone to love."

Susan walked to the credenza and refilled her cup. "I did that once."

"What's wrong with trying again?" Leila spoke over the whir of the vent fan. "I know Jim treated you like a child who was incapable of making decisions, but Patrick might be different. Also, remember how much you've changed."

"How many women choose the same type of man again and again? You've seen it happen."

"Joe's nothing like my ex."

Susan put her cup on the windowsill. Maybe Leila couldn't see the similarities. Joe didn't abuse Leila but he placed his own concerns first. Did love always create tunnel vision?

"Patrick is a lot like Jim. They grew up together and were closer than many brothers. He protects his children. He protects his ex-wife. I won't be swaddled again."

"Then let him know. Don't push him away before you try." Leila joined Susan at the window. "Did Barbara say anything Monday night about Joe and me?"

Susan glanced at the door. "Not about Joe. She was furious with you. Were you really going to recommend she be put on probation?"

Leila raked her hair. "I was going to and I would have even though she tried to blackmail me into turning over the material I'd collected. She spied on us. Even named times and places where we met."

"Did you destroy the things?"

"Not on a bet."

"Was Jim upset?"

"At me, not her. We had our first argument because I refused to give her the documents. He didn't understand that the next time she wanted something, she'd remember about us and make new demands."

"You were right about that."

"He planned to offer her money." Leila returned to the powder room. "I hated her. She tainted something special."

"Did he give her the money the police found?"

"I don't know, but who else could have. I didn't even know he had come to the hospital that night."

"Ask him." Susan cleared the table. "Not knowing would drive me crazy."

Leila shrugged. "He has too much to cope with these days."

"Mary?"

"Among other things. Her condition has deteriorated. She's due to be admitted for more tests. Mostly it's De Witt."

"What has he done? Seduced a patient."

"In a way."

"You're being cryptic."

"And that's the way it will stay. You know how Joe feels about gossip. If anyone heard what's going down, he'd blame me. I'm worried about the money, that's all."

Had Joe Barclay given the money to Barbara? Leila needed to discover the truth. Her fears made her appear fragile enough to shatter. "How did Barbara learn about you and Joe?"

Leila picked up the tray. "She may have known for years. I'm not sure what betrayed us. What really scares me is that the police will learn. Barbara's threats gave both of us a motive for her death."

"How would the police learn? I've never heard you and Joe linked by gossip."

"If she knew, there could be others. What if the wrong question sends me into hysterics and I let things slip?"

Susan walked to the door. "You're not the only jumpy person around here. Julie and Trish are so nervous they infect me. I'm glad they're off tonight."

"That kind of behavior will be the norm until the case is solved." Leila followed Susan to the door. "I need a favor for the weekend."

"Just ask."

"My new car wasn't delivered yesterday. Could I borrow yours? Mine is fine for local driving, but I'm afraid it will die in the mountains."

Susan frowned. "I thought you and Joe were going away."

"Separate cars. We usually travel that way. My idea."

"No problem. What time tomorrow do you want to meet?"

"Why not make the exchange tonight? That way I can pack when I get home and you won't have to rush in the morning. I have to be away by eight thirty to follow Joe."

Susan opened the door. "The parking lot at eleven thirty. If I finish early, will you give me permission to leave?"

Leila laughed. "How many times in the past year has that happened?"

"Twice."

"I've a better idea. I'll come down at eleven and let my presence act as a goad."

Susan chuckled. "Sounds good. See you then."

HE STOOD AT the window and stared at the street. A dark blue sedan with a MD license plate was parked at the curb across the street. Moments later, he saw Susan's sporty white sedan pull behind the other. For a moment, he hoped she had come to see him. His hopes were smashed when the doctor left his car and walked to Susan's.

A growl escaped. He knew the doctor. Mommy had liked him, but like Susan, the doctor had failed to protect Mommy. On the night Mommy had died, the doctor had stayed at home while those others had killed her. He watched the scene across the street and felt anger build. The doctor was married. So was Susan. Why would Susan want to be with a married man? Susan was like Mommy. Mommy would never have done a thing like that. After Daddy died, there had been no other men. The watcher smiled. Just me.

The cars pulled from the curb. Where were they going? He heard Mommy's voice. "Every Thanksgiving, Dr. Barclay goes to his hunting cabin, just like Daddy used to go. His place is just a mile from Daddy's."

Why was Susan going? She didn't like guns. Mommy didn't either.

They must have met by accident. Maybe Susan wanted to tell him about a patient. As he locked the door and strode to his car, he held tightly to that idea.

Slowly, he drove past Susan's house and peered into the driveway. Susan's car was gone. So was the other one. His anger changed to rage. How could she do this to him? She should know better. He had to think, to plan, to act but not yet. He knew where they would be but it was too soon to go.

After deciding he needed to practice, he drove to the shooting range. There, he chose a target, loaded and aimed his rifle. Instead of the circles, he saw Susan. A head shot. One to the body. Twenty-five rounds later, he examined the target. He was hot.

"That was some shooting. Do you ever miss?"

He turned and faced a large black man. "Very seldom, Detective Davies."

"Some of my buddies on the force could use your eye."

"Thanks." He strode to the car and fitted the rifle into its case.

"See you around," the police officer called. "Good hunting."

Tonight, he thought. Good hunting, indeed. Tonight he would find Susan and he would be free.

SUSAN SLUMPED on the couch in Patrick's living room. Bags and boxes littered the room. She rested her feet on a hassock and listened to the twins' report about the shopping expedition. They related every moment, except what presents they had bought.

"Burgers and fries for lunch," Adam said.

"Mom never lets us have them," Robin said. "She's always pushing salads. They're healthy."

"We can't have soda either. 'You have to watch your weight.'" Adam sat on the floor near the hassock. "I'll never be big enough for football if Mom has her way."

"We had sundaes," Robin said. "All gooey with hot fudge and caramel..."

"And topped with whipped cream." Adam rubbed his stomach. "It's been months since we've had ice cream. Mom's always dieting. She..."

"Thinks we should eat the way she and Rob do," Robin finished.

"I can't see that you've suffered," Patrick said. Susan opened her eyes. He winked. "You're spoiling them."

"And they're ruining me. I'm more tired than after working a double shift."

"Better you than me. Are you ready for dinner?"

Adam laughed. "Guess what Aunt Susan had for lunch?"

"A turkey sandwich," Robin said. "She threw it away and had a burger."

Patrick paused in the doorway. "Dinner is in fifteen minutes and no one's throwing their turkey away. I rented some moves for later."

"Scary ones." Robin and Adam spoke as one.

"What else?"

Susan decided to go to the grocery store after dinner. Scary reminded her of the hospital. She was glad she didn't have to be there this evening.

HE WALKED from the first tier of the parking lot to the third and checked every car. Susan's car was missing. He chewed on the inside of his lower lip. He had prayed she would be here. He didn't want to be angry with her. He smacked his fist against the hood of the last car and stumbled over the chain that formed the boundary of the cemetery.

A light rain misted on his face. When he reached Mommy's grave, he crouched and touched the tombstone.

"Help me, Mommy. Tell me what to do. She didn't come to work tonight and I know where she is. You told me. She's doing something you would never do."

He waited for an answer. No comfort came from the silent grave. He fled, nearly falling over the tombstones. He reached his car and sat behind the wheel.

He could go home but being alone wasn't what he wanted. Susan, he had to find her. He drove from the hospital to her house. Her side of the large house was dark. How could she do this to him?

He drove past unlit stores and past houses where lights revealed glimpses of people who weren't alone. The lawns broadened. Stone walls hid houses from view. He reached the dead end of the street and parked behind the statue at the end of the road.

Low-lying fog rolled from the river and hid the path to the Overlook. He strode into the mist and used the metal railing as a guide. On the day of Daddy's funeral, he and Mommy had come here. They had eaten lunch at one of the picnic tables. She had made her promise. That had been the best day of his life.

He emerged from the fog. Behind those bushes, grown taller now, two naked bodies had thrashed and grunted. Not fair. They shouldn't have ruined his special place.

The rising wind rustled leaves that clung to near barren trees. He paused beside the table where he and Mommy had eaten lunch. He closed his eyes and saw her. She shook her head, but he couldn't listen to her pleas.

He strode across the frost-killed grass until he reached the railing that guarded the edge of the sheer cliff that plunged hundreds of feet to the river. A million broken moons reflected from the dark water. The shifting patterns became the broken promise on which he had built his life.

"I'll never leave you. They'll have to kill me first. What will happen to you if I'm not here?"

"Tell me what to do."

He turned and raced across the grass. As he dashed down the steps, his left hand slid along the railing. At the car, he paused to catch his breath.

When he reached home, he climbed the stairs to Mommy's room. He paused beside the dresser and set the alarm for three A.M. That would give him time. Then he walked to the bed. Mommy's perfume bottle stood on the bedside table. He pressed the atomizer. The scent of roses enveloped him.

He lay on the bed. One hand kneaded the satin comforter. The other rubbed his hair. Rays of moonlight slipped between the slats of the Venetian blinds. As he closed his eyes, he caught a shimmer of Mommy's presence. He reached for her.

AT FIVE after twelve, Julie parked her car on the street near Larry's riverfront apartment. She stared at the low-lying fog that slithered across the flagstone walk leading to the terrace entrance.

"Use the terrace door." Larry had whispered just before he left the unit. On Wednesday, she had forgotten. A long lecture about how he hated her to use the front entrance where a security guard made her sign the guest book had been her punishment.

"I don't want my visitors treated like they're visiting a jail. No one needs to know whom I've been seeing."

"If privacy's so important, why not buy a house or a condo?" she had asked.

"Money. First I need the partnership. Don't fret, little bird. There'll always be a nest for you."

He meant marriage, didn't he? Doubt tickled her thoughts. She slumped against the car. He had to mean marriage. What would she do if he didn't? She couldn't stay away from him. A month ago, for three miserable days, she had tried and failed.

The fog shifted. As she slipped on the slick flagstones, she grasped the handrail. The river lapped against the retaining wall with a lulling sound. She reached the terrace and stared at the glass door.

Larry stood at the bar and tossed off a drink. She frowned. For the past month, his intake of alcohol had increased and he had refused to discuss the reasons. She walked toward the door.

Low slung jeans hugged his hips and thighs. He wore no shirt. When he replaced the decanter on the glass and chrome bar, his back muscles rippled.

Entranced by his movements, she traced his reflection on the glass. After a short time, she knocked. He turned and strode to the door. She ached to touch the blond curls that tapered to disappear beneath the waist of his jeans. He opened the door. The rhythmic beat of "Bolero" played softly in the background.

"You're late." He sipped his drink.

Julie unbuttoned her coat. "Narcotic count was off. Trish forgot to record a Valium." She frowned. Why the startled look so quickly masked? Was he worried about Trish? I'm not jealous, she silently repeated several times.

Larry set his drink on the glass and chrome table near the terrace doors. Julie kicked off her shoes and curled her toes into the deep pile of the carpet.

He slid her coat from her shoulders and pulled her into an embrace. His mouth met hers, explored and demanded. The rhythmic music changed to a soft and plaintive melody.

Larry released her. "Wine?"

She nodded. "Half a glass. I'm beat."

He picked up his drink and drained it. After crossing to the bar, he poured white wine for her and another drink for himself. She took the goblet and touched hers to his. "To us."

"To an affair destined to last longer than Uncle Joe's and Leila Vernon's."

"Ms. Vernon." Wine splashed on the pewter gray carpet. "What are you talking about?"

His eyes danced with a kind of excitement that made her wary. "Uncle Joe and Leila have been lovers for years."

"I don't believe you."

"I couldn't have learned at a better time. The partnership's assured."

Julie put her glass on the end table. "What do you mean?"

"Not for you to worry about, little bird."

"Is this part of what's been bothering you for weeks?"

He grinned. "I have no worries."

"Then why have you been drinking so much?"

He laughed. "Have I? Let's just say I have proof of this affair."

"Did Barbara tell you? I wouldn't trust a thing she said."

"She wasn't my source." He took her hand. "Don't worry your pretty self about anything." He pulled her closer. "When I tell him what I know, he'll give me a fifty-fifty split instead of the usual thirty-seventy for the first two years."

Julie stiffened. "That sounds like blackmail."

"Just a mutual secret-keeping agreement. Aunt Mary would be devastated to learn he's taken Leila to his hunting cabin for the weekend. I might just do a little hunting myself."

His smile caused a shiver to run down her spine. "Larry, please don't do this."

His mouth covered hers. Moments later, he led her to the bedroom.

BRIGHT RAYS of sunlight struck Julie's eyes. She wiggled across the bed seeking Larry's warmth. Peering from under half-hooded eyes, she discovered she was alone.

"Larry," she called.

She slipped to the edge of the bed. Her naked body was reflected from a half dozen mirrors. She reached for the robe slung over the foot of the bed and padded to the living room. "Larry, where are you?"

A glance at the clock told her it was just seven A.M. and a Saturday. Larry seldom rose early on weekends. She called again.

No answer. She frowned and crossed to the room he used as a study. She opened the door. Her lips curled in distaste. The walls, decorated with hunting trophies and guns, both new and antique, seemed to contradict the passionate lover she knew. Feeling like Bluebeard's wife, she crossed to the desk. A rifle was missing from the wall where it usually hung between two deer heads.

With a thud, she sat on the chair behind the desk. The chill that raised gooseflesh on her arms was part fear, part anger. Where was he? Why had he taken a rifle?

A stack of charts sat on a corner of the desk. Idly, she turned them over. Trish Fallon. The name seemed engraved in bright letters. As though she had brushed a snake, her hand flew back. Relief and curiosity mingled in her thoughts. Why was Trish Larry's patient? Though tempted, she pushed the chart away. As she left the room, she turned to stare at the empty rifle rack on the wall.

Chapter 5

SUNLIGHT STREAMED through the French doors into the dining room and warmed Susan's back. A stack of paid bills sat in front of her. She slipped the last check into the envelope.

When she put the pen down, her gaze strayed to the basket of chrysanthemums. She plucked a dead bloom from the arrangement. What was she going to do about Patrick? Her emotions bounced like a volleyed tennis ball. She enjoyed his company and valued his friendship, but she feared losing both if they moved beyond what they now shared.

The shrill sound of the doorbell broke into her thoughts. The bell sounded with staccato peals. As she crossed the room, she wondered who could be in such a rush. She opened the door and stared at Leila's blotched and swollen face.

"What's wrong?"

As though her name had been a signal for action, Leila brushed past Susan and collapsed on the couch. "He... Oh, Lord, Susan...he..." A paroxysm of wild sobbing cut off her words.

Susan closed the door. What was wrong? Just the other day, her friend had mentioned a quarrel with her lover. Had it erupted again? "You don't need him."

Leila looked up. "No...no..." Her wail rose in pitch.

The loud noise beat against Susan's eardrums. She stared at her friend. Leila was always calm and in control. The hysterical cries shocked Susan. Her hands curled into fists. If Joe Barclay had appeared, she would have slammed the door in his face. "Take deep breaths and tell me what happened."

Leila responded with a fresh outburst of weeping. Her slender body curled on itself.

Susan hurried to the kitchen and wet a paper towel. What had Joe Barclay done to devastate Leila so completely? Susan returned to the living room and handed the towel to her friend.

"I'm sorry if he let you down," Susan said. "I know it's hard, but there are other men."

Leila shuddered. "You don't understand."

"How can I when you haven't told me what happened?"

"Joe's dead." Body-racking sobs followed the words. Leila leaned against the back of the couch.

For a moment, Susan had difficulty grasping the meaning of her friend's words. "Dead, oh, Leila." She sat on the couch and reached for her friend's hand. "Dead... How? The car? A heart attack?"

Leila clutched the paper towel. "Joe's dead." Her wail rose like an infant's protest at being born. "How can I live with this?"

Susan frowned. Was Leila saying she was responsible? Susan couldn't imagine any situation that would drive her friend to violent action.

"How did he die?"

"He..." Leila's body sank deeper into the cushions of the couch. She inhaled several times. "Give me a minute. I have to think...Oh lord, what am I going to do?" She rose and began to pace. "What am I going to do?"

In an attempt to penetrate the fog of repetition, Susan shouted. "What happened to Joe?"

"He's dead."

"How? Where? When?" An image of the doctor's body slumped in the passenger's seat of her car flashed in Susan's thoughts.

"In the woods behind the cabin." Leila fumbled with the buttons on her red coat. Like a splotch of fresh blood, the coat landed on the brown carpet. "He gave me this." She held out her left arm.

Susan glanced at the gold watch and shook her head. How could she break through Leila's disjointed talk? Susan wanted to know about Joe, not admire his latest present.

"Tell me about Joe."

Her friend paced from the living room to the dining room and back in a series of abrupt stops and turns. "This morning, he left to go hunting. He never tries to kill the deer. Larry does. Joe had his camera." She paused at the French doors and stared into the yard.

Tears born of frustration filled Susan's eyes. Why was Leila being so evasive? What had she done? The singsong pattern of speech and the frenzied pacing made Susan wonder if her friend was in touch with reality.

"Are you sure he's dead?"

"He left. I fell back to sleep."

Leila sounded like a child reciting a memorized piece. Susan held back an impatient scream. Any interruption might push Leila into insanity.

"I got up. I made breakfast. Eggs, toast and sausage. Joe was late..." Her voice broke on the edge of a sob. "He was late. I went to look for him."

Susan grasped her friend's shoulders. The muscles felt like taut wires. "Tell me about Joe. Please. I want to help you. Did you try to resuscitate him?"

Primitive and shrill shrieks poured from Leila. She jerked away from Susan. "How? His face. The blood. I touched it with my fingers." She pulled off her gloves and exposed bloodstained hands.

For an instant, Susan caught a glimpse of the scene in the woods and shared Leila's terror. "Who shot him?"

"I don't know. I don't know. The blood. His face. The cabin was empty. I couldn't stay. What if someone found me? Barbara was going to tell. I was afraid Joe gave her the money. Or killed her. I couldn't let anyone know I was at the cabin so I packed my things and came to you. What am I going to do?"

"Call the police." Susan inhaled a breath. Another murder. Surely not.

"I did." Leila straightened. She gulped deep breaths of air. "I couldn't leave him lying in the woods until Monday when he was expected home. There were animals. I heard them rustling in the bushes." She shook her head. "What will Mary do?"

"She has friends and family. De Witt will take care of her."

"He won't. He'll cheat her. He's not a nice person."

"What do you mean?"

"He..." She put her hands over her mouth. "I can't tell. Joe hates gossip. If I tell he'll know I did."

Susan stared at her friend. Barbara knew. Dr. Barclay knew and they were dead. Fear for her friend rushed through her thoughts.

"What am I going to do?" Leila wailed.

"You're going to pull yourself together." Those were the words Leila had said the day of Jim's funeral. The wall clock struck two. "I'm calling in sick to stay with you."

As though Leila had just realized where she was, she looked at Susan. "On a weekend? Are you crazy? I'd better go." She tried to stand but fell back on the couch.

"I can't leave you to deal with this alone."

Leila gulped a breath. "Don't worry about me. I'll handle this."

"At least stay until I leave for work."

Leila nodded. "I'll be all right. I'm tough." Tears spilled down her cheeks. "Joe and I were so right for each other."

"I know."

"Don't tell anyone I was with him this weekend." Leila grasped Susan's arm. "Oh lord, the police."

"You didn't kill him. They'll understand how you panicked and ran."

"I'm safe. I didn't give my name." Leila walked to where her coat lay. "I'll leave so you can get ready for work." Her voice trembled. "I can't believe he's dead."

Susan stared into Leila's eyes. "Are you planning to do something foolish?"

"You know me better than that." A sound midway between a sob and a laugh escaped from Leila's lips. "I'll be fine, believe me. Go get dressed. You don't want to be late."

Twenty minutes later, Susan and Leila left the house. Leila's dark eyes brimmed with unshed tears. Susan shifted the suitcases from her car to Leila's. "Why don't I stop by after work?"

"There's no need." Leila looked up. "I know you needed people around you after Jim's death. I don't. I want to remember Joe and what we had. I'll be fine."

Leila's rigid calm frightened Susan as much as the earlier hysteria. She wished she could stay at home, but there was no chance a replacement could be found at this late hour.

Leila got into her car. "Will you go to the funeral with me?"

"Should you go? What about Mary? One look at you and she'll know."

"I don't care who knows. He's dead. I have to go."

"Think of what Joe would want."

"Please go with me. I don't want to go alone."

Susan frowned. Maybe tomorrow Leila would listen. "If I get a chance, I'll call you from the hospital this evening. If not, in the morning, we'll talk about the funeral."

Leila revved the engine. As the gray car shot out of the driveway and into the street without a pause to check for traffic, Susan gasped. She's tough. She'll be all right. Susan found no comfort in those words.

Though she wanted to follow her friend, she drove to the hospital. In the parking lot, she remained in the car and stared at the sky. Tension settled between her shoulder blades.

How could she hide her prior knowledge of Joe Barclay's death when the news reached the hospital?

SUSAN LET the locker room door slam shut. She wished her fears could be closed out as easily as the noise from the hall. What could she do to help Leila? Going to the funeral might be what her friend wanted, but attendance could only add new dimensions to Leila's grief. One look at her friend's face and the secret she had tried to keep would be known.

With a sigh, Susan stared at her reflection in the mirror on the back of the door. Did her face reveal the knowledge she had to hide? Her co-workers teased her about wearing her emotions where they could be seen. Patrick often said her feelings shone in her eyes. She practiced a poker player's face and failed.

With a laugh at her posturing, she walked to the second row of lockers where the deep shadows told her one of the overhead lights had burned out. She opened the locker. A package tumbled from the shelf. Uttering a cry of surprise, she jumped back. With a thud, the package landed on the floor at her feet. She sucked in a breath. Who had left this?

As she bent to examine the brown paper bag, her eyes widened. A note was taped to the bag. She opened the envelope.

"You were so good to her. I always bought her the latest books. I hope you like them, too."

Susan swallowed. The chocolate had been wrapped in a brown paper bag. The note—Was the writing the same? She wasn't sure what she had done with it. She drew the package closer.

During the fall, a corner of the bag had torn. She saw the edge of a book. Cautiously, she peeled the sealing tape and piled the books on the floor in front of the locker. She frowned. Why had someone sent her fifteen books from the latest New York Times bestseller list? Was there a meaning behind the messages?

Or was this some kind of practical joke? Candy. Books. Julie had teased her about a secret admirer. Were these gifts an extension of the teasing and designed to make everyone believe in a covert courtship?

The locker room door slammed. Susan yelped in surprise.

Kit popped around the end of the row. "It's just me." She stared at the books. "Planning to goof off tonight?"

Susan handed a stack of books to Kit. She picked up a second stack and rose. "These were in my locker." She shoved the books on the shelf.

"Maybe someone got the wrong locker. The night nurses read a lot."

"My name was on the bag." Susan shoved the second stack on the shelf.

Kit raised an eyebrow. "Another gift. Who do you think it is?" She laughed. "Aren't many interesting men around here unless you count the doctors and I can't see one of them doing something secret. Unless he's married."

"This isn't funny."

"Then get a lock and it won't happen again."

"The candy was left at the desk." Susan pulled off her boots and slipped into her white shoes.

"Doesn't this give you the creeps?"

"Should it?" Susan looked away to keep Kit from seeing the fear in her eyes. She wouldn't admit to anyone what the gift and the notes made her feel. She shoved her boots beneath her coat. "This has to be a joke. You and Julie, maybe."

Kit's eyes widened. "Me!" She shook her head. "I wouldn't play a joke on you. Besides, this isn't a cheap game. These books are new. On my salary, they'd be used."

"Sorry."

Kit dumped the books she held in Susan's arms. "When your secret admirer starts handing out money, jewels, or furs, let me know. I'll gladly share those." She flounced away.

The door slammed. Susan leaned against her locker. Jewelry, she thought. Why had that word caught her attention? Joe Barclay had given Leila a watch. That wasn't the connection. Maybe it would surface if she didn't push. She grabbed her stethoscope and hurried down the hall. In the lounge, she poured a cup of coffee and carried it to the nurses' station.

As she passed the census board, Joe Barclay's name seemed to be printed in bold letters. A gasp caught in her throat. He was dead and Leila shattered. Susan grabbed the chart rack for District Two. She had to pretend she didn't know.

The evening began with the admission of two patients. As Susan rushed to settle them, she found herself thinking about Leila. When one of the patients spoke about her brother's sudden and tragic death, Leila's tear-swollen face flashed in Susan's thoughts. While hearing a patient with cancer of the spine cry in desperation and agony, Susan heard Leila's repetitive wail.

A third admission arrived just as two patients returned from the Recovery Room. When Susan looked at the pages of orders, she groaned. With the push for better utilization of the hospital's facilities, Saturday surgeries were becoming the norm. Rumors circulated through the hospital about the operating room being used seven days a week.

While Susan checked the charts and talked to the admitting doctors for orders on the new patients, Faye took vital signs. Three phone calls later, Susan glanced at the clock. Though the time for her dinner break had come, she needed to assess the admissions and the two post-ops.

She rushed down the hall and stopped short. "Mr. Martin, why are you here on a Saturday night?"

"I promised five days a week and since I wasn't here on Thanksgiving, I came tonight."

"Thank you. We're busier tonight than usual."

"So I noticed. Isn't it time for your dinner break? You're usually in the lounge when I arrive."

Susan nodded. "No dinner break this evening. I'll eat while I chart."

"Would you like a cup of coffee?"

"That would be wonderful."

"I'll leave it at the desk. Milk, no sugar."

Ten minutes later, she finished checking the two post-ops and introduced herself to the third admission. She returned to the desk and reached for the coffee.

Faye approached. "Mrs. Chang wants something for pain."

Susan groaned. "I had hoped to finish these orders before seven."

"If not, I'll start evening care on my own."

"Bless you," Susan said. Since the regular staff practical nurses still followed Barbara's pattern, they never began without the RN.

In the med room, Susan reached for the narcotic cabinet's alarm and saw it had been switched off. Careless, she thought. Meg will have a fit if she learns. After taking a tube of Demerol, Susan locked the cabinet and activated the alarm. While she signed the narcotic book, Julie entered.

"Aren't you supposed to be at dinner?" Several strands of fair hair strayed from the silver clip at Julie's nape to curl around her face.

"I'll eat later. I may never catch up."

"You always do. Five admissions. Kit's going crazy at the desk. Aren't you glad they're not all yours?"

"They might as well be. I've three, plus two fresh from Recovery."

"Good thing they sent Faye. If we were five like last night, the evening would be a disaster. I have three pain meds to give. Maybe I should try Trish's method."

"What's she done now?"

"Put her patients on a schedule. She passes pain meds at five and nine." Julie took the keys from Susan. "When are they going to replace Barbara?"

Susan shrugged. "Meg has to interview the candidates and she's on vacation. Maybe they won't replace her. They might try a different pattern of care delivery like they have on the Surgical unit."

Julie opened the inner door of the narcotic cabinet. A shrill noise erupted. She sucked in her lower lip. "Who turned on the alarm?"

Susan flipped the switch. "I did."

"You're right. We should keep it on, but it's so inconvenient." Julie groaned. "Wait a minute. What's he doing here?" She stabbed a syringe at the window. "Isn't it Saturday?"

Susan's gaze followed the syringe. "You mean Mr. Martin. He takes his duties as a volunteer seriously, and since he wasn't here Thursday, he came tonight."

Julie fitted the tubex into the syringe. "I guess we have to be grateful."

Susan nodded. "When he saw how rushed I am, he brought me a cup of coffee. I'm glad he's here to do water and nourishments. My patients would have been out of luck." She turned to leave.

"Could I talk to you for a minute?"

"Problems?"

Julie blew a strand of hair that had strayed to touch the corner of her mouth. "Sort of. How can you love a man and not trust him?"

"De Witt?"

Julie nodded. "It's just...just...last night, he talked about doing something that's not...not right." She sighed. "It's kind of hard to explain."

"Are you sure you want to?"

Julie slumped against the counter. "I'm not sure what I want to do about anything. He's been pushing me to apply for the position that's opening on days."

"I don't see any reason you won't get it. I'm not ready for days. Trish prefers evenings. There's no one on nights who has more seniority than you do who might want to switch."

Julie fastened the keys around her slender waist. "I'm thinking about grad school. Evenings are best for that."

Susan looked at the clock. "Why don't we stop at the diner after work, or do you have a date?"

"No date. Larry's having dinner with his aunt. His uncle's away."

Susan stared at the floor. She couldn't reveal her knowledge.

"He's staying for bridge," Julie continued. "That's one game I'll never understand."

"Makes two of us. I'll rush to get done on time so I won't keep you waiting."

The door of the med room slammed against the wall. Susan turned.

De Witt strode in and closed the door. "Julie, we have to talk."

Julie crossed to him. "What happened? Where did you go last night?"

"Uncle Joe's dead."

Julie's hands dropped to her sides. "Why, Larry? Was that where you went? How did it happen?"

Susan edged past the refrigerator. Was Julie accusing De Witt of being responsible for Dr. Barclay's death? Was this what the younger nurse had tried to tell her just moments ago?

De Witt grabbed Julie's shoulders. "It was a hunting accident. Of all the times for this to happen."

"What are you talking about?"

Susan silently echoed Julie's exclamation. She eased along the wall where a window looked into the station.

"The practice. My plans. Aunt Mary will have to sell the practice. Where am I going to get that kind of money?"

"Why worry about that now?" Julie asked. "When did you learn he died?"

"This...afternoon. I stopped to check on my aunt and took the call from the police upstate. They said he had an accident. Since she couldn't go, I drove up and discovered he was dead. I don't know what I'm going to tell her."

Julie's mouth gaped. "You haven't told her yet? What were you doing all this time?"

"Um... Nothing that matters. It's a long drive. I had to go to the cabin to see if anything was missing. You know, his female companion didn't leave a trace."

"Did you tell the police who she was?"

He looked away. "What purpose would that serve? How am I going to break the news?"

Susan whirled. "Your aunt's probably frantic."

He glared. "What are you doing here?"

Julie caught his arm. "She's right. You've got to go to your aunt."

He shook his head. "We need to talk first."

"I'm busy."

"Just for a few minutes. We'll go to the lounge. We have to talk without an audience." He grabbed Julie's arm. "I need your help."

His selfish attitude made Susan itch to slap him. Didn't he care that his invalid aunt was alone and probably worried sick? Julie stroked his arm as though she soothed a fretful child. What was wrong with her? Not long ago, she had questioned her faith in him. Didn't she see she was being manipulated?

Susan stepped into the station. Her shoulder muscles tensed. The anger in De Witt's eyes and his rigid stance frightened her. She could imagine him battering Barbara. She could picture him shooting his uncle. Would he remember all the things he'd said before he realized she was there?

"Susan, could you medicate my patients," Julie called. "The list is on the counter."

Before Susan had a chance to refuse, Julie dashed after De Witt.

"What's the matter?" Kit drawled. "Did the lovebirds have a quarrel?"

Susan sucked in a breath. The news had arrived and the need for secrecy had vanished.

"Well." Trish tapped her foot in an impatient beat against the carpet.

"Dr. Barclay was killed in a hunting accident this morning."

The chart Trish held dropped and hit the edge of the desk. The contents spread across the dark green carpet. "What amazing luck. Trust De Witt to come up with another prize."

Susan stooped and picked up some of the papers. "What do you mean?"

"This isn't the first time he's been in the right place at the right time to benefit from someone's bad luck. That's how he became chief resident."

Kit rose from her chair at the desk. "Did I hear right? Is Dr. Barclay dead? What happened? Tell me everything you know."

"Very little," Susan said. "There was a hunting accident upstate."

Kit flipped her red hair back. "Come on, give. Tell me more."

Susan clenched her teeth. "That's all I heard." She walked away. Let Kit discover the details from another source.

The three practical nurses gathered at the desk. Kit edged between them. "Did you hear? Barclay's dead. That's all Susan knows, but I know where we can learn more."

"Kit," Susan said. "Let Julie and De Witt alone." She saw the stack of charts on the secretary's desk. "Finish the orders first."

Kit flounced back to her chair. "Some people were born without curiosity."

Susan hurried down the hall to Mrs. Chang's room and gave the medication. As she returned to the station, she encountered Mr. Martin.

"Such dreadful news," he said. "Are they sure Dr. Barclay had an accident?"

Susan continued walking. "I'm afraid I don't know what happened."

He trailed her. "What will his patients do?"

"I'm sure Dr. De Witt will keep the office open." Susan reached the station and entered the med room. Before she continued her own work, she had to find Julie's list.

Mr. Martin stood at the door. "I noticed on the schedule in the lounge that you're off next Saturday. Would you like to go to dinner with me?"

Susan tried to think of a way to discourage him without hurting his feelings. Then she remembered Patrick's invitation. "I have plans. Maybe another time." She closed the door and picked up Julie's list. She groaned. The younger nurse had the keys around her waist. Susan walked to the lounge, knocked and opened the door.

Julie turned. Tears glistened in her eyes. Her mouth twisted into an angry grimace. "Do you need me?"

"Just the keys."

De Witt leaned against the wall near the windows. Susan glanced at him. What had he said that upset Julie?

WHEN THE door closed behind Susan, Julie's shoulders slumped. She refastened the silver clip at her nape. "I won't lie."

"Then say what you want. It's no big deal."

"You want me to tell anyone who asks that I spent the night with you. I want to know why."

"Because it's the truth. You were at my place and in my bed. You might never be asked. When the police upstate asked me, your name just slipped out."

"But you lied." Hot tears ran down her cheeks.

"Not exactly. If you hadn't taken off so early, you could have had coffee and doughnuts with me. I slipped out to buy them. Why did you leave?"

Was he telling the truth? Her trust in him had dissipated like wisps of fog. "Because one of the rifles was missing from your study and you talked about going hunting...I'm so confused I don't know what to think. I can't be with you again until my head's straight."

He walked toward her. "Remember how it was between us last night, little bird."

"Wonderful and exciting." Julie raised her chin. "Did you go to your uncle's cabin? I need to know the truth."

"I didn't kill him." He narrowed the gap between them.

"I'd like to believe that."

He put his hand on her shoulder. "Okay, I went to the cabin, but armed with my camera. I'll even show you the pictures I took when they're developed. Don't you see? I did this for us."

Julie closed her eyes. "The rifle."

"Went out for repairs weeks ago."

Had it been? She seldom went into his study. He could be telling the truth. She stepped back. The edge of the bulletin board jabbed her. She loved him, but she wasn't sure she believed him. "It's the same thing. You were planning on blackmail. I can't trust a man who would do that."

Gently, he massaged her shoulders. "I know it was a stupid idea, but I wanted all the things a partnership would bring us." He touched her hair. "Look, little bird, I know the practice isn't important. You are and how you feel about me."

"Please. Give me a few days, a week. I need to sort through my feelings."

His lips brushed her cheek. "You're mine. I'll never get enough of you."

Could she believe him? She wanted to send him away. She wanted him to stay. He pulled her close. When his lips met hers, the few seconds of hating herself for being weak vanished.

He stepped back. His fingers stroked her throat. "You're right. Blackmail was a bad idea." He kissed the tip of her nose. "Little bird, with you around, I'll be fine."

Julie looked away. Why did his kisses always make her forget how much their values differed? "You'd better go to your aunt. She'll need you."

He put his arm around her shoulders. "The apartment when you're finished here. The terrace door. I need you."

"I—"

The door closed behind him. Julie leaned against the wall. She had to think. Could she believe him?

TRISH STOOD in the hall outside the lounge. Maybe she should go in and congratulate De Witt on his good fortune. Some people, she thought. During his last year in the residency program at the city hospital where they had worked, the chief medical resident had been injured in an automobile accident. De Witt had stepped into the position. Now he would inherit a lucrative practice.

Her foot tapped against the carpet. Would he brush her off the way he had the last time she'd approached him? With just a few words she could ruin his future prosperity.

The lounge door opened. De Witt strode out and rammed into her. She stumbled backward and would have fallen except for the hands that caught and steadied her.

"Watch where you're going," De Witt snapped. He strode down the hall.

"Miss Fallon, have you the injury? Did he hurt your foot?" Dr. Mendoza asked.

"I'm fine." She stared after De Witt.

"Why did he not stop? He has no politeness."

"Most of the time I'd say you were right, but he received some tragic news today."

"How so?"

"His uncle, Dr. Barclay, was killed today."

"Was he murdered like the fat nurse?"

Trish shook her head. "Why would you think that?"

He shrugged. "Is it not said one violent death breeds another?"

"He was killed in a hunting accident."

"Then I will not change my opinion. How easy it would be to make the shooting in the forest seem like an accident."

"You could be right." Trish linked arms with Mendoza. They walked around the nourishment cart. "De Witt could have killed his uncle. He's a crack shot and collects guns and hunting trophies."

Mendoza laughed. "I thought he only hunted the deer with two legs."

"He does that, too." Trish entered a patient's room.

AT ELEVEN-THIRTY, Susan sat at the desk to give report to the night nurse. Julie slung her purse over her shoulder and left the station. "Be right back." Susan followed the younger nurse. "Julie."

The fair-haired nurse turned. "Susan, sorry. I know we had plans to go to the diner, but Larry needs me."

"What if he's still with his aunt?"

"I'll wait. The terrace door will be open. I always use it."

"Oh?"

"You have to sign a guest book if you use the front entrance. He says he doesn't want his guests to feel they're visiting a prison."

Susan frowned. Or he doesn't want a record of his visitors. Julie walked away. Though Susan wanted to caution the younger nurse, she didn't know how. Was Julie afraid of losing De Witt if she wasn't on call when he needed her? She wished Julie could see what she was doing to herself. Susan walked back to the station. This wasn't her problem.

A short time later, Susan finished report and walked to the lounge to call Leila. Two earlier calls had gone unanswered. They needed to talk about Leila's determination to attend the funeral.

Susan dialed the familiar number. After twelve rings, she hung up. Where was Leila? Why didn't she answer? Susan swallowed. The icy calm that had followed the hysterics this afternoon troubled Susan. As she put on her coat and boots, she wondered what she should do.

When the security guard left her at her car, she knew she couldn't sleep until she was sure her friend was all right. Ten minutes later, Susan pulled into the driveway of Leila's ranch house. Lights shone from the kitchen window. The rest of the house was dark.

For several minutes, Susan sat in the car and wondered what to do. Finally, she walked to the front porch. Her finger stabbed the bell with the same impatience as Leila's had done that morning. After a short period, Susan realized the bell wasn't sounding in the house. She rapped on the door.

There was no answer so she walked to the side of the house and peered into an empty kitchen. Through the window, she could see into the family room. Bright lights burned. The television flickered. Before she had time to walk to the patio door, Leila entered the kitchen.

Feeling like a peeping Tom, Susan backed away from the window and hurried to her car. Why had she come? Leila wanted to be alone.

When Susan reached home, the lights on Patrick's side of the house beckoned. More scary movies, she wondered. Last night, she had watched one scene before escaping to the grocery store.

She paused on the porch and considered her options. The desire to be part of a family would have to remain unsatisfied tonight. Patrick would sense her uneasiness and she would tell him about Leila and Joe. His curiosity might elicit answers she didn't want to give.

Chapter 6

ON SUNDAY morning, at a few minutes before nine, Patrick left the house. He walked across the porch to Susan's side and studied the clump of rhododendrons beside the porch. Last evening, Robin had chased Adam into the thicket. Patrick wanted to see how much damage they had done. As he strode down the side steps, the glint of sunlight on metal momentarily blinded him.

He edged into the cluster, squatted and stared at a small handgun. How long had the derringer been here? Last spring, he had removed the debris from beneath the bushes. The gun hadn't been there then. With a tissue, he lifted the pistol and wrapped it in several more before dropping the packet into his jacket pocket.

Should he mention the gun to Susan? Jim had been avidly anti-gun and Patrick couldn't imagine Susan owning one. He returned to the porch. He should report this to the police, but who? Several years ago, he would have called any number of men, but since becoming Arts and Leisure editor for the News, he had lost touch with the local police. He rolled names in his thoughts. Then he went inside and picked up the phone.

"Jane, it's Pat Macleith... Yes, I know it's been ages...Is Greg around?" He leaned against the counter. "He has... I'll try to catch him there... I know... Soon."

Instead of walking as he had planned, Patrick jumped into his car. Uptown, he found a parking space across from the News Shop.

"Pat... Pat Macleith," a deep voice called.

Patrick saw Greg Davies standing outside the shop. He crossed the street and slapped his friend's hand. "Just the person I wanted to see." Greg was one of the few men who made Patrick feel small. There was little difference in their heights, but Greg outweighed Patrick by fifty pounds and tons of energy.

"Planning a crime?" Greg asked.

Patrick didn't want to pull the gun out on the street. "Not these days. What's new at the cop shop?"

"The usual. A lot of crime and little punishment. Some days, all we do is spin."

The wind beat against Patrick's back. "Coffee?"

"Why not?" Greg grinned. "How's the editing business? I can't imagine you hanging with an artsy crowd."

"They're no different from most people."

Greg walked facing Patrick. "Are you still friends with Susan Randall? Met her Monday night at the hospital. A very pretty lady."

Patrick turned to open the coffee shop door. "She's my landlady. How's the family?"

"Turning me into a pauper. Two in college and two to go. Just wait. Your turn's coming. We miss you at the shop. Sometimes you saw things we missed."

Patrick chose an empty booth across from the long counter and signaled the waitress. "I miss you guys but not the hours."

When Patrick had covered the police beat for the News, his hours had been long and erratic. Though he had made the rounds of the village stations, more of his work had been with the town detectives. Greg was one of them.

The waitress slid two cups of coffee across the table. Greg opened four packets of sugar. Patrick raised an eyebrow. "What happened to the diet?"

"Sugar in my coffee is my only treat. This is my first cup of the day." Greg added milk and stirred. "What does your friend say about the Denton woman?"

"Very little. She's worried one of her coworkers is the killer."

"Any particular one?"

Patrick shook his head. "She's not talking about her suspicions. She just wants the case solved and for things to get back to normal."

Greg placed a folded napkin in the saucer to blot the overflow of coffee. "So do we. Do me a favor. Ask her what she knows about Dr. Barclay."

Patrick's brow wrinkled. "Is that the Dr. Barclay who's so involved in local charities?"

"The same, only it was. Read your paper. Not the Times, but the rag you work for. The doctor was killed upstate yesterday. A hunting accident."

"A suspicious one?"

"Aren't all hunting accidents, especially when no one owns up?" Greg reached for his coffee. "An old buddy's on the force up there. Asked me to nose around a bit. Seems some woman who wasn't the doctor's wife was at the cabin. She reported the accident."

"Do they think she's the one?"

Greg shook his head. "No sign there'd been a rifle at his cabin. Also, they found a dead deer several hundred yards from his body. They figure someone wounded the deer and chased it onto the doctor's property. They shot again and hit the doctor instead of the deer. When he yelled, the hunter panicked and ran."

"What do you want from Susan?"

"The name of the woman. Surely it's common knowledge at the hospital. I've got a feeling about this one."

"I'll ask her, but I'm not sure she'll say much." Patrick reached for his jacket. "I called your house this morning and hurried here to catch you." He removed the tissue-wrapped gun and pushed it across the table. "Take a look at this. Found it in a clump of bushes at the house."

Greg unwrapped the derringer. "Couldn't have been there long. Too clean. Any robberies in the neighborhood?"

"Not that I know of."

"I'll check." Greg looked up. "Good lord, it's loaded. Why did you carry it in your pocket without checking?"

"Though I covered the crime desk, what do I know about guns?"

"Evidently very little." Greg frowned. "This looks almost old and clean enough to have come from someone's collection. There's an antique gun dealer in town. I'll drop by his place. Maybe he can dig up something."

"Let me know what you learn." Patrick lifted his coffee cup. "Makes one wonder if this is connected to the Denton woman's murder."

Greg leaned forward. "How so?"

"Maybe the killer was hanging around when Susan found the body and is afraid she saw something. Somehow, he could have discovered where she lives and come after her."

"Could have been a woman. One of her coworkers."

"I don't think so."

Greg chuckled. "The artsy world has certainly stimulated your imagination. I wish she *had* seen something. We've next to nothing to go on, not even the weapon." He signaled for a refill.

An hour and several cups of coffee later, Patrick arrived home. He crossed the porch and rang Susan's bell. She opened the door. "I'm on the phone. Be with you in a few."

Patrick unzipped his black ski jacket. The swaying movements of the light brown caftan drew a silent whistle. How much longer could he wait before making a move? He dropped his jacket on the couch and followed her.

"Tuesday at ten... I don't think you should go. Why put yourself in what could be an awkward position... I know you loved him... Look, I have company. I'd rather wait until we have time to discuss the funeral. I'll call you back." She hung up and turned to face Patrick. "Coffee?"

Patrick straddled a chair. "Only if you join me. I've a couple of questions to ask you."

"Sounds serious." She filled two mugs and carried them to the table.

"Curiosity. What's the gossip at the hospital about Dr. Barclay's death?"

"I didn't hear any last night."

"Not even about the woman at his cabin?"

"No." She looked away, but not before he saw a hint of panic in her eyes. "I heard there was one." She turned a mug in slow circles on the table. "His nephew dates Julie. He came to tell her about his uncle's death and he mentioned the woman."

Patrick reached across the table and put his hand over hers. "I think you know more."

"She had nothing to do with his death."

"I'm not looking for a story. She might have noticed something. There was a delay in finding the body. I ran into Greg Davies this morning. The police upstate have to view this as a murder until they learn differently. Tell her to call Greg."

Susan studied the table. "She loved him. The fewer who know about them, the less gossip there'll be. She needs time to grieve so she can get on with her life."

Patrick squeezed her hand. "Try."

"I will." For several minutes, Patrick savored the coffee. Should he tell her about the gun he had found in the yard? Since he didn't want to frighten her, he decided to wait until he heard from Greg.

He looked up. "You never answered me about dinner and the concert next Saturday."

"I'd like to go."

"Great. We'll do something your next weekend off, too."

"Let's see what happens Saturday before you plan my life."

He caught a note of annoyance in her voice and knew he had jumped ahead too far, too fast. "I didn't mean...Actually, I guess I did. There's an Arts Council Gala coming soon. There'll be great food and dancing."

"I'm sure there are dozens of women you could ask."

The only one he wanted was seated across the table. "Just how long has it been since you went dancing?"

"Don't ask. You know how Jim hated loud music and crowds."

The living room clock chimed. As Patrick counted them, he rose. "I'd better go. I left the twins asleep but that was nearly two hours ago. I'll send them over with turkey quiche for your dinner."

"And for a few minutes peace," she teased. "Their energy level amazes me. I covered more territory on Friday than in one week at work."

"Did Adam bug you about the Denton woman?"

"Robin, too. I told them what I saw and said that was all they'd hear from me."

Patrick raised an eyebrow. "And they listened?"

"Of course."

"You have a knack I must learn." He saluted. "See you."

SUSAN CARRIED her coffee to the living room. Talk to Leila, Patrick had said. Ask her to call the police. An effort in futility. Leila would never call Greg Davies for fear the affair would be revealed. A sudden thought occurred and brought a frisson of fear. What if Leila was in danger? She knew about the problem between De Witt and Joe Barclay. So had Barbara. Susan sucked in a breath. This fact turned Leila's determination to attend the funeral into a dangerous decision. She should call her friend, but she needed to marshal her arguments first.

Susan curled on the couch and picked up the local newspaper. The headline produced a groan. "Local Doctor Shooting Victim." The story began in an equally aggravating way. "A second member of the staff at Bradley Memorial Hospital died violently yesterday. Dr. Joseph Barclay was possibly murdered at his hunting cabin upstate."

Though the reporter went on to clarify that hunting accidents were listed as manslaughter, the intent seemed the same. In the second paragraph, Susan read about Joe Barclay's position in the community and his wife's illness. The third paragraph was full of speculations about the woman who had reported the death. The words brought an uncomfortable feeling. She hoped Leila would read the article and change her mind about the funeral.

The story ended with a statement that disturbed Susan. "Though the police have stated that while the doctor's death was a tragic accident, there is a common denominator between his death and that of Barbara Denton — the hospital."

And with De Witt, Susan thought.

She crushed the paper and jumped to her feet. She had to call Leila. Before she reached the kitchen, the doorbell rang. She opened the door. Adam and Robin burst inside.

"Hi, Aunt Susan," they said in unison.

Robin handed Susan a plastic container. "Your dinner. Dad said you're not to forget it this time."

"Don't you ever get tired of working nearly every evening?" Adam asked.

"Sometimes."

Robin smoothed the paper. "Dad got upset, too. He said he wouldn't have handled the story this way. Did you know the doctor, too?"

"Not very well."

Adam pulled off his jacket. "A hunting accident isn't nearly as exciting as a murder. I'm starved. All Dad has are cereal, eggs and turkey. We have to go shopping. Do you have any of those chocolate chip cookies you always make?"

"In the freezer. I'll zap a few in the microwave." Susan walked to the kitchen. Once the twins were settled at the table with milk and cookies, she refilled her coffee mug and joined them.

"Do you think Dad will like the sweater and shirt we bought him?" Robin asked.

"I still think we should have gotten Rob something different," Adam said.

"Like that expensive golf club Mom suggested?" Robin asked.

Adam looked at Susan. "She always wants us to treat him better than Dad. Except Dad's the one who buys things for us." He deepened his voice. "You should be grateful for the roof over your head and the food you eat."

Robin made a face. "Is it wrong to love your dad more than your stepfather?"

"Especially when he thinks you're a pain?" Adam added.

Susan put her mug down. "You know it's not. Are you sure Rob doesn't like you?"

"He's different when Mom's around." Adam reached for the last cookie on the plate. "These are great. Mom doesn't bake cookies."

His wistful smile made Susan grin. "I'll give you the rest to take home."

Adam eyed the bag. "Thanks. I wish we lived with Dad. Then we could come for cookies every day."

Robin sat on the edge of the chair. "I have a better idea. Why don't you and Dad get married? Then we could come and live with you. I think Rob would be glad to get rid of us."

"That would be great but we wouldn't want Aunt Susan to marry Dad just because she was sorry for us."

Susan walked to the sink. The twins were as bad as their father about making plans for her future. "Your dad and I are friends." She handed Robin the bag of cookies. "I'll see you the next time you come to visit."

"Will you spend Christmas with us?" Robin asked.

"If I'm invited."

"You will be. We'll tell him he has to," Adam said. "Thanks for the cookies."

Susan closed the door behind them. She needed to talk to Patrick about the things the twins had said. Maybe concern for his children would divert him from wanting to arrange her life.

As she walked upstairs to iron uniforms for the week, she grinned. Why did she feel the pair had just manipulated her?

The smile faded. She had to call Leila and convince her to stay away from Joe Barclay's funeral. The phone rang. She dashed up the rest of the stairs and picked up the phone in the master bedroom.

"Have you seen the newspapers?" Leila's voice rang shrill. "How do they get away with saying things like that?"

"Calm down. Your name wasn't mentioned."

"You know how everyone at the hospital will react when they read this."

"With gossip and speculation about the identity of the woman." Susan let out a breath. "Now do you understand why you can't go to the funeral? One look at you and everyone will know you're the woman. Do you want people thinking you killed him?"

For a long time, Leila didn't answer. Susan hoped her comment had reached her friend.

"I have to go. I have to tell him goodbye."

Susan slumped on the bed. "Think of your future. Joe's dead. Attending the funeral won't change that."

"I'll think about what you've said. Talk to you tomorrow."

The phone went dead. Susan opened the ironing board. Would

Leila listen?

GENTLY, HE placed the pine grave blanket over the place where Mommy slept. Should be roses, he thought, but the cold would kill them. For a long time, he stared at the grave. Mommy was alone, but Susan would join her soon. In his head, he heard Mammy's protests, but he refused to heed them. Susan had to be like Mommy.

He had his plans. The seeds of the plan sown on the Overlook had sprung to life today. This morning, he had found the perfect place to lie in wait for her. How easy the matter had become once he had decided what to do.

"You like Susan," he whispered. "You told me that. Won't it be nice when she's there to take care of you?"

A smile turned the corners of his mouth upward. His laughter shattered the silence of the cemetery.

ON TUESDAY evening at six thirty, Susan entered the nurses' lounge and stopped just inside the door. Leila huddled in a chair at the round table and stared at the window. Susan caught her lower lip with her teeth. The depth of her friend's grief touched and made her feel helpless.

"I tried to call you this morning." Susan crossed to the credenza.

Leila turned. Unshed tears glistened in her dark eyes. Carefully applied makeup couldn't hide the shadows beneath her eyes. "You were right. I shouldn't have gone." She lit a cigarette.

Susan's protest remained unspoken. She couldn't scold Leila today. "I wish I could help you."

Leila shook her head. "I'm glad you didn't go. One word of sympathy and I would have fallen apart."

"What happened?"

"Nothing overt." Leila tapped her cigarette against the edge of a saucer. "Mary looked frightened. I didn't speak to her. She would have known."

Susan nodded. "I'm glad you realized that."

"De Witt stood behind her wheelchair looking like a palace guard. You should have seen the way he glared. Made me feel like a tax form being scrutinized by the IRS."

Susan studied her hands. She didn't tell Leila that De Witt knew she'd been at the cabin. "Did you stay for the service?"

Leila shook her head. "I had to leave before I broke down. I didn't even get to see him. The casket was closed. It took me twenty minutes after I left to calm down enough to drive home."

"I know how hard it must have been." Susan touched Leila's hand. "Have you slept since he died?"

"I've slept."

Susan studied her friend's face. "I'm not sure I believe you."

"Two sleepers and several gin and tonics give me three or four hours a night."

"Leila! Do you realize how dangerous that is?" Susan's warning exploded in a shout.

"I know, but I'm careful. I've moved to the family room to sleep. There are too many memories in the bedroom."

Susan recalled her own long and lonely nights. "I slept in the guest room for months after Jim died."

As soon as Leila's cigarette burned to the end, she lit another. She took a deep drag and placed the cigarette on the saucer. Smoke curled toward the ceiling. "I think De Witt knows about Joe and me."

"How?"

Leila shook her head. "I have no idea. He glared and smirked at the same time."

"Do you think he'll make trouble?"

Leila shook her head. "I can make more for him."

Susan leaned forward. "Maybe you should go to the police and tell them what you know."

Leila shook her head. "Joe's dead. I have to protect his memory." She carried the saucer to the powder room. "Back to work. Thank heavens for routine. That's what keeps me going."

Susan understood the sentiment. Routine had been her shield for a long time. "I'll call you in the morning. Maybe we'll go to lunch."

"I'll be all right."

The sharp edge in Leila's voice honed Susan's concern. "Take care of yourself, please."

Leila touched Susan's arm. "I'll be fine. Just give me time."

Though Leila's attempt to smile failed, the gesture warmed Susan. Her friend walked away. Rounded shoulders made her appear old.

Trish stepped out of a patient's room. "What's with Leila? She looks like a puppet whose strings have been cut."

"She has some personal problems."

"Don't we all. Speaking of which..." Trish turned. "When you have a few minutes, could we...could you...oh, forget it."

"Is something wrong?"

Trish's bony shoulders hunched. "I thought I was ready to talk, but I'm not. Maybe some other time." She pivoted and entered the room she had just left.

Susan frowned. After evening care, she would find an excuse to pull the other nurse aside for a talk. Did Trish's problems have anything to do with Barbara's death? Did the other nurse know something about the killer? After pushing her questions aside, Susan walked to her district and found Faye.

"Why don't you start at one end and I'll begin at the other?" Faye asked. "There's no one requiring heavy care and if I have a problem, I'll call you. For pin care, it's peroxide and sterile swabs?"

"That's right." Susan grabbed two draw sheets and walked into 501. The moment she entered, she knew there was a problem. The elderly woman in the first bed sat in an upright position and grasped the side rail. Pain contorted her features. Drops of perspiration dotted her forehead and ran down her cheeks.

"Mrs. Greene, what's wrong?"

"My chest. The pain." The elderly woman gasped for breath.

Susan elevated the head of the bed. Four days before, Mrs. Greene had a hip pinning. Because of her obesity, she ambulated poorly. The day nurse also reported the patient's refusal to practice deep breathing exercises. As Susan began an assessment, she considered the possible complications.

"I need to know about the pain. Does it hurt all the time?" Mrs. Greene shook her head. "Is the pain worse when you breathe in or out?"

"In."

"Does it move to your arm or chin?"

"No."

Susan pressed the bell of her stethoscope to Mrs. Greene's back and heard a crackling noise in the lower right lung. When Susan checked the elderly woman's legs, the right calf was red, swollen and hot.

"What's wrong?" The patient convulsively grasped Susan's arm. "Am I going to be all right?"

Susan wiped the woman's forehead. "I won't let anything happen to you. I'll have the house doctor come to check you. You'll soon be more comfortable." Before Susan left the room, she took a series of vital signs. She strode to the desk.

Kit looked up. "There's a problem. I can tell by the look on your face. A bad one?"

"It could be. Call the house doctor. Mrs. Greene in 501 has chest pain. Put in a call to her medical doctor."

"Will do." Kit groaned. "De Witt's her doctor. He doesn't like the house staff to see his patients."

"I don't care," Susan said. "We can't wait for his service to locate him. If he has a problem with my actions, refer him to me. Don't let him bully you."

Susan dashed down the hall. When she located Faye, she called the practical into the hall. "I'll be with Mrs. Greene in 501."

"Do you want me to come? Will there be a code?"

Susan shook her head. "My guess is a pulmonary emboli. Once treatment is initiated, we may have to transfer her to ICU. She's anxious and tachycardic. Right now, she needs reassurance."

"Go," said Faye. "I'll manage. If I need help, I'll grab one of the others."

Susan hurried to 501. Mrs. Greene shifted her position in a restless dance. Her eyes were wide. Tears spilled down her cheeks. "I'm dying." She held out a tissue. "See. Blood."

Small flecks of red dotted the tissue. Susan reached for the elderly woman's hand. "I know you're frightened but it's important for you to remain calm. Looks like blood, but it could be the cranberry juice you drank earlier." She pointed to the empty container on the bedside stand.

Mrs. Greene slumped against the raised head of the bed. A shadow crossed the sheets.

Susan turned. "Mrs. Greene, this is Dr. Mendoza. He'll check you and begin treatment. Your doctor's been called." She patted the patient's hand. "I'm going to tell the doctor what happened. If I forget anything, let me know."

With a minimum of detail, Susan described Mrs. Greene's symptoms and what the assessment had revealed. A brief history of the patient's surgery and the course of her recovery followed.

Dr. Mendoza examined Mrs. Greene and nodded. "Get the arterial blood gases, EKG, partial prothrombin time and prothrombin time, cardiac enzymes and portable chest X-ray. You should start the intravenous of 5 percent dextrose in water at thirty cc's an hour. Oxygen at five liters and give the sixth of morphine for pain."

Susan noted the orders on a piece of paper. Before leaving the room, she read them back. At the desk, she handed the paper to Kit. "Make the ABG's, blood work, EKG and chest X-ray stat. Have you heard from De Witt?"

"His service paged him. They're waiting for a call back." Kit reached for the phone. "I called her orthopod. He said to let De Witt handle the treatment."

When Susan returned to the room with the morphine and the intravenous, the respiratory therapist was leaving. An oxygen cannula was in place. Mrs. Greene's color had improved. The lab technical drew blood. Susan gave the injection and started the IV. When the EKG technician arrived, Susan scooted to the desk. "Have you reached De Witt?"

"Just talked to him. He'll be here in twenty minutes or so. I asked if he wanted to talk to you and he didn't. Here are the ABG results."

Susan looked at the clock. Forty-five minutes had passed since she had discovered Mrs. Greene in distress. "Did you tell him what had been ordered?"

"Didn't get that far. When he heard Mendoza was with the patient, he exploded." Kit grinned. "I won't repeat what he said. Looks like there'll be an interesting scene ahead."

Susan inhaled. "If he creates a scene, notify the supervisor immediately." She strode away. Kit's eager anticipation of trouble made Susan want to slap the girl.

Outside 501, Susan paused to take a series of calming breaths. She hoped De Witt would maintain a professional attitude in the patient's presence. Susan handed the blood gas results to Mendoza. He studied the paper and put it on the over-bed table.

The X-ray technician guided the portable machine into the room. After positioning the patient, Susan retreated to the hall and joined Mendoza. "What does the strip show?" she asked. "From the gases, I'd say an emboli."

"You are absolutely correct. Would you call the laboratory for the blood work results? I would like to see the baseline first, but I think you should give the patient ten thousand units of heparin by the push. Then order the lung scan."

Susan nodded. "De Witt's on his way in. Would you like to hold the heparin until he arrives?"

Mendoza shrugged. "He will complain if I do nothing or something. We will act for the patient. The tests will support my actions. The pulmonary emboli can be dangerous. The patient, she is lucky to have you for the nurse."

"Thank you." Susan smiled. Compliments from Mendoza were

rare. "What schedule do you want for the heparin boluses or do you want a continuous drip?"

"De Witt will tell you when he arrives. I must take the chart and write the orders I have said."

Susan rooted through the drawers in her med cart until she found a vial of heparin. After withdrawing the ordered dose, she checked the emergency tray for the antidote. She paused in the doorway of 501, and for a moment, observed Mrs. Greene. The elderly woman's respiration had slowed and her expression revealed her anxiety had decreased.

The patient stared at the syringe in Susan's hand. "What's that?" Her voice tightened.

"Did Dr. Mendoza explain your problem?" The elderly woman nodded. "This medicine will help your body dissolve the blood clots and prevent new ones from forming."

"Won't I bleed too much?"

"We'll check your blood levels frequently." Susan smiled. "I have an antidote that works in minutes." She wiped the injection port on the IV tubing and pinched off the clear plastic to prevent back flow. "Let me know if this burns and I'll stop the push."

"If what burns, Mrs. Randall?"

Susan turned her head and saw De Witt. "A loading dose of heparin." As she spoke, she slowly depressed the plunger. "Nearly an hour ago, Mrs. Greene complained of chest pain."

"Who wrote the orders?" His words were clipped.

"Dr. Mendoza."

The blond doctor whirled and left the room. Susan completed the push and remained to make Mrs. Greene comfortable. Before she returned to the nurses' station, she straightened the bed of the second patient. When she stepped into the hall, the sound of two male voices raised in anger caused her to hurry to the desk.

De Witt stood beside the doctors' desk. "Why did you initiate treatment? You should have known I'd come."

"Did you not have the funeral for your uncle today?" Mendoza asked. "Mrs. Randall could not be sure how soon you could be reached. It has been one hour since she called for me."

"My service knew where I was. You should have waited for all the test results including the lung scan before starting treatment."

Mendoza rose. "I do not agree. The complaints of the patient, the assessment of the nurse and myself and my own examination were enough." He thrust the EKG strip and the lab slips at De Witt. "You will read these and know I was right."

De Witt grabbed the chart. "She's my patient. I'll order treatment."

Mendoza stepped back. "I will miss your uncle. He was a gentleman and a good doctor. When this patient returned from surgery, he would have ordered the prophylactic doses of heparin. The weight, the age, the immobility make this necessary. I am thinking the wrong doctor is dead and I am believing he did not have the accident."

Susan strode to the doctors' desk. "Gentlemen, this is not the time and place for this discussion."

Mendoza nodded. "Mrs. Randall, you are correct. My apologies."

"Not so fast," De Witt said. "What did you mean by your last crack?"

"The nurse says you shoot a gun real good."

"One of these days, you'll push that white Porsche too fast and it'll be all over." De Witt whirled to face Susan. He raised a hand as though he planned to hit her. "Just what do you know about my shooting ability?"

"Nothing and I never mentioned them." She turned to Mendoza for confirmation but the house doctor had left.

"Just make sure you don't or you'll be sorry." De Witt tucked the chart under his arm. "From now on, no house doctor to see any of my patients. Do I make myself clear?"

"I'll inform the supervisor." Susan walked to Kit. "Let Ms. Vernon know about Dr. De Witt's latest order."

Kit's eyes danced with excitement. "Told you there'd be sparks."

"You should have called the supervisor the instant they started. What's wrong with you tonight?"

"Sorry, but De Witt jumped Mendoza before I knew what was happening. Good thing Julie's off. What would she think of her hero if she had seen him? Wait until I tell her."

Susan hurried to find Faye. A good thing Julie was off. Though the younger nurse would have seen another side of De Witt, Susan wasn't sure Julie would have recognized that De Witt had been in the wrong. In Julie's eyes, the man was perfect.

Chapter 7

THE NEXT afternoon when Susan arrived in the lounge, the atmosphere crackled with hostility. She tried to catch the door before her retreat was blocked but her attempt to escape failed.

Julie stood in the middle of the room with her hands on her hips. "I don't want to hear your opinions. You're making this up."

In a pose reminiscent of Barbara, Kit lounged on the loveseat. Trish moved from the window. "He's using you," she said. "He always finds some innocent to corrupt. Back off before you get hurt."

"You're jealous," Julie said. "Just because he dropped you doesn't mean he'll do the same to me."

"Jealousy is the furthest thing from my mind. You have no idea about the wonderful experiences he'll induce you into sharing, except he cheats."

"Name one."

"You wouldn't want to know."

Kit undulated from the loveseat. "It's a good thing you weren't here last night. De Witt raked Mendoza but good when the man hadn't done a thing except give excellent care to a patient. He was way out of line."

"I don't want to hear this," Julie said.

"Susan was there. I thought he was going to hit her." Kit joined Susan at the credenza. "Tell her what happened. Maybe she'll believe you."

Susan heaved a sigh. "Stop this, all of you. I thought the pettiness around here had expired with Barbara." She ignored the quick intakes of breath. "If things don't change, I'll request a transfer." She picked up her coffee and strode to the door.

Julie followed. "Why are they trying to make Larry look like the bad guy?"

"You're asking me when you know how I feel about him?" Susan turned to the younger nurse. "What I do know is if things continue to escalate the way they are, Meg will step in and we've all seen her solutions."

"Too often," Julie said. "Why did they say he attacked Mendoza?

Larry wouldn't do a thing like that without a good reason."

Susan halted outside the utility room. "He verbally abused Mendoza and Mendoza retaliated in kind. Neither man looked good."

"I bet Larry didn't start it."

"I've no further comment. What's wrong with you? Just the other night, was it you or your twin who didn't think she could trust De Witt?"

Julie quickly glanced around. "You're right, but when he's around, I can't think of anything but him. What am I going to do?"

"Start thinking about your own goals for a change."

"I guess so."

With only five staff members on duty that evening, Susan ate dinner at the desk while she picked up orders. The atmosphere from the nurses' lounge invaded the station. By the end of the evening, she felt as though she had been trapped in a city under siege. When the night staff arrived, she still had charts to complete.

At five to twelve, she left the unit and hurried to the ER exit. The sound of angry voices startled her. One belonged to Mendoza. Was the other De Witt?

"Calm down, Ramon. So I owe you a couple of hours."

Susan turned the corner. Mendoza and Zeller, another house doctor, stood near the doors.

"I was doing you the favor," Mendoza said. "You should have been here by eight. The time is almost midnight."

"I got tied up. What's pending?"

"The house is quiet."

"Then what's the big deal. Don't burn the roads on the way home. You can't afford another speeding ticket."

"This would not be the worry if you had been on time. In my country, the police would never give the ticket to the doctor."

Zeller shrugged. "Different countries, different rules. I'll cover for you one evening next week. Just let me know when."

Susan attempted to edge around the pair. Mendoza turned. "Mrs. Randall, what has kept you here this late?"

"Too many patients and not enough help. I had tons of paperwork to complete."

He nodded. "For me as well. How is the lady I saw last night?"

"She's improving." She groaned and saw the security guard had left the desk.

"Your husband, is he late?"

"No." Susan shook her head. "I have to wait for a security guard to walk me to my car."

He held out his arm. "May I be the escort?"

"I'd appreciate the company." Susan stepped outside into a swirl of snow. "I hope this doesn't keep up all night."

As they crossed the street, Mendoza held her arm. "Since you work on the orthopedic unit, you should have the happiness. The snow will be good for business."

"The unit is full but I guess if there are accidents, we can transfer some of the medical patients to other units." She held the metal railing with one hand. "I'm on the second tier."

"I have parked there as well. The doctor's lot was full from the meeting."

When Susan reached her car, she turned and smiled. "Thanks."

"To escort you was my pleasure." He grinned. "I would challenge you to the race."

She laughed. "You've never seen me drive. There'd be no contest. You really shouldn't drive so fast."

"That is my nature. I have never had the accident."

Before she pulled out of the parking space, Susan let her car warm. She stopped at the gate behind Mendoza's white Porsche. He waved a challenge. The thought of a race brought memories shimmering to the surface. She motioned him on.

"I'll beat you home." As they had left their summer cottage, Jim had called the challenge. Since that night, she had become a cautious driver.

HE STOOD between two maples at the edge of the earth embankment overlooking the Thruway. The wind gusted and drove fat snowflakes against his face. Branches of the barren trees creaked in a skeleton's dance. He stared through the falling snow and felt satisfied with his choice of tonight for Susan's death.

The wet roads made the possibility of a fatal car accident believable. He looked at his watch. She was late. Could he have missed her sporty white sedan?

He shook his head. His vigilance had been constant. No cars had passed his hiding place for ten minutes. Susan was late, but she often was. If he remained patient, she would come.

Thankful for the arctic jacket that shielded him from the biting wind, he left the shelter of the trees and squatted on a ground cloth.

After adjusting his cap, he raised the rifle and peered through the telescopic lens. Aloud he repeated the number of her license plate. "709AMO."

The intensity of his concentration was so strong, he nearly forgot to breathe. Headlights approached. A white car. He saw the M and fired. A split-second too late he realized he had shot at the wrong car. Susan didn't drive a Porsche. He dropped the rifle.

For several seconds, he thought his marksmanship had failed. Then the right front tire disintegrated and the speeding car spun out of control. The sound of the car's impact against the overpass abutment reverberated like the roar of a crowd cheering a spectacular athletic event. He reveled in the applause for a hand of seconds. Then he walked to the edge of the embankment and stared at the crumpled car.

Not Susan's car. It should be. Why had he failed? She led a charmed life. Three times he had tried and failed. Three deaths and she was still here and not with Mommy. Barbara Denton. Dr. Barclay. Now a stranger. Had they died to keep Susan safe? That must be the answer.

The sound of sirens alerted him. He stepped behind a massive oak. Two police cars with lights revolving and sirens blaring pulled off the road. The officers left their cars and converged on the Porsche. One spoke into a microphone.

He stared without really comprehending the scene. Susan was alive. Mommy, why? Are you protecting her? Wind whistled around him. He had to find a different plan. Maybe he should listen to Mommy.

AS SUSAN approached the tollbooths, a police car flew past. A second followed before she paid the toll. Snow swirled through the air. Fat flakes melted as soon as they touched the ground. When Susan left the toll plaza, afraid the snow had made the roads slick, she cautiously increased her speed.

Less than a half mile beyond the booths, she saw red flashes from the domes of two police cars. Convinced there had been an accident, she slowed and shifted lanes. When she saw the white Porsche against the abutment, she gasped. Mendoza's car.

Her car slowed to a crawl. She eased into the right-hand lane and pulled onto the shoulder just beyond the second police car. An officer approached. Susan rolled down her window. "I'm a nurse. Is there anything I can do?"

He shook his head. "The driver's trapped. I've sent for the Jaws, but I think it's too late."

Susan bit her lip. "I think I know the driver...from the hospital...one of the house doctors. He walked me to my car. Are you sure there's nothing I can do?" She pressed her lips together to stop the hysterical scream that crept into her voice.

He shrugged. "Go ahead. If you can identify him, that's a start."

As she got out of the car, she looked toward the wooded area above the road. Her eyes narrowed. Was someone there?

"Lady, what's wrong?"

"I thought I saw someone up there." She waved her hand toward the trees.

"Shadows." He shone the beam of his flashlight over the area.

Must have been my imagination, she thought.

Susan followed the officer across the rubble-strewn shoulder. When they were a few feet from the abutment, she saw the way the front end of the Porsche twisted to fit around the concrete barrier. Nuggets of glass from the shattered windows glittered among the gravel and on the near lane of the highway.

Her footsteps faltered. She had walked this way before. Though the season had been summer and there had been no police cars, the similarity of the situation stirred ghosts. Jim's smashed car had been empty. Identification of his body had been delayed until she had found a phone and learned where he had been taken. She paused beside the Porsche and blinked her eyes to clear away the memories that blocked her from the present.

Carefully, she slid her hand through the jagged mouth of the side window and probed Mendoza's throat for a pulse. His skin felt cold. The revolving lights created an abnormal ruddiness on his cheeks. She found no heartbeat.

"He's dead." She withdrew her hand. The officer rose from a crouch beside the right front tire. His face wavered. Susan's knee buckled. Strong arms guided her away from the wrecked car.

She leaned against the door of her sedan and gulped air the way an asthmatic sucks oxygen. The officer spoke into a hand mike.

"Send someone to check the patch of woods above the Thruway. Found a bullet in the tire."

His voice faded in and out. When her head cleared, Susan straightened.

"Is he the doctor you mentioned?"

The officer's deep voice made her jump. "Dr. Mendoza. We left the hospital at the same time."

He flipped open a pad. "When was that?"

"Around midnight. The security guard was gone. He...Dr. Mendoza walked me to my car. He always drove too fast but he never had an accident...What do you think happened?"

The officer looked away. "Too soon to tell. Must have been hitting better than eighty. When the tire blew, he spun out of control."

Had the officer mentioned a bullet or had she imagined the word? Should she ask?

"Do you know anything about him?" the officer asked. "His address, phone number, anything?"

The clump of fear lodged in her chest forcing Susan to close her eyes. She thought about her knowledge of Mendoza. When he didn't allow petty problems to annoy him, he was an excellent doctor. At some point during the past five years, he had alienated most of the nurses at the hospital. Speeding tickets angered him. Slights from other doctors evoked bitter complaints. These weren't the sort of details the officer wanted.

"He was a house doctor. We weren't friends. I'm sure the supervisors at Bradley Memorial will have the information you need." As she opened the car door, a siren sounded in the distance.

"Thanks for stopping. Sorry you couldn't help." The officer walked to the edge of the road and guided her car from the shoulder.

A bullet, she thought. Fear spread through her body. Last night De Witt and Mendoza had quarreled. Mendoza had practically accused De Witt of killing his uncle. Should she have mentioned this? But the words had been spoken in anger. Mendoza had no way of knowing what De Witt had done.

As Susan drove away, she saw an ambulance and a tow truck arrive. The officer waved. Her thoughts reverted to the hospital parking lot and Mendoza's jaunty wave. The roll of memories continued until she saw her husband's car shattered almost beyond recognition.

She bit her lip to staunch the tears that burned her eyes. She gripped the steering wheel. Her car swerved toward the middle lane and back again. Stop it, she told herself. Exhaustion swamped her. If she pulled off the road to wait until the memories vanished, she might still be there in the morning.

Her car crept past several exits before she reached her turnoff. Relief that the trip had nearly ended allowed her to grip the wheel with less than a wrestler's hold. A short time later, she pulled into the driveway at home.

The lights from Patrick's side of the house were like a lighthouse beacon promising safety and peace. Susan bit her lip. Was she so conditioned to dependency that she couldn't face her memories alone? Was it fair to lean on Patrick when she wasn't sure she could promise anything? A crisis in their friendship approached and she feared she would hurt him.

WHEN PATRICK saw Susan's car pull into the driveway, he rose from the couch. In hopes she would stop by, he walked to the door. Five minutes later, her headlights still shone through the darkness. What was wrong?

He grabbed his jacket and opened the door an instant before the headlights went out. Susan stood beside her car. The night the Denton woman had been murdered, Susan had stood with the same forlorn posture. Had another nurse at the hospital died?

He left the porch. "What's wrong?"

"There was an accident on the Thruway."

He gathered her into his arms. "Were you involved?"

"No." As she shook her head, her hair brushed his face.

He kept his arm around her waist and guided her up the steps to the porch. She shivered. From the cold or the accident? His lips found hers. His tongue traced the curve of her mouth. Slowly, her tension ebbed and her response to him began.

He freed her and trailed kisses across her chin and neck. Her arms lightly circled his shoulders and her fingers toyed with the hair at his nape. His lips met hers again.

He felt a current of energy sizzle along his nerves. His body responded to her nearness. Just as the other time they had embraced, her body molded to his. She rocked against him. He slid his hands beneath her uniform shirt and released the clasp of her bra. Her tongue clashed with his, thrusting and probing. She was all he had imagined and more.

Patrick lifted his mouth from hers. "Susan." He stepped back and drew her with him toward the living room and the couch.

She shook her head. "Patrick, I'm sorry. I can't." She broke free and walked to the kitchen door. "This is so much like the night..."

Had her response been driven by memories of the night she'd found solace in his arms? If so, what chance did they have to find a time for themselves?

"Did you stop at the accident?" The words emerged like a groan.

She nodded. "I knew the driver. One of the house doctors. Just tonight, he walked me to the parking lot. He challenged me to a race."

"You didn't?" Patrick blurted. That might explain the intensity of her reaction to his kiss. Jim had challenged her. Patrick remembered how guilt had colored her grief. He leaned against the kitchen counter.

"Of course not. You know how I feel about speeding." Susan's voice shook. "He drives—drove like the devil clung to his tailpipe. I followed him to the Thruway, where he took off."

Patrick listened to the remainder of her story. During the recitation, a short hesitation made him wonder if she had left something out. "Stopping took a lot of courage."

"I'm a nurse. I couldn't pass by."

"Did the police have any idea about the cause of the accident?" Patrick drew her from the door.

"One of the front tires blew." Again, she hesitated. "He skidded out of control."

She stood in the circle of his arms. He took comfort that she didn't move away. He hadn't meant to rush her. He massaged her shoulders. A question lunged from the recesses of his mind. "Denton, Barclay, Mendoza, could there be a connection between the deaths?"

She looked away. "How? Dr. Barclay died in a hunting accident upstate. Mendoza, when his car went out of control."

"Perhaps the two were intended to look like accidents."

"Don't talk like that." She shook her head. "Dr. Barclay and Mendoza had nothing to do with Barbara. Except—" She closed her mouth, but not before Patrick saw something in her eyes that made him doubt her statement. An uneasy feeling lay like a block of cement on his chest. What was she hiding?

"With the Denton woman's love of gossip and blackmail, she might have known something about them."

"Then why would someone kill the three of them?" She shook her head. "You're not making sense."

He nodded. "You're right." He had allowed his concern for her to control his thoughts.

She stepped back. "I have to go."

"Are you sure you'll be all right?"

She nodded. "I can't keep running to you every time I'm upset. It's not fair." She picked up her coat.

"I don't mind." He followed her to the door. "See you Saturday." He touched her cheek. "I won't push you for what you're not ready to give."

SUSAN OPENED the door on her side of the house and switched on the lights. Her emotions churned. Just like the night of Jim's death, Patrick's kiss had ignited her. Had the similarities caused her to react with passion? Until she knew, she had to hold herself away from Patrick. Though she hadn't run to him, when he had appeared, she had stepped eagerly into his arms. She wished she could find an easy answer.

Upstairs, she stood beside the bed and lifted Jim's portrait. "You were right about Patrick. What should I do?"

For a moment, she studied the picture. Her lips brushed the glass. With a sigh, she carried the photograph to the hall and placed it with the other family portraits.

Her gesture didn't mean she was ready to fall into Patrick's embrace. She just felt ready to consider the possibilities.

SUSAN DROPPED a basket of uniforms beside the ironing board. Since this wasn't her favorite chore, she searched for a way to avoid the job. There was no cleaning to be done. She had no desire to complete her Christmas shopping.

With a sigh, she opened the drapes. Last night's snow had melted under the bright morning sun. A new realization arose. The panic she'd felt when she'd driven away from the white Porsche still lingered, but as a dull ache.

A smile crossed her lips. In the interval between last night and this morning, something had freed her from the desperate need to cling to memories of her husband.

Her hands touched the cold glass. She could have told Patrick about Barbara's threat to reveal the affair between Joe Barclay and Leila. But for what purpose? Joe Barclay's death had been an accident. Barbara's a murder. The practical's death had been a climax to the life she's lived. Gossip. Threats. Blackmail. Susan turned from the window.

She reached into the clothes basket. Last night, Patrick had been wonderful. Even though she had responded with desire to his kiss, he had accepted her withdrawal. How long would his control last? A week, a month? She straightened the leg of a pair of white slacks. Be honest. She feared her own reaction more than his.

The thought of Saturday, of dinner and the concert, brought fear and anticipation to mingle in her thoughts. During the fifteen years of marriage, she had forgotten much about the interplay of dating. She wanted the evening to be fun, to be an adventure and the chance to learn more about who she was becoming. To keep from thinking about Patrick, she switched on the radio. Soon the movements of her body as she plied the iron matched the tempo of the music.

Music changed to news. A pleasant voice droned a summary of the national and international news.

"Now for a look at the local scene. Is there a jinx operating at Bradley Memorial Hospital? Staff members must be asking that question. In eleven days, three of their colleagues had died tragically. The first death—"

As the voice recalled the deaths, Susan froze. Her eyes focused on the wall, and though she wanted to change the station, she relived the terror of finding Barbara, heard Leila's shrill cries and saw the crumpled white Porsche.

The smell of scorched fabric broke the spell. She lifted the iron. A large brown spot scarred the back of a white top. She rolled the shirt in a ball and tossed it in the wastebasket. As she turned the radio to a different station, a thought occurred. There had been no mention of a bullet in the report of Mendoza's accident. Did that mean the police were keeping the fact a secret or that she had imagined the policeman's words?

SUSAN PULLED into a parking spot on the second tier. She stared across the street at the hospital. After collecting her purse and salad container, she left the car.

"Wait for me," Julie called. "Did you hear about Mendoza?"

Susan paused at the top of the steps. "Yes."

"I nearly fell out of bed when I turned on the radio this morning. That's the first thing I heard. Doesn't surprise me a bit."

"He said he never had an accident."

"Now that does surprise me." Julie stopped and fastened the silver clip around her hair. "I've followed him to the Thruway a couple of times. I'm not a slow driver, but there was no way I could keep up with him."

"We're jinxed." Kit ran down from the third tier to join them. "I'm looking for a job as far as possible from the hospital."

Susan made a face at the glee in Kit's voice. "Just remember what they say about threes."

Kit moved past Susan. She held the rail and backed down the steps. "It's been one murder and two accidents. The way I figure it, we've one accident and two murders to come."

"The accident will be yours if you don't watch where you're going," Susan said.

Kit halted. "I just want to know what's going on around here, and let me tell you, I'm going to learn."

The unit secretary's broad grin reminded Susan of the one Barbara always wore when she was about to begin a story. "Why don't you let it drop?"

"I have a right to be curious."

Trish waited at the bottom of the steps. "Curious or just plain nosy. A person could get hurt that way."

"Are you threatening me?"

"Hardly," Trish said. "You're not Barbara. In fact, your imitation is rather comic."

"Hear, hear," Julie said.

"I heard Mendoza was drunk and he wasn't alone," Kit said.

"Where did you come up with that?" Julie asked. "A radio report from Mars."

Susan clenched her hands. "Cut the inventions. You don't know anything."

"And I suppose you do." Kit flipped her hair back. "What I really want to know is the identity of the woman. Maybe she's the same one who was at Dr. Barclay's cabin."

"What woman?" Trish asked.

Kit smirked. "Didn't you hear that Mendoza's body was identified by a woman who vanished by the time the reporters arrived."

"Into thin air on the Thruway? Spare me," Trish said. "If you're going to invent stories, at least see that they make sense."

"You're sick, both of you," Julie said.

Susan ran across the street with the others on her heels. "There was no woman with him."

"How would you know?" Kit asked.

"I identified the body."

Julie grabbed Susan's arm. "Really?"

"Don't tell me you and Mendoza were—" Kit pushed the ER door open.

Susan exhaled. "I saw his car against the overpass abutment and stopped to see if I could help."

Trish grimaced. "Sounds like something you'd do. You'd never catch me stopping at the scene of an accident. Aren't you afraid of being sued?"

"No," Susan said.

"Was he gross?" Kit asked. "You sure have all the luck. First Barbara and now Mendoza. What did he look like? Was there a lot of blood?"

Susan pushed the elevator button. "I've said enough." She closed her eyes. Would Kit's harassment continue all evening?

"Stop bugging her." Julie held the elevator for the others. "It couldn't have been pleasant."

The doors closed. Kit pressed five. "Funny how this happened just the way De Witt predicted."

"What's that supposed to mean?" Julie asked.

"Want me to quote?" Trish asked. "Someday you're going to push that white Porsche—"

"Stop it," Julie snapped. "I'm tired of snide remarks and nasty comments. If you have a quarrel with Larry, confront him."

Trish's laughter exploded. "Now that would be an interesting scene."

The elevator doors opened on five. Susan dashed to the locker room and hoped to escape before the others arrived. As she tied her shoes, Julie, Kit and Trish burst into the room. The door slammed behind them.

"Did De Witt really drop me?" Trish asked. "You don't know what went down between us. Ask him to level with you. His answer might be a real eye-opener."

Kit's eyes glittered with avid interest. Julie shoved her coat into the locker. "What does this have to do with Mendoza's death?"

Susan slammed her locker door. "I've had it with the three of you. We're here to do a job. Forget this nonsense and start thinking about the patients."

"I will as soon as you tell me what happened," Kit said.

Susan strode to the door. "It was an accident. He was speeding. The roads were wet. A tire blew and he lost control." She opened the door. "That's all you're going to hear from me."

"Wasn't that the way your husband died?" Kit asked.

Tears welled in Susan's eyes. "Enough, Kit."

"Sorry. Me and my big mouth. I didn't mean to remind you."

"What do you think I've been remembering since last night? I'll be at the desk."

"Do you want me to bring you some coffee?" Julie asked.

"I don't want to see any of you until three o'clock when we're officially on duty." She clutched her purse and strode down the hall. The time had come to bury herself in orders, reports and other people's problems.

AT QUARTER to six, Susan stood in the med room and prepared an injection for one of the new patients. The door closed with a click. She turned. Leila crossed to the sink and lit a cigarette.

"Aren't you pushing your luck a bit?" Susan raised an eyebrow.

"I'll take my chances."

"You're early."

Leila nodded. "I'm due in the OR in fifteen minutes. Surgery on a battered child."

Susan made a face. "That's a bad one."

"The worst." Leila sighed. "How can a parent do that to a child?"

"I wish I knew."

"How are you holding up? I hear you stopped at Mendoza's accident."

Susan shook her head. "News sure travels fast around here."

"With the speed of light. Kit's been burning the phone wires with a secondhand assessment of the accident."

"She's becoming obnoxious in her quest to take Barbara's place as gossip queen."

"As long as she sticks to gossip." Leila tapped an ash in the sink. "How's the unit tonight?"

"Sullen. I blew my cool with Kit, Trish and Julie earlier. They're so busy sniping at each other, I'm afraid the patients will suffer. I don't want Meg to hear about the problems and act in her dogmatic way."

"You're more patient with the situation than I'd be. Why didn't you call me last night? I'm sure being a witness to Mendoza's accident upset you."

"Patrick was waiting for me. He let me talk."

"And?"

"When I finished talking, I went home." She wasn't ready to talk about the kiss and the desires that had been stirred. "He has this weird theory about the deaths."

"What are you going to do about him?"

Her failure to divert Leila made Susan smile. "Let's say that I'm ready to consider the possibilities."

"That's the best news I've heard in months."

Susan picked up the syringe. "Don't rush me. I don't want him to start acting like he's my husband. How are you?"

Leila turned on the water and doused her cigarette. "Living each day as it comes. I'm thinking about moving to California or New Mexico."

"I'd hate to see you go." Susan tucked a handful of alcohol wipes in her pocket. "What about your parents?"

"They're one of the problems." Leila dropped the butt in the trash. "They won't leave the farm. Don't worry. I'm not making decisions until I finish my Master's."

Susan walked to the door. "I'm thinking about a transfer to days."

"You have seniority. Why not go back to school? Then you can have my job."

"I'll leave that for Julie."

"Has she applied to any school?"

Susan shook her head. "First she has to get her mind off De Witt."

"How long have they lasted?"

"Four months."

"That's about two more than usual. Maybe this time he's serious." Leila started down the hall and stopped outside the utility room. "Are you free for dinner tomorrow night?"

"If you want to eat here. I'm working and off the weekend. Do you want to meet me at the diner after work tonight?"

Leila shook her head. "And have to wait until eleven thirty when I'm always out of here at eleven?"

"Some people are lucky. See you."

"What about Sunday brunch?" Leila asked.

"Sounds good. Where?"

"O'Quill's. I'll meet you there."

SUSAN FINISHED report and headed to the locker room in hopes of catching up with the others. The room was deserted. With a sigh of exasperation because they hadn't waited for her, she pulled on her boots and coat. In the elevator, several nurses from other units joined her. She walked to the parking lot with them.

On the steps, the group dispersed and headed to cars on all three levels. Susan dug her keys from her purse. At the car, she halted so abruptly she nearly dropped the keys.

A brown paper bag sat on the hood. This is becoming less than a joke, she thought. No wonder they didn't wait for me. Why are they playing these tricks? Her hands shook. The trembling spread to her legs. She leaned against the car to keep from falling. Why? A surge of anger restored her equilibrium. She grabbed the bag, unlocked the car and slid behind the wheel.

Three gifts. Three deaths. The coincidence of the arrival of the presents shook her. Could there be a connection?

She shook her head. "It's a joke." Her coworkers had to be doing this. Nothing else made sense.

Her thoughts ran wild with speculation. With unsteady hands, she pulled the note free.

"She always wore this perfume for me. I want you to wear it, too."

Susan swallowed and extracted the bottle from the bag. She sniffed. Roses. Where had she smelled this perfume before? The memory was as elusive as the one concerning Barbara.

What if her co-workers weren't playing a joke? The impact of this thought stunned her. If they weren't, these gifts were a subtle threat and she didn't understand why.

Chapter 8

PATRICK STOOD in front of the mirror in his bedroom and for the fifth time, tied his tie. Four jackets lay in a heap on the bed where he had discarded them. He wanted to laugh at his retreat into adolescence, but the anxiety he felt couldn't be easily dismissed.

This evening's dinner and concert with Susan was a first. They had never appeared in public as a couple unless a chance meeting at the food court in the mall counted. They had eaten meals at home together, they had barbecued in the back yard and had joined forces for projects around the house. They had kissed. Once they had made love. They were friends and he loved her.

With a groan, he stepped back from the mirror. This tie would have to do. If he dawdled another minute, he would be late.

He took the stairs two at a time. After buttoning his overcoat, he lifted the scarlet poinsettia from the counter. He shook his head. Buying the largest plant in the store hadn't been his intention but he seemed to have succeeded. When he left his side of the house, the leaves brushed his face. With the pot braced between his body and the doorframe, he rang the bell.

When Susan opened the door, he peered between the leaves. He whistled softly. The rust-colored silk dress made her skin glow and her eyes to appear more brown than hazel.

He held out the poinsettia. "A little gift."

"Did you have to buy a tree?" Laughter punctuated her words.

Patrick chuckled over the ridiculous picture he must make. "It is a bit large. Where do you want me to put it?"

"On the coffee table for now." She moved a stack of magazines. "Proper placement will take creative thinking. You know, I could forget the idea of a real tree and decorate this instead."

Patrick studied her face. Did her desire to have a real tree have significance? She and Jim had always decorated an artificial one. This seemed to be another step away from the past. "Have a tree, too." As he deposited his burden in the space she had cleared, he understood her amusement. The plant dominated the spacious room. He turned. She stood at the door and buttoned her coat.

"Not fair," he said. "You've cheated me out of the chance to prove I'm a gentleman."

"You don't have to prove anything." She opened the door.

Since there wasn't time for a leisurely dinner, Patrick had made reservations at the Pub. Once inside the restaurant, Susan slid onto one of the church pews used as benches and studied the menu. After they ordered, he grinned sheepishly. The bar was double lined with men watching a football game. Their loudly voiced comments and their friendly shoving made Susan smile.

"Sorry," Patrick said.

"At least it's not wrestling. The spectators are more fun to watch than the game."

The waitress brought their salads and a basket of breath. He lifted his fork. "Are they more interesting than your patients?"

She nodded. "The hospital's not a great place to be these days. There's a lot of sniping among the people I work with. Sometimes it gets nasty."

"Did they bug you about Dr. Mendoza's accident?"

"And that led to innuendoes and accusations until I lost my cool." She put her fork on the plate. "I fear the sniping is behind the odd things that are happening to me." The fear she had felt on finding the third gift resurfaced. Once again, she was almost sure one of her coworkers was responsible for the gifts and Barbara's death.

Patrick looked up. "Tell me."

"Maybe it started as a joke, but it's not funny anymore. When I came back from vacation, Julie teased me about hiding something from them. Some kind of relationship." She told him about the candy, books and perfume and where she had found them. "The giver knows my schedule. That's why I think it's someone I work with."

"What about one of the doctors?"

She laughed. "I'm not the kind of woman to attract one of them. Most of the doctors are married. They wouldn't choose me for a fling."

He nodded. Susan brought thoughts of home and family. "Any other men around?"

"Patients, visitors, security, maintenance. To them, I'm just a nurse."

Patrick reached for a piece of bread. "You're probably right about your coworkers being the culprit." As he spoke, an uneasy feeling arose, one he refused to voice. Was she being stalked? "Who left the hospital before you did the night you found the perfume?"

"All of them. I was late."

"What about a group prank?"

"Before Barbara's death, maybe, but I can't imagine them cooperating on anything these days. All they do is bicker."

"As long as the gifts are benign, I wouldn't worry." He speared the last bite of salad.

"It's just...the gifts..." She shrugged. "I wish I could discover why I've been chosen."

What had she been about to say? Was there something sinister about the gifts that made her think of them as a threat?

"What were you going to say?"

"It's nothing."

The waitress brought their steaks. Patrick cut a piece. "Lisa called this morning to inform me of the current holiday schedule. The twins will arrive Christmas Eve and stay for a month."

"Will Lisa and Rob be in Europe that long?"

He nodded. "She's fighting for her marriage. That's more than—" He cut off a bitter remark. "She's lucky I can keep the twins."

Susan looked up. "There are some things I need to tell you." She toyed with her food. "When the twins were here, they talked to me about their stepfather. I guess he doesn't hide his resentment of them when Lisa's not around."

"Damn. Lisa insists he loves and wants the twins. What do you think I should do?"

"Take them as often as you can. I'm sure Lisa won't believe you if you say anything."

Patrick groaned. If he petitioned for custody, the twins would be forced to choose. He didn't want to put them in the middle of a custody fight. He looked up. "I'll take your advice for now, but I'm going to talk to Lisa when they come back."

"You'll find the answer." She pointed to their steaks. "Let's eat before these get cold."

Patrick nodded. The problem of the twins was his. His relationship with Susan hadn't progressed to where he could ask her how she felt about becoming part of a family.

HE SAT IN the kitchen of the house he shared with Mommy. Her presence lurked at the edge of his awareness. He felt her disappointment as strongly as he had the night he'd crouched above the Thruway and waited for her white car. As he ate a solitary supper, he muttered to himself.

"Her life is charmed. Mommy, I don't understand why you don't want her with you." He looked up. *"That's not fair. She has to be with you. I don't want her to tell."* He scowled. *"You can't protect her forever."* He struck the tines of the fork against the plate. His plans were made. Since Mommy protected Susan, he had to choose another. He rose. The fork clattered on the floor.

At ten o'clock, he sat in the Emergency Room waiting area and stared at the clock. Each sweep of the second hand cut into his well-timed plan. The self-inflicted wound was deeper and had bled more than he had expected. Finally, a nurse called his name. He followed her to the examining room screened from others by green curtains.

After describing the accident and moaning about his clumsiness, he waited for the doctor.

At ten minutes to eleven, the nurse bandaged his thumb. She handed him a printed instruction sheet. He jammed the paper in his pocket and hurried outside to look for a pay phone. He located one outside the Emergency Room doors. He put in the money and dialed.

"Ms. Vernon, please."

When he heard her voice, he began a lengthy and convoluted complaint about how badly the nurses were treating his mother. His tirade continued until he saw the other evening supervisors leave the hospital. After promising to come in the next afternoon to make a formal complaint, he hung up and walked to the door.

Several minutes later, the door opened and Leila Vernon strode outside. He moved to intercept her. *"Good evening."*

She looked up. *"What are you doing here tonight?"*

He displayed his bandaged thumb. *"A dumb workshop accident."* He frowned. *"I thought there was a security guard assigned to escort the nurses on the evening shift to their cars."*

"He's not due until eleven thirty. I usually leave with the other supervisors, but tonight, a phone call delayed me."

"Can I be your escort?"

"Thank you."

Her smile made her cheeks flush. Until they reached the steps, he walked beside her. Two cars left the parking lot. Had the drivers noticed him, and if they had, could they identify him? He had to take the chance. Mommy had blessed tonight's action.

"I'm on the second tier," Ms. Vernon said. *"You don't have to go with me."*

"I don't mind." He reached into his jacket pocket and grasped the weight.

When she paused beside her car, he pulled the weight free. A rush of anticipation energized him. She bent to fit the key into the lock.

He smashed the weight against the base of her skull. Her face hit the car window. He struck again. She toppled to the ground and nearly knocked him over. He knelt on the asphalt and smashed the weight again and again against the back of her head.

His breath came in ragged gasps. The heat of accomplishment coursed through his veins. He stared at the way her coat sleeve had ridden up to expose her pale arm.

The glitter of gold on her wrist entranced him. How did she get Mommy's bracelet? The bracelet had spanned a different arm. His fingers fumbled with the clasp.

Moments later, he hurried down the steps. When he reached the safety of his car, he thought of Susan. Would she guess what he had done? Would she know he was the one? Mommy did. Would she tell?

THE NEARLY full moon competed with the lights in the parking lot outside the community college auditorium. Susan slipped her hand into Patrick's. The chill of the night vanished. All evening, the music had formed a background to her awareness of the stirring chords he made her feel. Though the pressure of his fingers on hers was a sign the night was real, she felt as though she walked in a dream.

His touch lingered and then disappeared. He unlocked the car. Their gazes met, Susan looked away. The need reflected in his eyes stirred a similar response in her. Was she ready to make a choice between fears generated by the past and her hopes for the future?

By the time they reached the house, she had pushed her mixed feelings aside. She handed him the key to her front door. "Would you like to come in for coffee and dessert?"

"Yes."

His eyes held desire for something more. She felt heat streak through her body.

Inside, he took her coat and pulled her into his arms for a quick and demanding kiss. She looked up. When he stepped back, she was sure he'd read the uncertainty in her expression.

When she stood at the kitchen counter cutting thick slabs of gingerbread baked on a bed of peaches, her awareness of him grew. After carrying the cake to the table, she returned to the counter and filled two mugs with coffee.

This time when she turned, his head was bent. He wrote in the notebook he had held during the concert. The mugs she held kept her from touching his skin, his hair, the rough texture of his tweed jacket. The moment of desire held her paralyzed.

With deliberate movement, she set the mugs on the table and sat across from him. Her senses seemed enhanced. The pungent aroma of coffee and spices, the sweet and tangy taste of the gingerbread, the feel of the polished surface of the table, the frown on his face captured her attention. The change in their relationship had begun on Thanksgiving with her realization that he wanted more than friendship. Could she meet his needs?

He put the pencil on the table and slipped the notebook in his pocket. "Had to make my notes while the music was still fresh." He tasted the cake. "Delicious. A new recipe?"

She shook her head. "A childhood favorite that I'd forgotten until Mom made one while I was there."

"I'd like the recipe. The kids would like this."

"It's simple. Brown sugar, butter, a can of peaches and a box of gingerbread mix."

"My kind of baking."

They lingered over coffee, lifting mugs and forks with mirrored movements. Susan sought his eyes, but when their gazes met, unsure of her answer, she looked away.

Finally, he rose. "I have to turn my notes into a column for Monday's paper."

Susan followed him to the living room. He turned and put his arms around her waist. His lips met hers, his hands moved on her back. The caress of silk against her skin sent her thoughts toward the bedroom, toward love and commitment.

"I'd stay longer," he said. "All you have to do is ask."

The invitation wedged in her throat. She wasn't ready to test her fear or to explore her growing desire for this man.

He cupped her face. Their lips met in a kiss that nearly made her forget her fears.

"Susan." His breath flowed over her lips. "I'll call you in the morning. We'll go to brunch."

"I can't. I promised Leila I'd meet her." She stood at the door and watched him cross the porch. If she called, she knew he would return. They could spend the night making love, this time without guilt. He entered his side of the house. She closed the door. While savoring the anticipation of what lay ahead, she regretted sending him away.

JULIE AND Trish dashed past the security guard and raced across the street. Trish paused at the foot of the steps. "Do you think we should have waited for the guard?"

"I never do." Before Julie plunged up the steps, she glanced over her shoulder. "With the mob behind us, any mugger would run. Imagine being pummeled by fifteen or more nurses and their oversized handbags."

Trish chuckled. "You know, I always wondered if Barbara invented that story."

"She sure took it seriously."

"But she was the star of the piece. Her ability to inject herself into that tale is what convinced everyone this wasn't a fantasy."

Julie left the steps at the landing of the second tier. "See you tomorrow." She had to hurry. Larry hated when she arrived late.

As she ran to her car, she stumbled and quickly recovered her balance. A woman's handbag lay on the ground. Then she saw the body sprawled on the asphalt between two cars. Her scream continued like a siren out of control.

"What's wrong?" Trish appeared at her side.

Julie pointed. Her scream died to a whimper. "It's Ms. Vernon. She looks worse than Barbara."

"Move," Trish said. "I want to see."

"I'm going to be sick."

"Move first."

Julie edged away and stumbled to the steps. Several nurses halted just below her. "What's wrong?" they shouted.

"There's been another attack." Julie swallowed several times.

"Are you alone?"

"Trish Fallon's with the body. We need help."

Two of the nurses pushed through the cluster of women. "We'll get Security."

Julie grasped the railing. Women shoved past her. Her heart pounded. She felt faint. After gulping deep breaths of cold air, she stared at the group of nurses who stood near the cars that partly concealed Leila's body.

She had to leave or she would be late. Larry would be upset. His uncle's death, the lawyers, the attempt to cover the large medical practice alone had made him easily angered. Instead of joining the others, she ran to her car.

The engine started instantly. She backed out of the space. A thought occurred. Susan will be devastated when she hears. She and Leila were good friends. What if Susan was alone when she heard?

Julie's car shot between the gateposts. Her thoughts flipped from Larry to Susan. After deciding Susan shouldn't be alone when she learned about her friend's death, Julie sped to the Thruway. She could call Larry from Susan's house.

WHEN TRISH heard a car engine, she turned. "What the—" she shouted. Why was Julie leaving? The police were on the way. They would want to talk to her.

Trish moved closer to Leila and scanned the ground. The only reason Trish could figure for Julie's flight was that she had seen something to link De Witt to the death. The suspicion Trish had dismissed the night of Barbara's death returned. Trish studied the body without discovering a clue.

"Move," a stern male voice ordered. "Let me through. Someone reported another mugging. Which one of you lost her purse?"

"Leila Vernon," someone said.

"She lost more than her purse." Trish joined the retreat.

"Dear lord," the guard said. "All right, ladies, I want the lot of you to stay here until the police arrive." He spoke into his radio.

Trish collapsed against a car. The effects of the last amphetamine she had taken several hours before had worn off. "If I don't get away, I'm going to be sick."

"What's your name?"

"Trish Fallon. Julie Gilbert and I found the body."

"Where is she?"

"Gone. I don't know where." Trish closed her eyes. She had a good idea where Julie had gone.

"Damn. Trust you women to panic." He pulled a pad of paper from his pocket. "Give me your name and phone number. Did you see anyone running away?"

Trish shook her head. "The mugger's long gone. The supervisors leave at eleven." Her legs trembled. As she scrawled the information he'd requested, her hand shook. "I really have to go."

"Me, too," chorused a group of women.

"Okay, okay. The rest of you leave your names and phone

numbers. The police will be in touch."

"What about my car?" one of the women asked. "I can't move it without hitting her."

The guard glanced at the body. "Then you'll have to stay or hitch a ride with someone. Can't be destroying evidence."

Trish reached her car. She had to get away before she crashed. She drove to the gates. By the time the gate lifted, a surge of energy banished her exhaustion. What had Julie seen? Trish smiled. She planned to find out.

AS SUSAN turned out the kitchen light, she thought about Patrick. Why hadn't she invited him to stay? The doorbell rang. She smiled. Had he noticed her hesitation and returned? As she ran to the door, she remembered the prowler. "Who's there?"

"Julie. Let me in."

The panic in the younger nurse's voice startled Susan. Why had Julie come at this hour? Susan opened the door. Julie pushed past. Susan read fear and sorrow in the other nurse's expression.

"What's wrong?" Susan asked.

"I didn't want you to hear when you were alone. It was ghastly. I nearly vomited." Julie collapsed on the couch.

"What are you talking about?" Susan closed the door and stood with her back against the firm surface.

"She was mugged. Barbara didn't lie."

"Who?"

"Leila."

A scream rose from Susan's toes but she choked it back. "What are you talking about? You're not making sense."

Julie straightened. "Leila was mugged in the parking lot tonight. Trish and I found her. Whoever did this must be crazy. Her head was worse than Barbara's."

Susan moved to the couch. Her legs buckled. She crossed her arms over her chest and rubbed the upper parts. She felt cold and though she didn't want to believe what Julie had said, the words had to be true. "Tell me what happened from the beginning."

Julie touched Susan's hand. "I'm late. Could I call Larry? He'll be upset but I didn't want you to be alone."

Susan stared at her hands. Who was doing this? First Barbara and now Leila. They both had known the same secret.

The chance of a mugger being in the hospital parking lot,

especially after the hospital had initiated precautions, seemed monumental. De Witt. She had to warn Julie.

Susan covered her face. The sound of Julie's voice came from the kitchen. "I can't leave her now... Why are you being so rude...Well, *if* that's the way you feel, I'll see you tomorrow."

When Julie appeared in the doorway, anger filled her eyes and tightened her mouth. "Are you all right?" she asked.

"Not really," Susan said.

"Men! Sometimes I think they're a different species."

"You could be right." Susan shifted her position. "Tell me everything you can remember about Leila."

Julie slowly repeated the story. "Her watch was gone."

Susan bolted to her feet. A gold watch. A gold bracelet. That was what she hadn't been able to remember.

"What's the matter?"

"Barbara's bracelet was missing," Susan said. "I knew there was something wrong with her body."

Julie nodded. "Then that proves the mugger killed Barbara."

Susan shook her head. "How could a stranger know about the storage room or even be in the hospital?" She paced the room. "What did the police say?"

Julie twisted a strand of hair around her finger. "I didn't wait for them. Trish did. I wonder what she told them?"

"Ask her tomorrow." Susan returned to the couch. "You'd better call the police in the morning."

"I promise. Is there any way I can help? I know you and Leila were close. I could stay if you want."

Julie's words echoed Patrick's, but Susan knew she needed to be alone to release the tears that choked her. "Thanks for coming. I'll be all right."

"Are you sure?"

"Go home, please. I hate to cry in front of anyone. Even when Jim died, I couldn't." Instead, she had sought refuge in Patrick's arms. But not tonight. She needed to grieve alone—one more step toward her goal of strength.

"I'll call you in the morning."

"After the police."

Susan locked the door behind Julie. Tears gathered but remained unshed. What's wrong with me? Leila was my best friend. Instead of grief, she felt anger. Why had Leila been killed? Because she knew a secret? That had to be the reason. Why hadn't Leila told her the reason De Witt wasn't being offered the partnership? Why hadn't there been a security guard to escort Leila to her car?

Her hands clenched so tight her fingers cramped. First thing in the morning, she intended to call the Nursing Office and vent her anger.

She couldn't understand why Leila had lost her usual caution and walked to the parking lot alone. Where had the other evening supervisors been?

As Susan remembered the days of friendship, one tear became a stream. Rather than go upstairs to a too large and empty bed, she curled on the couch and pulled the afghan close.

PATRICK STOOD at the kitchen counter and buttered a piece of toast. A bright sun promised a cold but beautiful day. The radio, tuned to the local station, played a soft accompaniment to his actions. After breakfast, he'd deliver his column to the paper.

At eight, the news began. He poured a glass of orange juice and sat on a stool to eat.

"A second nurse was murdered last night at Bradley Memorial Hospital. Leila Vernon, one of the evening supervisors, died as a result of injuries sustained during a mugging. The attack occurred around eleven P.M. in the hospital parking lot."

The toast dropped on the counter. Susan will be upset. Leila had been her best friend. He reached for the phone and dropped his hand to his side. What could he say that wouldn't frighten her?

He rose. How could he keep her safe without making her resent his intentions?

In the past year, she had become a different woman from the one who had married Jim. Stronger, more self-assured. He liked her strength though her rigid hold on independence sometimes exasperated him.

The gun, he thought. Would she believe she was in danger if he told her about the gun? He needed to call Greg and discover what his friend had learned from the antique dealer. Again, he reached for the phone and just as quickly, changed his mind.

Was she up? Because she worked evenings, she usually slept late in the morning. He wanted to be with her when she learned about her friend. With resolute steps, he returned to the counter. He would call and see if she was awake.

THE PHONE woke Susan. She groped for the bedside stand and nearly fell off the couch. Her hand hit the edge of the coffee table. In confusion, she looked around. Why was she on the couch? The reason hit like a lethal virus. Last night, Leila had been murdered.

Susan untangled her legs from the afghan and ran to the kitchen. The phone continued to ring. She grabbed the receiver. "Hello."

"I'm on my way over."

"Patrick, not now." The last word was spoken to the dial tone.

She splashed cold water on her face and combed her fingers through her short curls. As she smoothed her wrinkled dress, the doorbell rang. She went to the door.

Patrick strode into the room. He stared. "You know."

She nodded. "Fifteen minutes after you left, Julie arrived to tell me."

"Why didn't you call me?"

"I can't keep running to you every time something upsets me."

"Upset. I'd say you were more than upset." His gaze focused on her wrinkled dress. "I want to take care of you."

"No."

He groaned. "I just want to share your troubles and have you share mine. Leila was your best friend. I'm sure you're feeling hurt and lost."

"More like angry." She strode to the kitchen and filled the coffee maker. "I needed to cry and if you had been here, I wouldn't have allowed myself." She looked up and caught the flare of passion in his eyes and knew he remembered the night Jim had died.

He straddled one of the kitchen chairs. "I think you're in danger. That disturbs me."

She looked away. She had thought the same thing, but she couldn't let fear rule her. To do so would mean a return to the woman she had been before Jim died.

"How can I be in more danger than any of the other nurses on the evening shift?"

"I... " He sucked in a breath. "You know everyone who has died."

"So do about 90 percent of the evening staff. The hospital is like a small town. As she poured coffee into mugs, her annoyance with his attitude grew. "Why have you decided this is a personal vendetta against me?"

"You needed equipment from the storage room. Leila borrowed your car to go to Dr. Barclay's cabin. You and Mendoza left the hospital in white cars at the same time."

A chill snaked up her spine. And the gifts had arrived after each death. She hadn't told him that and now she wouldn't. His protective instincts had already gone into overdrive.

"Then how do you explain Leila's mugging? There's no way she could have been mistaken for me."

He shrugged. "I'm sure there's a connection. I just haven't found it. Call the hospital on Monday and request a leave of absence."

She gripped the back of a chair. "That's what Jim would have said. Do you want me to leave town and the country? If I've suddenly become the target, the person could find me here." Her fingers tightened. There had been a prowler. She gulped a breath. "Why are you doing this to me?"

"I love you. Isn't that reason enough?"

She turned away. "Love would allow me to be myself. The decision to continue to work is mine. I let Jim make decisions for me, but never again."

Patrick put his hands on her shoulders. "Don't ask me not to worry. Don't ask me not to want to protect you. I know I can't make decisions for you, but we could share."

"Not today," she said.

A few minutes later, she heard the door close. They could share decisions if he allowed her to express her views. But he had demanded. He believed love gave him that right.

ALL DAY, Patrick's theories troubled her. By evening, she wondered if she should call him. For what? To apologize, to give in to his demands? Did he know something he hadn't told her? He knew Greg Davies. Had the police officer given Patrick some piece of inside information?

The bracelet. Should she call the detective and tell him about the missing piece of jewelry? Surely one of the others had mentioned it.

The poinsettia reminded her of Patrick. So did the concert program. His gifts, his company, the way they had worked together in the yard this past summer had been times of enjoyment. Tonight, she had realized he had never forgotten the exciting and frenzied sexual encounter the night Jim had died. Neither had she, but her reasons had been different from his. Even then, he had loved her. She had been reaching for life. She wasn't sure she could explain the difference. Did she even want to try? Why, when he had made demands and ruined her growing ease in his presence?

She shook her head. She didn't want Patrick as a substitute for her husband. A partnership with equal sharing of decisions and responsibilities. Breaking the habit of dependency had been hard and she refused to allow herself to slide into the trap again.

With a sigh, she walked to the kitchen and loaded the dishwasher. The calendar on the refrigerator caught her eye. A star marked December twenty-eighth. Leila's birthday. Tears filled her eyes and spilled over. Why had she pushed all thoughts of her friend to some dark corner? Would the funeral be held here or upstate? When would it be?

In that instant, she understood Leila's desperate need to attend Joe Barclay's funeral. Even if it meant taking several days off without pay, she intended to attend her friend's funeral.

She hurried to the desk for her phone book. Under L for Leila, she found the Vernons' number. While she drank a glass of orange juice, she wondered if anyone in the Nursing Office had the information. She reached for the phone. Though she hesitated to intrude on the Vernons' grief, she needed to talk to someone who had also loved her friend.

A half-hour later, glad she had called, Susan hung up. No one from the hospital had spoken to Leila's parents. Susan's eyes were moist, her cheeks wet. The Vernons had needed to talk about their daughter.

She dialed the hospital. One of the evening supervisors answered. "Grace, this is Susan Randall...I'm still in shock...The funeral will be Tuesday at ten thirty...Powers...No, the burial will be upstate. I need Tuesday and Wednesday off. There are some things I need to do for her parents...Just Wednesday...All right, I'll see who I can trade for Tuesday. Thanks."

The call was transferred to Five Orthopedics. Trish answered and quickly agreed to trade days.

Susan put the receiver in the cradle. Trish's questions had made her wonder if Patrick's idea of a leave of absence had merit. Not because of danger but because of her coworkers' curiosity. Facing them would be a trial.

"I'm strong. I can handle this." The echo of Leila's words after Joe's death brought a fresh storm of tears.

Chapter 9

WHEN SUSAN entered the med room to organize her nine o'clock rounds, she groaned. The evening had dragged and allowed her too much time to think about Leila's death. Trish was off, Kit subdued and Julie looked as though some dark problem had infected her with insomnia.

And I have two problems, Susan thought. Having too much time to grieve for Leila and wondering what to do about Patrick. She didn't want the pair of problems to become entwined so tightly she could never unravel them.

"Are you all right?" Julie asked.

Susan turned. "Two and a half hours left. I'll never make it through them. What about you? You look like you're ready to cry."

"Larry, what else? I can't stop wondering what's been bothering him lately."

Susan nodded. "There's too much empty time tonight."

"Most of my thoughts aren't pleasant." Julie leaned against the sink. "Can we stop at the diner after work?"

"What, no date?"

"Larry's having dinner with Mrs. Barclay and her lawyer to discuss the sale of the practice. I'm not sure I care if he takes over or not."

"Is he still upset about Saturday night?"

"Let's talk at the diner. I don't want to say anything around here that could be misunderstood, misinterpreted or misused." She waved at Kit who stood outside the door with her face pressed against the glass.

"Good thinking. She's probably practicing the act of lip-reading. Why she wants to emulate Barbara, I'll never understand." Susan pushed the cart to the door.

SUSAN FINISHED report and closed the care plan book. "Have a good night," she said to the oncoming nurse. She reached for her purse. Julie waited beside the doctors' desk.

As they neared the locker room, Susan tensed and her steps faltered. There had been another death. Would there be a brown paper bag with her name printed in block letters and a present inside waiting in some unlikely place?

Julie reached around Susan and pushed the door open. "What's wrong? Finding it hard to enter because you're five minutes early?"

The teasing words failed to erase Susan's apprehension. She tried to smile and failed. When she reached her locker, she eased it open.

"There is something wrong," Julie said. "Is it more than Leila's death?"

Susan fitted her right foot into a boot. "Every time there's a death, I've found a present." She pulled on the left boot.

"You mean like the chocolates?"

Susan nodded. "Candy at the desk. Books in my locker. Perfume on my car."

"When?"

"After each death." Susan reached for her coat. "I'm surprised Kit didn't tell you. She was here for the books and I accused her of playing a joke."

"Weird." Julie's eyes narrowed. "You don't think I'm the one, do you?"

"I considered the possibility."

Julie shook her head. "I know I teased you about having a secret admirer, but I'd never pull a trick like that on you."

Susan slammed her locker door. "I figured that." But she also wondered if the gifts had been left to frighten her. "I can't think of anyone who'd leave gifts for me."

"What about Patrick?"

"He'd hardly sneak in here when he lives next door."

"Mr. Martin?"

"He leaves coffee for me at the desk."

Julie shrugged. "Maybe someone wanted to cheer you up. Since you found Barbara's body, you've been kind of jumpy."

"Haven't we all?" Susan walked to the door. She didn't mention the notes that had accompanied the presents. That would only give Julie more data for speculation and Susan had done enough of that herself.

As they walked to the elevator, Julie spouted a dozen names of men who worked at the hospital in the evening from pharmacists to maintenance.

By the time they reached the ground floor, they were joined by a number of nurses. The crowd headed for the exit and crossed the street to the parking lot.

Julie paused beside her car. "Meet you at the diner. I'll go in and order for us."

"Wait in your car for me."

"Not tonight. I'm starved. Coffee and a cheese omelet for you?"

"What else?"

FIFTEEN MINUTES later, Susan reached the diner and pulled in beside Julie's car. A brisk chill wind pushed against her back. When she opened the diner door, a blast of hot air hit her face. A quick glance around showed several men seated at the counter. She scanned the high-backed booths. Julie waved. Susan reached her friend and hung her coat on a hook jutting from the divider between the booths. She slid across the red plastic seat. Moments later, the waitress arrived with their order.

Julie ate with relish until half the omelet had disappeared. She looked up. "Kit was quiet tonight. No gossip. No wild tales. Do you suppose someone issued a warning?"

"I don't know, but the break from her pseudo-Barbara imitation was welcome. One stupid question or one inane comment would have finished me."

"Maybe she's afraid of Grace Rodgers. Our new supervisor reminds me of a drill sergeant."

Susan laughed. "She's reached her level of incompetency. I remember when Grace was a staff nurse. She hasn't changed."

Julie cut several pieces of omelet with her fork. "Why don't you put in for supervisor? You know a lot about nursing, the hospital and getting along with people and you have a BS."

"Thanks for the compliment, but I have no desire to go back to school. You know the rule. To obtain the position of supervisor, the candidate must be enrolled in a Master's program." Susan rested her form on the edge of the plate. "I've been thinking about requesting a transfer to days on another unit."

"I'll withdraw my request for the day position. I might have to any way."

"Don't. By the time I decide what to do, there'll be other positions. I'm not about to rush into anything."

"Lucky you. I wish I didn't have someone pushing me for a decision." Julie moved pieces of the omelet around the plate.

"De Witt?"

Julie nodded. "He wants me to resign. Since a friend has agreed to join him in buying the practice, he thinks I should work in the office full-time."

"Wouldn't you be bored?" Susan looked at her omelet. Why was Julie even considering that type of move?

"I'd be doing things like drawing blood, doing EKG's, taking histories and doing patient teaching. I'd even have my own patients."

Susan picked up a piece of toast. "You'd be working as a practitioner without the credentials. Won't he wait until you have a Master's?"

"I haven't mentioned school to him." Julie's fork tapped the plate. "Since his uncle died, we've hardly seen each other. That's why he was upset Saturday night. He spends a lot of time with his aunt."

Or another woman, Susan thought. "Just don't end up with nothing. Working in a doctor's office distances you from the latest in hospital care."

Julie continued to scramble her omelet. "I know that. I also know you don't trust Larry. I'm not sure I do either. I love him, but how long can love last without trust?"

Susan stared at her hands. Could love even take root without trust? "I don't know. Just think about your goals and options before you choose."

"I'm trying.' Julie leaned back. "How come you asked Trish to trade with you for tomorrow? You should have heard her gripe after she hung up. You'd think she had a command performance somewhere."

"She answered the phone," Susan said. "I'm taking Wednesday as a personal one. Leila's parents asked me to go through her things."

"Need any help? I could come for the morning."

Susan shook her head. There were things of Joe's at Leila's. Though Julie wouldn't intentionally gossip, Susan felt the need to protect her friend's secret.

"Do you think Leila was mugged?" Julie asked.

Susan shrugged. Did Julie share her suspicions? If Leila hadn't been mugged, she had been murdered, perhaps to protect someone's secret. "I don't know what to think."

"Me either. I always thought Barbara made up the story about the parking lot, especially when she injected your name into the telling. I wish the police would find who killed her."

"And who gave her the money." Susan held the cup for the waitress to refill. "Did you call them?"

Julie nodded. "They kept insisting I must have seen something and was deliberately hiding information."

Susan leaned forward. "I think someone frightened Barbara in the parking lot and the same person killed Leila." Even as she spoke, she felt doubt creep into her thoughts. "I'm also convinced Barbara's death is connected to the money."

Julie's voice dropped to a whisper. "I was afraid you'd think that."

"Why?"

Julie stared at the window. "I'd rather not say right now."

"Patrick has an odd theory. He thinks someone is after me."

"Why you?"

"Who knows." Susan didn't intend to air Patrick's views. Though they made sense, she didn't want to believe he might be right. There was no reason she could be the target. "He wants me to take a leave of absence. He has this idea he's my keeper."

"Aren't you afraid of losing him?"

"As a friend?"

"As more."

"Maybe I don't want more. Friendship is enough."

"I wish I felt that way. With Larry, it's all or nothing."

"Would nothing be that bad?" Susan leaned forward. How could she tell Julie her suspicions without Julie telling De Witt? If the younger nurse said anything, Susan believed she would be in the same danger as Barbara and Leila. "About De Witt—"

Julie reached for her coat. "I don't want to hear any more about him tonight."

Susan closed her mouth but Julie had already headed for the door. With a shrug, Susan reached for her coat. The next time she worked with Julie, she had some questions about De Witt she wanted to ask.

HE DROVE past Susan's house. Lights shone from the upper windows on one side. He parked at the curb across from the driveway and waited. When the house was dark, he opened the box on the passenger's seat.

The aroma of pine filled the car. The wreath had been made that afternoon. Last year, he'd bought a smaller one for Mommy and she had known whose death he had honored. Would Susan guess the Christmas wreath studded with red bows and silver bells were for the evening supervisor?

He frowned. The scent of pine failed to evoke Mommy's memory the way her perfume did. He inhaled and thought about the grave and the coverlet of green he had placed there.

Wishing he could mute the bells, he carried the wreath across the street. What if Susan or her tenant looked out the window? Stealth and secrecy were needed to complete his mission. As he crept down the driveway, pine needles scratched his face.

At the foot of the steps, he paused to check the street. He climbed the stairs and crossed the porch. Where should he hang the wreath? A hook embedded in the wood of the door provided the answer. He smiled. She knew.

After hanging the wreath, he stepped back to admire the door. He chewed the inside of his lip and rocked from his heels to his toes. In his imagination, he saw Susan's face and heard her exclaim pleasure over the gift. Though he wished he could watch her, he couldn't stay that long. He reached into his pocket. After tucking the glittering gold watch in the greenery, he smiled. When Susan found the watch, she would know why he had left the wreath. He turned and strode to his car.

SUSAN OPENED the door to check the temperature before she chose an outfit to wear to the funeral. The lilt of bells surprised her. For a moment, she stared at the wreath. Dread filled her chest. Then she saw no telltale note fastened to the greenery. The tension ebbed.

Patrick, she thought. The wreath was his apology. She started across the porch to thank him, but saw his car was gone. Tonight, she would drop by and offer her own regrets for the quarrel.

At a few minutes after ten, she stood in front of the gaunt Victorian house that had been converted into a funeral home. The irony of the choice struck her. Joe Barclay's service had been held here, too.

After Susan closed the door, she checked the board to see where the service would be held. She paused to sign the book on the lectern beside the door. How many people would attend? Leila had many acquaintances but few friends. As the pen formed the letters of her name, Susan felt as though she had just sealed the end of an important part of her life.

For a few minutes, she stood in the threshold of the Lilac Parlor. Though she had talked to the Vernons on Sunday night, she wondered if they would remember her. During one of their rare visits to Leila's, Susan had been invited to dinner. What she remembered from that evening was their pride in their only child and how inarticulate they had been about expressing their love.

A dark casket dominated the room. Susan's gaze slid past the bier to focus on the Grant Wood "American Gothic" couple seated on a plush sofa beside the flower stands. Slowly, she passed the rows of chairs. The elderly couple rose.

"Mrs. Randall, we're glad you came," Mr. Vernon said. As she shook his hand, she felt the calluses that spoke of years of hard work.

"I wish we were meeting for some other reason." Her voice sounded tight and thin.

Mrs. Vernon looked up. "She was coming home for Christmas. We got the letter yesterday." She wiped her eyes.

Susan clasped the elderly woman's hand. Rage arose toward the nameless assailant who had caused these people pain they couldn't express. She wanted to strike something or someone. The dark eyes that met hers were reminiscent of her friend's eyes. They glistened with tears the way Leila's had so often since Joe Barclay's death.

"Why?" Mrs. Vernon asked. "It makes no sense."

Susan shook her head. "I don't know." She put her arms around the older woman. "I loved her, too."

Mr. Vernon cleared his throat. "While you're at the house, if there's anything of hers you'd like, take it. Let me give you a key."

"I have one and she had one for my house. I know where she kept it so you don't have to worry. I'll take any important papers and bills to her lawyer and have her clothes ready for the Thrift Shop." Susan turned her head.

Trish approached the casket. With jerky movement, the thin nurse knelt, crossed herself and bobbed to her feet. She moved to the Vernons. "Hi, I'm Trish Fallon. I worked with Leila. She was an excellent supervisor."

Trish's arrival drew the Vernons' attention away from Susan. The cadence of the thin nurse's speech and the jerkiness of her movements made Susan wonder what Trish had taken before she arrived. While pondering the question, Susan moved to the foot of the casket. She hadn't expected the coffin to be open. Barbara's had been closed. Then Susan remembered Julie saying Leila's injuries had been to the back of her head.

Susan's gaze traveled along the white blanket. For a moment, her attention lingered on the spray of violet gladioli and the bouquet of white roses. She inched toward the head of the bier and forced herself to look at Leila's face. Heavy makeup hid the bruises Susan had expected to see. Her friend's pointed features had lost their acuteness. In some ways, Susan felt as though she gazed at a stranger.

Tears stung her eyes. Leila would never smile, never laugh, never cry again. This last thought allowed Susan to bank her tears. During the final days of her life, Leila had cried too many times.

Susan felt a hand brush her arm. She turned and saw Julie. With a quick movement, Susan stepped aside so the younger nurse could approach the casket. "I didn't know you planned to come."

"I knew you would need someone with you. Sorry I ran out last night, but I just wasn't ready to hear someone else put Larry down. Are you all right?"

Susan released her held breath. "I will be when some time has blunted the shock."

Several nurses and a half dozen members of the hospital's administrative staff arrived. Susan and Julie found seats in the last row.

"It's hard to believe she won't stop by for coffee while I'm eating dinner. We were supposed to go to brunch on Sunday." Susan gulped a breath. "She wanted to talk about her plans for the future."

Julie patted Susan's arm. "I know it won't be the same, but would you like to have lunch with me today? There are some decisions I'd like to talk about."

Julie was right that lunch with her wouldn't be the same as going with Leila, but Susan didn't want to be alone. "That would be nice." To keep from staring at the casket, she closed her eyes.

She felt someone slip into the seat beside her. She opened her eyes. Patrick handed her a tissue. She wiped the tears that trickled down her cheeks. Then she looked from Patrick to Julie. The presence of these friends eased her grief.

HE STOOD in the shadows near the door of the Lilac Parlor. He hadn't been able to resist coming to the funeral home. When he saw Susan, he had thought about slipping into the seat beside her. Would she guess he had been the one?

A strangled cry made him glance around to see if he'd been noticed. Who was that man and when had he arrived? Why was that man holding Susan's hand?

The watcher wanted to snatch the tissue the man gave Susan. His mind clamped on the raging emotions that threatened to explode. How dare Susan be with a man?

No one had the right to offer her love disguised as sympathy. She shouldn't let that man hold her hand. He slid from the shadows and crept into the hall. His shoes hit the hardwood floor in a thudding rhythm.

He wanted—he couldn't—he should—A thought unbidden and unwanted arose. He couldn't touch, not Mommy, not Susan, not anyone.

His emotions rose and fell like a boat on a stormy sea. He couldn't stop the tempestuous images of Susan and Mommy that abounded in his thoughts. How could she? Why did he feel this way?

His heavy steps jarred his body. He marched down the street and flung open the door of his shop. The bell above the door jangled in a wild melody. With giant strides, he tramped to the door leading to the basement workshop.

As he started down the stairs, his hand missed the switch. He paused at the bottom and flipped on the lights. A flash of brightness brought tears to his eyes. He blinked them away and crossed to the worktable.

With a groaning cry, he lifted the derringer the police officer had brought him. He hadn't told Detective Davies that he owned the gun or where he had lost it. He aimed at the target at the end of the room and clicked the trigger several times. Then he held the small pistol at eye level. How could something so small express his rage?

He loaded a target pistol. Gunfire cracked in the empty room. He fired at the target and emptied the pistol. After reloading, he shot again and again until the sound reverberated in his head.

With his rage spent, he walked to the target. His smile tightened. The bullets had obliterated Mommy's photograph. His head felt light. His body ached. He gulped deep breaths and waited for his composure to return.

SUSAN AND Julie stood on the steps of the funeral home and waved to Patrick. He had refused their invitation to join them for lunch. Instead, he had invited Susan to dinner.

Julie bounced down the steps. Susan followed. She wondered where the younger nurse had found the energy. Sadness washed over Susan. She would never go to lunch with Leila, never sit with her friend and people-watch. Susan pushed her grief aside and walked with Julie toward the craft and antique shops. Feathery clouds streaked the brilliant sky. When the wind blew, Christmas decorations danced on the light poles.

"That was terrific of Patrick to come," Julie said. "I wonder if you appreciate him." She paused to look at a window where a collection of antique toys spilled from Santa's sack.

"He's one of the best friends I've ever had."

"He's in love with you."

Susan stared at a mass of red and white poinsettias in the window of a florist's shop. "I know he is. He's also overprotective."

Julie grinned. "Aren't all men? I'd grab him before some other woman does."

As they strolled down the street, Julie stopped to admire and exclaim over every holiday window. Susan continued ahead.

"You've got to see this." Julie stood with her face pressed against the window of the Potter's Wheel. "Would you look at the teapot? I'm buying one for my mom."

Susan smiled. The lid had been fashioned to make it appear as though a person crawled from inside to escape the hot water in the pot. She entered the shop on Julie's heels.

While the younger nurse examined the selection of teapots, Susan browsed in the alcove off the main room of the shop. A set of pottery wine glasses caught her eye. She lifted one and liked the way the stem was molded into ridges that fit her fingers. The pale clay streaked with rusty tones matched Patrick's dishes. The set would make a nice and neutral Christmas present for him.

After several stops, they reached O'Quill's and were shown to a table at the rear of the long narrow room. Julie tucked her packages beneath the chair. "You know, we should have left the packages at the car. We walked right past where I parked." She craned her head. "Can you read the special board?"

Susan recited the list. "I'm having quiche and salad."

"With coffee," Julie said. "We'll make that two. Let me see what you bought."

Susan unwrapped one of the goblets. "For Patrick. They match his dishes."

While Julie admired the piece of pottery, the waitress took their order. "I like the way it fits my hand," Julie said. "Maybe I should buy a set for Larry. The way he's been drinking lately, he needs a firm grip on his glass."

Susan raised an eyebrow. "Could be the stress of his uncle's death and having to handle the practice alone." She frowned. Why was she defending De Witt?

Julie giggled. "I don't believe you said that."

"Neither do I."

The waitress arrived with their food.

Julie handed the goblet to Susan. "That's not the reason. I've been thinking about the things you said last night." She paused until the waitress left. "You know, his uncle wasn't going to make him a partner."

Leila had mentioned the same thing but the reason had died with her. Susan leaned forward. "Do you know why?"

"Larry wouldn't tell me." Julie lowered her voice. "There's something odd. I saw some charts in his study. One belonged to Trish. I was tempted but I didn't look."

"You did the right thing."

Julie picked up her fork. "He knew about Leila and his uncle. He planned to use her to threaten his uncle into making him a partner. I tried to talk him out of that, but I think if Dr. Barclay hadn't died, Larry would have."

Susan swallowed. Did Julie realize she had just given De Witt a motive for Leila's murder and for his uncle's as well? "Do you think he had anything to do with his uncle's death?"

"Larry?" Julie's eyes widened. "How could you think that?" She choked and coughed. "You know, Barbara had me deliver a lot of cryptic messages to him. I think she tried to blackmail him but he didn't bite."

"Are you sure?"

Doubt filled Julie's eyes. "I don't want to believe he did."

"What did Barbara know?"

Julie shook her head. "He never said. Neither did she." She pushed her plate away. "I can't eat another bite."

Susan tucked away the bits of information Julie had told her. She needed time to sort through them and fit the facts into a theory about the deaths. When the waitress brought the bill, they paid and left.

"I'll see you Thursday," Susan said.

"Do you want me to drive you home?" Julie asked.

Susan shook her head. "I'll walk. I've some thinking to do."

"That makes two of us. I have to tell Larry it's over and I'm not sure I can."

Susan strolled down the street. One by one, she reviewed the things Julie had said. She wasn't sure how they fit into the puzzle of the murders, but she planned to learn.

As she passed the Pub, she halted and backed a few paces. Trish and De Witt sat at one of the window tables. The thin nurse wore a uniform. Trish's mouth twisted and the stormy expression on De Witt's face spelled a quarrel. De Witt slapped several square pieces of paper on the table. Trish snatched and shoved them in her purse. When De Witt rose, Susan hurried home.

Another piece of the puzzle, she thought. The papers looked like prescriptions. He had a chart at his apartment with Trish's name on the cover. Barbara had blackmailed him. Once again, Susan wished Trish hadn't backed away the evening she had begun to talk about her problems.

Susan frowned. Drugs? With Trish's erratic behavior that seemed to be the answer.

PATRICK ARRIVED at Susan's twenty minutes early. He looked at the height of her heels and revised his plans.

"You're early," she said. "Where are we going?"

"I thought we'd walk."

"Next time, warn me." She walked to the stairs. "Be right back."

"I'll be here." He stood at the foot of the stairs and admired the way the forest green dress clung to her slender hips. Moments later, she returned. Then, holding hands, they walked to the center of town.

Outside the Japanese restaurant, Susan stopped to admire the window. A pair of silk screens were set in a bed of white pebbles. Several aged bronze lanterns had been placed near a large black rock. "Every time I pass, I stop to admire the screens."

"They belonged to the owner's grandmother." Patrick held the door for her.

A short Oriental man stood at the desk. "Mr. Macleith, we have not seen you for many weeks. Please to enjoy your dinner."

After Patrick hung up their coats, the man led them to a small table beside a woven bamboo screen. A waitress wearing a blue kimono offered them hot washcloths and menus.

Susan opened hers. After a few minutes, she looked up. "What would you suggest?"

"Tempura or Negamiaki. That's beef wrapped around scallions."

"Sounds delicious."

"Someday when you feel adventurous, we'll come for Sushi."

She shook her head. "I'll take an eternal raincheck on raw fish." She studied the delicate arrangement of flowers. "What a restful place. I've always wanted to eat here, but Jim hated to eat out."

Patrick wondered if she had used her husband's name to place a barrier between them. "Would you like plum wine or saki?"

"Do I have to choose? I've never tasted either."

"Order plum wine and I'll let you try my saki." He gave their order to the waitress and turned back to study Susan's face. "How are you feeling?"

"Tired...sad...maybe resigned."

He reached across the table and took her hands in his. "I know how it feels to lose a good friend."

She nodded. "Time is what it takes to dull the ache."

He smiled. "Your young friend is delightful."

"Julie's a good person. I wish she wasn't involved with De Witt."

"What's wrong with her seeing him?"

"I'm not sure, but he treats her in a strange way. At the hospital, he makes no secret of their relationship, but he makes her use the terrace door when she visits. He lives in one of those luxury apartments on the river."

Patrick shook his head. "Worrying won't help. She has to make her own decisions."

A smile lit her face. "Can you remember that?"

He laughed. "You got me. How was lunch?"

"When we finally ate, good...Julie's idea of forgetting problems is to shop. I think we visited every shop in town."

The waitress brought their drinks. Patrick poured saki into a small cup and offered it to her.

Susan sipped. "Interesting. Is it always served hot?"

"No, but this is my preference."

During dinner, their conversation touched on many subjects. Patrick's gaze followed Susan's movements—the way she held the wineglass, her attempts to eat with chopsticks, the changes in her expression as she tasted each new food.

As they walked home, he held her hand. He didn't want to leave her tonight the way he had so many other times. Their lips met. She responded by stepping into his embrace. In that moment, he knew he would spend the night.

SUSAN TOOK the key from her purse and opened the front door. She turned to smile at Patrick. His hands rested on her shoulders. He smiled and she knew she wanted him to stay tonight. The bells on the wreath jingled. She remembered the warmth and the feeling of being loved that his gift had brought.

As she turned to thank him, she caught a glimpse of gold tucked behind a red bow. She stepped closer and froze. Leila's watch. A chill rode her spine and jolted her heart into rapid action. Not Patrick. The secret gift-giver had left the wreath. As a warning? As a way of gloating?

"Is something wrong?"

She heard a sharp note in Patrick's voice and forced herself to smile. "Just a little nervous." And a lot afraid, but if she told him he would react. She would solve this puzzle on her own. She unbuttoned her coat and draped it over the arm of a chair. Patrick's coat covered hers. She turned. His eyes held an invitation and she needed the warmth he offered. She stepped into his arms. Her fears were swept away with the rush of emotions raised by his kiss.

"I love you," he said.

She raised her head and met his gaze. In that instant, she laid the past to rest and opened herself to the future. Her lips met his. He caressed her gently. His fingers moved in circles on her back. Myriad sensations swept along her skin.

Her fingers stroked his nape and brushed over his hair. She wanted to rush to completion where pleasure conquered and all sense of reality disappeared.

Slowly, he released her lips. "Are you sure this is what you want?"

The hesitancy in his voice charmed her. She caught his hand and led him to the stairs. "Oh, yes."

He laughed and put his arm around her waist. "You're all I've dreamed of for years." He shook his head. "I would never...I didn't want..."

She put her fingers on his lips. "I know, but I want you tonight."

"And every night?"

She swallowed. "Nothing is forever, and until that moment arrives, yes."

They reached the bedroom. Susan slipped out of his embrace and began to unbutton her dress. Patrick leaned against the doorframe. His eyes watched her every move. The desire she saw fanned her need for him. Her dress fell to the floor. Her underclothes followed. For several seconds, she felt self-conscious about her nudity, until she saw his expression.

Patrick loosened his tie, removed his jacket and shirt. His hands went to his belt. Susan watched as he took off the rest of his clothes. Lean, muscular and fully aroused. She stepped toward him. He met her

Janet Lane Walters

in the middle of the room.

His hands caressed her skin. She massaged the muscles of his back. Their mouths fused and their tongues thrust with questing movements. Patrick groaned and freed her lips. He edged her toward the bed.

He laved her nipples. Sharp, almost painful sparks sizzled along her nerves and gathered in her lower abdomen. She felt her memories fading until all she knew was the touch, the taste, the scent of him. Long dormant responses awoke. For the first time in months, she felt alive.

"Now," she said. With a cry of joy, she welcomed his penetration.

THOUGH PATRICK felt sated, he couldn't sleep. He shifted position. Susan stirred in his arms. Her curls tickled his chest. He controlled the desire to laugh aloud for fear he'd wake her.

His gaze swept the room. Jim's picture was missing from the bedside stand. As Patrick pondered the absence, he smiled. Hope became a soporific lulling him to sleep.

At sunrise, he woke to find Susan leaning on one elbow. Her lips brushed his chest and moved to his mouth. He groaned and pulled her on top of him. The kiss deepened. The day began with love and whispered confidences.

He yawned and curled around her softness. When he woke, she was gone. He sat up. The aroma of coffee told him where she was. A man's robe was draped over the end of the bed. Jim's? Her father? Not wanting to appear in either man's clothing, he pulled on his trousers and went downstairs.

When he entered the kitchen, Susan flashed a smile. "Coffee's ready. Pour me a cup, too. How many pancakes do you want?"

"Four to start." He kissed her nape. "What would you like to do today?"

Susan spooned batter onto the griddle. "What I'd like to do is different from what I'm going to do. You have to go to work and I'm going to Leila's to pack her clothes for the Thrift Shop."

"What about this evening?"

"I should be home by dinner time."

"Where do you want to go?"

"Let's wait and see." She took a deep breath. "Today isn't going to be fun."

Chapter 10

SUSAN DROPPED a soggy tissue in the nearly full wastebasket and reached for a dry one. Today's tears made up for the ones she'd held back so often since the night Leila had been killed. She took the last article of clothing from the closet. Memories of the day she and Leila had bought the dress surfaced and produced a fresh spate of tears.

She blew her nose and opened the dresser drawers. Nightgowns, underwear, sweatsuits and sweaters were added to the boxes beside the bed. Though the Vernons had suggested she take something for herself, she hadn't, not even a piece of costume jewelry.

A gasp escaped and she remembered last night's discovery. Patrick's presence and the emotional release of making love had driven tears and questions from her thoughts. Who had left the wreath?

Candy, books, perfume. The wreath could be considered flowers. This time, there hadn't been a note. Somehow, that was more frightening than the cryptic messages.

What was the meaning of this bizarre courting ritual? She shivered. For a moment, she felt exposed. She was alone in Leila's house. She shook her head. This wasn't the time to consider the connection between the gifts and the deaths. Later, when she was at home, she could make a list.

Before leaving the bedroom, she checked the dresser and the closet again. Everything except the clothes in the dryer had been packed.

Susan tucked the photograph of Joe Barclay and the album that documented the affair under her arm. She planned to take them home. She saw no reason for the Vernons' image of their daughter to be tarnished.

Papers next, she thought.

The dryer buzzed and diverted her attention. On her way to the small laundry room, she paused in the kitchen and poured a cup of coffee. While she folded the lab coats, slacks and sweaters, she sipped coffee and remembered all the things she and Leila had done together. With a sigh, she wondered if there was any place in the county they hadn't been together. She folded the last item and drained the cup.

Would memories of her friend remain vivid as long as those of Jim?

On her return to the kitchen, she found a paper bag and dropped the evidence of Leila's affair inside. She strode to the living room and sat at the Queen Anne desk. In the drawer, she discovered several packets of letters and cards from Joe Barclay. She added them to the bag and tackled the desk. The pigeonholes were neatly labeled. The bills, the checking and saving account books, the insurance policies and a copy of Leila's will filled a manila envelope.

Susan looked at the clock. Nearly three thirty. She stretched to ease the kinks in her shoulder muscles. After she closed the desk, she picked up the bag and the manila envelope and returned to the kitchen to wash the cup and clean the coffee-maker. .

Her tears began again and continued until she locked the door and walked to her car. After drying her eyes, she backed out of the driveway. Was Patrick home yet? She needed the comfort of his arms. Last night, she had found that and more. Their lovemaking had filled her with a desire to embrace life rather than live in the shadows.

She drove home and parked her car. When she saw Patrick's empty space, she frowned. Then she shook her head. She couldn't use him as an anodyne for her grief. He was the future.

She lifted the manila envelope from the seat. In her haste to reach the house, she had forgotten to stop at the lawyer's office. She strode up the drive and walked uptown.

There, she delivered the envelope and relinquished the keys to Leila's house and car. When she left the building, the sky looked as dull as she felt.

"Mrs. Randall, are you all right?"

Susan turned and saw Mr. Martin. "I will be."

"You've been crying."

She nodded. "Just some sad thoughts."

"Your friend. Wasn't her funeral yesterday?"

"Yes." Susan turned to walk away.

"Wait," he said. "Would you like to go somewhere to eat? I know it's early for dinner, but I bet you didn't eat lunch. Grief ruins the appetite."

"You're right. I didn't." She hesitated. "I'm not hungry."

"Then coffee. You might be better for the company."

I might, she thought. Though she would have preferred to be with Patrick, he wasn't home. Mr. Martin understood grief and she didn't want to be alone with all the memories of Leila that had been stirred today.

Mr. Martin opened the door of the coffee shop. "All those deaths. Such a sad thing."

Susan nodded. She ordered coffee and closed her eyes. Why had she come here with him? She wasn't ready to respond to anyone's curiosity.

"Have the police any idea who killed Ms. Vernon?"

His question jolted her. She opened her eyes. "I haven't heard anything other than what's been in the news." She reached for the coffee cup. "Do you mind if we don't talk about the deaths?"

He shrugged and dug into a piece of pie the waitress brought. "They say talking helps."

"I'm not ready yet." At least to talk about Leila during a meeting with someone she barely knew. "I'd like to thank you for the hours you spend as a volunteer. I'm afraid we take your help for granted."

He looked up. "It helps fill the hours."

She nodded. "That I can understand." She looked at the clock. "I've got to go."

"Let me drive you home. You look exhausted."

"Thanks."

WITH THE movements of a child whose fingers have brushed the hot burners of a stove, Patrick dropped the edge of the living room curtain. Who was this man who had brought Susan home? Where had she been? For a moment, he considered storming from the house and demanding an explanation and an introduction.

Whoa, he thought. He had no reason for jealousy. He and Susan had made love, but she had spoken no vows of love. She'd accepted his declaration and remained silent. Though she had promised to stay with him, she had also said nothing lasts forever. How could he experience this dreadful fear of losing her when there was no commitment?

He rose from the couch. At the kitchen counter, he reached for the phone. Had she invited the man inside?

With a groan, he halted the impulsive action. If he called her, she would know he'd been spying. He paced to the kitchen door and back again. He'd planned to call Greg and ask about the derringer. What better time than now?

"Pat, what's up?" Greg asked.

"Have you learned anything about the gun I found?"

"Nothing. No prints, no registration. The guy I mentioned is checking with other antique dealers. He'll call when he has something."

Patrick reached for a pen. "I wonder—"

"What?"

"Just a notion that's been bugging me."

"Is this one of your wild theories? Spit it out."

Patrick doodled on the pad he kept by the phone. "Why not have four murders by the same unknown person? Maybe for some kind of revenge."

"Have you been drinking?" Greg asked. "We're pretty sure the same weapon was used on the nurses. That's off the record." He paused. "What do you mean four murders?"

"Barclay and Mendoza."

"Barclay died upstate. He was shot. And Mendoza, that was an accident."

"Are you sure?"

"If I'm not, I'm not telling. The squabble over who's responsible for the hospital's parking lot is making me prematurely bald. They want the town to post officers but it's the hospital's property and they're responsible for security."

"You're right."

"Got to go. Talk to you soon."

Patrick hung up. Almost instantly, the phone rang. When he heard Susan's voice, he grinned. "Are you all right?" he asked.

"Not really."

"Are you too tired to go to dinner?"

"Let's eat in. I'll broil some chops and make a salad."

"Be right over to help." He hung up and grabbed his jacket.

THE MOMENT Patrick entered the house, Susan stepped into his arms. She pressed her face against his jacket.

He lifted her chin with his fingers. "Bad day?"

The concern in his voice warmed her. "The worst. I feel numb."

"Want to talk?"

She shook her head. She wanted to feel his head and savor his passion. "Love me."

"I do. I will." He drew her to the couch.

The warmth of his hands on her skin removed the chill that had settled there the moment she had entered Leila's empty house. His mouth moved from her lips and left a trail of fire behind. She felt alive and rejoiced in that feeling. When they were joined, she moved in harmony with him until her body exploded and came together again.

THE NEXT afternoon, Susan entered an empty lounge and wondered where her co-workers were. Trish was off, but Susan had expected to find Julie and Kit engaged in one of their sniping sessions. Susan filled a cup with coffee and carried it to the nurses' station. The cluster of women around Kit and Julie caused Susan to wonder what new scandal had erupted.

"Susan, what's your opinion?" one of the day nurses asked.

"About what?"

"Trish," Rhonda said. "Kit believes she knows why Barbara and Leila were killed and she's afraid she'll be next. Doesn't explain what she tried to do, though."

"What are you talking about?" Susan checked the patient board and reached for the chart rack for her assigned district.

"Trish was admitted to ICU early this morning." Kit flipped her red hair over her shoulder. "She overdosed on sleepers."

Guilt assaulted Susan. She had sensed Trish was troubled and had planned to talk to her the next time they worked together. "How is she?"

"Stable." Kit followed Susan across the station. "I hear she panicked and called for help. Good thing the media hasn't heard. They'd be nosing around for a story."

Susan placed her coffee on the desk. A thought jolted her. Sleepers. Prescriptions. She had seen De Witt hand Trish papers that looked like prescriptions. Had he suspected what would happen and deliberately given Trish the means? Before the shift ended, Susan hoped she'd have time to visit Trish and demand answers.

One of the day nurses reached for the care plan book. "Julie's testy this evening. Wonder what's eating her?"

"Trish and De Witt were seen together on Tuesday." Rhonda leaned against the counter.

Susan looked up. "I don't have time for gossip."

"You sure won't have time later." Rhonda cracked her gum. "You and Julie have to split the floor for meds and orders. They're sending a practical but there are no RN's available."

Susan counted the cluster of nurses at the desk. "Doesn't look like you were short on days. Meg's known for a month we were short this evening. Is it budget time, or was there an Inspection today?"

"Direct your complaints to the Nursing Office. Since Meg's on vacation, they're in charge."

By the time Susan made rounds and gave out five o'clock meds, she had fielded a dozen complaints and calmed several patients who demanded immediate attention. If she heard one more comment beginning, "During the day, they always come as soon as I ring," she would scream.

She looked at the stack of charts in her order basket. "Have that many doctors been in?"

Kit swivelled in her chair. "Left from days. You know, the more help they have, the less work they do."

"I believe you." Susan reached for the top chart.

"Guess what I heard in the cafeteria?" Kit's voice dropped to a whisper.

"I'm not even going to try."

"Someone tried to poison Trish's drink at the Oasis."

"Wrong. Trish never goes out after work."

"Then how about this? Trish knew the killer and he entered her apartment and doctored her liquor supply."

"Not even close. Give it up." Susan signed one chart and reached for another. "You'd better be careful. Gossips don't have a long shelf-life around here."

"I'll think about what you just said." As Kit walked to the end of the desk, she made a face. "Life won't be as much fun, though."

Julie put a tray on the counter. "Here's your salad." She frowned. "Didn't they do anything on days except gossip?"

"Doesn't look that way," Susan said.

Julie picked up half a sandwich. "Guess you heard about Trish and Larry. The vultures on the day shift couldn't wait to tell me."

"I heard, but I don't think it's what everyone suspects."

"Doesn't matter. On Tuesday night, I told him it was over."

Susan frowned. The tightness of the younger nurse's voice made her wonder if Julie meant what she said. "Do you really want to discuss this here?" She directed Julie's attention to Kit.

"You're right."

Kit turned. "Hide the tray. Here comes Grace Rodgers and you know how rule-bound she is."

Julie picked up the tray. "I'll put it in the med room until she leaves."

Susan put her hand on the tray. "Leave it. Grace should realize it's better for us to eat here than to put in for overtime."

When the gray-haired supervisor arrived, she looked at the tray. "I'm surprised, Mrs. Randall. You know the rules. No eating in the nurses' station."

Susan smiled. "I'm writing a complaint. We're short tonight. Meg knew about the problem a month ago. Since she's on vacation, you're responsible for the unit. Kit, how many charts with orders were left from days?"

"A dozen and they had an extra nurse on duty."

Grace nodded. "All right. I'll make an exception this time, but no complaints. If you want overtime, just call. Any problems pending?"

Susan gave report on the two post-ops and the pair of admissions. Julie mentioned a new patient.

"Grace, if you have time, talk to Mrs. Levy, Room 512. Maybe she'll respond to a little TLC from the supervisor." She reached for the remainder of the charts.

A short time later, Tina came to the desk. "Could you help me with Mrs. Price?"

"Be glad to."

When Susan returned to the desk, Kit was gone. Julie and De Witt stood at the doctors' desk. The younger nurse stood with her hands on her hips.

"Didn't you get my message?" Julie asked. "I thought I was perfectly clear."

"Don't act like this." De Witt smoothed his ash blond hair and picked up a black leather jacket. "Meet me at the Oasis when you get off. We'll talk."

"No."

"Then come to the lounge."

"I'm really too busy right now and I have nothing to say to you."

"If you want, I'll meet you in the parking lot. You can drive and bring me back for my car."

"I'm not going anywhere with you." Julie bolted from the station and dashed into one of the patient rooms.

De Witt paused in front of the small kitchen where nourishments were kept. "Eleven thirty at the Oasis. Be there."

Susan reached for the last chart. After signing the order sheet, she went to help with evening care. At nine fifteen, she entered the med room and leaned against the door.

"My sentiments exactly. Want to stop at the diner after work?"

Susan shook her head. "Patrick will be waiting for me."

"That's a switch. I take it you're an item."

"We're exploring the possibilities."

"That's great. I really liked him." Julie pushed her med cart to the door. "See you later."

There was no time to talk before the night nurses arrived. Susan had just reached for the care plan book when Kit announced a patient with a hip fracture was on the way.

The night nurse groaned. "Can you show me how to set up Buck's traction?" She glanced at the other night nurse. "Mavis won't help me. She thinks I'm dumb."

Susan saw a glimmer of tears in Amy's eyes. "After report." She opened the care plan book.

A short time later, Susan and Amy walked toward the storage room. Julie joined them. "Am I ever glad this evening is over," she said. "Maybe we can talk on the way to the parking lot."

"I'm giving Amy a hand."

"I'll wait."

Amy entered the storage room hall. "Be with you in a few."

Susan breathed a sigh of relief. "Saved again. I haven't been in there since I found Barbara's body. You don't have to wait. I'll grab a security guard."

"There are a couple of things I want to ask you and I'm off tomorrow."

"Lucky you." Susan looked up. De Witt strode down the hall.

Julie gasped and backed away. He grabbed her arm. "I said we need to talk." De Witt's voice was harsh. "I know the rumors upset you, but they're absolutely false."

"That's not the reason. I broke off before I heard about you and Trish."

"Don't trash what we have. I'm depending on you."

Julie nodded. "Are you afraid of what I might say? Don't worry. Just leave me alone." She pulled away and ran toward the locker room.

Susan felt torn. She had promised to help Amy, but she didn't like De Witt's mood. She moved into the storage room hall. What had Julie meant? "Amy, I've got to go."

"Just five minutes, please?"

LIKE THE fingers on a multitude of hands, streamers of fog drifted from the cemetery toward the hospital parking lot. The lights set around the perimeter resembled shadow suns. He crouched beside the steps and waited for the evening nurses to finish their shift.

Since Mommy protected Susan, Julie was his target tonight. She never waited for the other nurses or the security guard. He had often seen her dash across the street alone. A grin contorted his mouth.

He thrust his hand in the pocket of his black jacket and touched the weight. Then he peered into the billowing fog. Time crept. He counted to one hundred and checked his watch again. The chill of the December night reached his bones. His heart raced. He forced himself to breathe slowly and evenly.

Loud voices startled him. He edged toward the chain. A group of nurses started up the steps. They moved in and out of the haze. Had he missed Julie? She was usually the first to arrive.

Cars left the parking lot. Susan's remained. So did several others. Which one was Julie's? Had she left? Four women emerged from the fog and paused directly in front of him.

"Are Julie and Susan coming to the diner?"

"I doubt it. De Witt ordered her to meet him at the Oasis and Susan never joins us."

"Julie said she wasn't meeting him. His car's still in the doctor's lot. You know, I don't blame her for seeing him. Imagine going places in a Jag."

"Dream on. He's only interested in RN's."

Moments later, four cars left the lot. Three remained. He crossed the chain and stood on the steps. The sound of shoes tapping on the concrete alerted him. He drew the weight from his pocket. He had to be ready for her. Julie appeared on the step below him.

The instant she reached him, he grabbed her. His left forearm tightened across her throat. For someone so slender, her strength surprised him. She twisted and kicked at his shins. Her elbow rammed into his gut. He caught her flailing arm with one hand and raised the weight.

She pulled free. Her eyes widened. "You!"

He lunged and struck a glancing blow with the weight. She pushed him away. He grabbed her. Her teeth clamped on his hand and the weight clattered on the steps.

"Help!" she cried.

AS SUSAN hurried down the hall, she could barely control her fear for Julie. When the younger nurse had refused De Witt's demand for a meeting, his eyes had flashed with anger. Why hadn't Julie waited in the locker room? Where had the girl gone?

Susan ran past the deserted security desk and stepped outside. Fog blurred her view of the parking lot. She stared at the billowing grayness. Had someone shouted? Like a bubbling cauldron, patches of fog twisted and churned. She gasped.

On the steps across the street, she saw a struggling couple. One of them wore a black jacket.

Fog shrouded the struggle. Susan pushed open the ER doors. "Help! Across the street. Someone's being attacked," she yelled to the guard who strolled down the hall. She let the door bang closed and ran across the street. The fog lifted. She saw Julie and her attacker. The man had light hair. De Witt, Susan thought. "Help!" she cried again and started up the steps.

"HELP!" THE CRY from the street penetrated his concentration. He pushed Julie away. She fell and her head hit the steps. He bellowed his rage.

"Stop! Would someone help?"

Susan. What was she doing here? Mommy protected Susan. She mustn't see him. She was like Mommy and she would tell everyone how bad he was.

Panic froze him. He stared at Julie. She was dead. She had to be. The weight. Where was it? He searched the steps. Everything was falling apart. He jumped and leaped over the chain.

A MAN'S VOICE rose in an angry roar. Susan ran up the steps. By the time she reached Julie, the mugger had vanished. Susan knelt beside the younger nurse. "Julie, Julie, are you all right?" A strong pulse beat against her fingers.

Julie groaned. Her eyelids fluttered open. "He...he..." Her blue eyes were unfocused. She sighed and closed her eyes.

"Julie, Julie." This time Susan's cries brought no response. "Would someone help?" she shouted.

While she waited for an answer, Susan unbuttoned her coat and searched her uniform pocket for her penlight. She shone the beam into the younger woman's eyes. "Does anyone hear me?" Julie needed help but Susan feared leaving. The attacker might return.

"What's wrong?" A man's voice cut through the fog.

"I need help. There's been another mugging."

Moments later, a figure appeared at the bottom of the steps. When she realized his hair was as dark as his jacket, Susan swallowed her scream.

"What did you say?"

"There's been another attack. I interrupted it. Get a stretcher. She's hurt, I'm not sure how badly."

"Hang on, I'll be right back."

Susan noticed the way Julie's left leg was bent beneath her. Until help arrived, the younger nurse couldn't be moved. Susan slipped her hands under Julie's head and felt a large hematoma.

Two security guards and a nurse from the ER arrived. They moved Julie on a lift board and carried her down the steps to the gurney.

"What happened?" one of the guards asked. "How did she fall?"

"She was attacked. I saw her struggling with a man."

"Thought you nurses were supposed to wait for an escort?" A belligerent tone entered his voice. "Are you sure you didn't imagine the attack? Visibility's not too good what with the fog and all."

"There was a man. I yelled and ran across the street. He pushed her and ran into the cemetery."

The ER doors opened. Susan and the ER nurse pushed the gurney into a treatment room. Mary Brady, a friend of Susan's, followed them. "What happened?"

Susan related the event she'd witnessed. "She must have hit her head on one of the steps. There's a hematoma on the right occipital area. For a few seconds, she responded and then lapsed into unconsciousness." She gulped a breath. "Pupils are equal and sluggish. There's a possible fracture of the left tib/fib."

While Susan spoke, the ER doctor completed his exam. "Start an IV, routine labs, X-ray skull, cervical spine and left leg. Ortho and neuro consults, stat."

Mary caught Susan's hand. "Why don't you wait outside? I'll let you know what we find. She'll be fine."

"I'll call her parents. You'll need consents." Susan stopped at the desk and dialed Julie's home number. After six rings, a sleepy voice answered.

"Mrs. Gilbert, it's Susan Randall. Julie's had an accident and she's in the Emergency Room...not her car. She hit her head on the steps in the parking lot...I'll stay until you arrive." And when they did, she would tell them what had happened. She opened the door and stepped into the hall. A policeman sat on the edge of the security desk.

"There she is," the security guard said. "She's the one who found her."

The officer opened a notebook and motioned to Susan. "Tell me about the attack you thought you witnessed. Start with your name, address and phone number."

The tone of his voice made Susan wonder if he was skeptical about the attack. What had the security guard said? His absence from the desk was responsible for Julie's danger, but so was the younger nurse's impulsive nature. Susan stated her name and then recounted the scene she'd witnessed.

"Did you get a look at the assailant?"

"I didn't see his face. He was taller than Julie. He had light hair and wore a black jacket. He—" She stopped. Before she accused De Witt, she needed proof. Right now, Julie was the only one who could identify her attacker.

The officer placed a gray metal object on the desk. "Any idea what this is?"

"A traction weight."

"Any idea why your friend was carrying it?"

Susan frowned. "It's not something you'd drop in your pocket and forget."

"Would make a great weapon." The officer nodded. "Maybe your friend can tell us."

"She's unconscious," Susan said.

"Any connection between her and the other nurses who were attacked?"

"She worked with Mrs. Denton and Ms. Vernon was our supervisor."

"Think she'd know anything about their deaths? Maybe who killed them?"

Susan shook her head. "She knew as much as any of us."

"What about common enemies? Maybe some patient who had a grudge?"

"Not that I can think of." She frowned. De Witt was the only person she could think of who had a connection to the three women.

"Guess that's all for now." The officer turned to the guard. "Have someone call the station as soon as the nurse is able to talk." He tapped his notebook. "Your statement will be ready Friday if you want to read it. If you think of anything else, call." He strode to the door.

His words reminded Susan that she hadn't called about Barbara's bracelet—or Leila's watch. She needed to tell someone. Not Patrick. He would overreact.

She walked to the machines for a cup of coffee. Then she carried the steaming liquid to the waiting room.

AT MIDNIGHT, Patrick opened the front door and checked for Susan's car. Late again. He stared toward her side of the house and wondered how she'd react if she came home and found him in her living room. He shook his head. Though they had gone beyond friendship, she wasn't ready for total togetherness.

To let her know he was still awake, he switched on all the downstairs lights. He turned on the television and stretched out on the couch.

When the mantle clock struck two, he sat up and looked around in confusion. He hadn't meant to sleep.

Susan, he thought. He must have missed her. Then he saw the porch light through the curtained windows. Where was she? Had she gone to the diner with Julie? Even so, she should be home. He opened the door and saw an empty space where her car usually sat.

For several minutes, he allowed the winter air to chill the heat of his panic. After closing the door, he walked to the kitchen and snapped on the radio and picked up the coffeepot.

The announcer's first item sent chills down his spine. "A third mugging at Bradley Memorial Hospital has left a nurse in critical condition. Her name is being withheld pending notification of her family."

Coffee filled the mug and flowed over the counter. Were they talking about Susan? Was that why she hadn't come home? Should he call the hospital? He pulled on his jacket and headed for the door. Phone reports from any hospital were always less than satisfactory.

As he started down the steps, headlights shone down the driveway. Relief flooded his senses. He was at the driver's door before Susan opened it. Once he had her in his arms, he kissed her, hard and demanding. "Don't ever do this to me again."

"What are you talking about?" she asked.

"I fell asleep and woke to find you weren't home. When I heard about the mugging, I was afraid you were the victim. Who was it?"

Susan pressed her face against his jacket. "Julie. I interrupted the attack and stayed until her parents arrived and learned she was responding. She was admitted to ICU."

"Why didn't you call? Didn't you realize I'd be frantic?" He

couldn't keep fear and anger from his voice. When she stiffened, he
regretted the questions.

"I didn't think of anything but Julie. She was unconscious when I
found her. If I'd been a few minutes earlier, he wouldn't have grabbed
her."

"You could have been killed."

She shook her head. "If there had been two of us, it wouldn't have
happened."

"Don't blame yourself."

"I'm not." She shivered. "Let's go inside before I freeze." She
pulled him to the steps. "I'm drained. Even before the attack, the
evening was a horror." She opened the door and turned on the lights.

Patrick closed the door. He turned Susan to face him. "Is she all
right?"

"So far." Susan slumped on the couch. "A concussion with loss of
consciousness and a fractured leg." She rubbed her arms with her
hands. "When I left, they said she was responding to treatment." She
put her hands to her face. "Pat answers. I'll never use them again."

Patrick walked to the bar and filled a snifter with brandy. "Did
they catch the attacker?"

"By the time help arrived, he was gone." Her voice rose in pitch.
"De Witt tried to force Julie to go out with him." She accepted the
snifter and sipped. "If Amy hadn't needed help, I would have left with
Julie. I ran to catch up with her. The security guard wasn't at the desk. I
saw her fighting with a man. I screamed and ran to help her."

Patrick organized her narrative into logical order. He joined her
on the couch. "You're brave and wonderful. You must have been
terrified."

"I was too angry to be scared."

"Did you get a good look at the man?"

She shook her head. "Taller than Julie. Light hair. Black jacket.
That's all I saw."

He looked at her. "But you have suspicions?"

"In a way."

Patrick pulled her into his arms. "Tell the police what you suspect.
If he's capable of harming Julie, what do you think he'd do if he knew
you suspected him?"

"If I tell them, he'll know I did. I'm sure he has an alibi. Without
proof, what can the police do?"

"I don't know. Why do you think he's the mugger, other than his physical description?"

Susan closed her eyes. "Julie said Barbara tried to blackmail him. Leila knew why Joe Barclay wasn't offering him a partnership. He wanted Julie to alibi him for something. I'm almost sure he gave Trish prescriptions and she tried to kill herself."

Patrick straightened. "You have to tell Greg. Tell him everything you know or suspect."

"I have to talk to Trish and Julie first."

"Tomorrow, first thing, you call Greg." He took her silence for agreement. "What's wrong with a doctor writing prescriptions?"

"Because she's addicted. If he's her supplier—" She exhaled. "I would have had proof *if* the evening hadn't been so hectic."

Patrick grasped her hand. "Tell the police."

"Of course."

He tightened his grip. She was in danger. How could he protect her if she refused his help? "Please be careful."

"I will."

He stroked her throat with his thumbs. His tongue traced her lips. "Let's talk about this upstairs." He pulled her to her feet.

Instead of eagerness he felt her hesitate. "This is happening all too fast," she said.

He kissed her forehead. "I love you. Are you sure you want to be alone tonight?"

Her smile heated his desire. "Maybe not."

Chapter 11

SUSAN CRUSHED the front page of the newspaper and tossed it at the wastebasket. "Local Nurses Decimated." The latest news headline imitated a supermarket tabloid. Instead of producing a chuckle, this aping made her angry.

Several minutes later, she retrieved the wadded paper. At least someone had believed her report about the mugger. Last night, she had feared the police officer had agreed with the security guard and decided Julie had an accident. After smoothing the sheet, she settled on the couch to read the article.

"Last night, despite increased security measures, the Bradley Memorial parking lot was the scene of yet another mugging. Twenty-three-year-old Julie Gilbert suffered multiple injuries and is listed in satisfactory condition. The quick action of an unidentified nurse prevented this from becoming another tragedy. Where were the police?"

Susan scanned the rest of the page. Each paragraph ended with a question pointing to police neglect. She frowned. That wasn't how it had happened. Where had the security guard been when Julie had run past his desk. He hadn't been at his station when Susan had arrived either. She put the paper on the table. Had the hospital's publicity department hidden that fact?

Wait until I see Patrick. Had he noticed the semi-sensational reporting style that had crept into the pages of the News? Was there anything he could do about it? She laughed at herself. What power did the Arts and Leisure Editor have over the front page?

With a sigh, she lifted the basket of dirty clothes from the floor beside the couch and walked to the basement door. The kitchen radio blared the opinions of a local psychic.

"I see the face of the killer covered by a shroud. If I could touch an article worn by one of the victims during the attack, the veil would be torn and his aura captured. Though I've informed the police of my willingness to aid in the search for this evil man, they haven't responded to my offer."

"No wonder," Susan said. She closed the basement door and went down to the laundry room. "And I have my suspicions and no proof."

After loading the washer, she returned to the kitchen and stood at the counter to make a shopping list that included the extras she needed for Christmas baking. The radio program had now turned to a pair of psychologists who stated their opinions regarding the psychological profile of the killer.

"A very disturbed man," a deep voice said. "A gray soul who had difficulty expressing his emotions. He sees the hospital as a symbol of authority, as the giver of life and death, and is rebelling against this power. He will present himself to others as the man next door."

"Disturbed, I agree," a second voice said. "But I disagree with my esteemed colleague's assessment of the killer's character. In my opinion, the killer is the product of sexual abuse. Killing gives him a sense of power and allows him to express his hostility toward women and to his mother in particular."

Susan snapped off the radio. "What about a greedy doctor who's earning cash on the side by writing prescriptions for addicts." She closed the pantry door and pinned the list to the bulletin board.

AT ONE-THIRTY, Susan stopped at the deli and bought a sandwich. With Trish and Julie as patients, the unit would be short staffed. A sandwich would be easier eaten on the run than a salad.

After she pulled into a space on the second tier of the hospital parking lot, she stayed in the car and devised questions to ask Julie and Trish. If these answers confirmed her suspicions, she would call Greg Davies and tell him about De Witt.

A few minutes later, Susan entered the Intensive Care Unit. She scanned the visible section of the desk that formed a circle around a central core to find her friend, Marge. Her search failed so Susan walked to where she could see the rest of the desk.

Before she moved five feet, a petite black nurse grabbed her arm. "A float... Thank heavens they got you to come in early. With three patients, we're pushed."

Susan shook her head. "I'm not a float. I'm here to see Julie Gilbert. We work together on Five Ortho. If I'm lucky, I won't have thirty-six patients tonight, just eighteen. Have you seen Marge Inglasia?"

"You'll find her somewhere between four and six. Have you ever considered transferring here?"

"Sometimes, but I think I'd be bored." Susan spotted Marge's black curls and headed for the cubicle where her friend regulated an intravenous. She paused in the doorway.

Marge turned. "She's in four. Stop on your way out and we'll talk."

"Will do."

Susan entered Julie's cubicle. For several minutes, she studied the younger nurse with a professional eye. Julie's eyes were closed. Her skin color was good. The fractured leg remained in a soft cast. The lines on the monitor above the bed showed a normal heart rhythm. Susan exhaled and walked to the bed.

"Julie, it's Susan."

The younger nurse's eyes opened. "Hi." Her voice emerged in a hoarse whisper. Her hand moved to touch her throat.

"It's all right," Susan said. "You don't have to make conversation. You look so much better than you did last night."

"Thanks."

"I'm glad I arrived in time."

Julie smiled. "Me, too. Mom told me." She coughed.

Susan poured a glass of water and positioned the straw so Julie could sip. "Don't talk. A yes or no will do. Do you remember who attacked you?"

Julie frowned. "I..." Her eyes closed over a look of frustration. "He...he..." A coughing spasm ended with a hoarse intake of breath.

Susan squeezed Julie's hand. "Don't let this upset you. You'll remember. Is there anything you need?"

Julie grinned. "Out of here."

"Will be awhile." A few minutes later, Susan rose. "I want to see Trish before I head upstairs. I'll try to run down after nine o'clock meds."

As Susan left the cubicle, Marge motioned. "She's doing great."

"Why can't she talk?"

Marge walked to the end of the desk. "Let's go in the break room. I don't want everyone in the world to see how angry I am."

Susan followed her friend into the small break room. Marge poured a cup of coffee and looked at Susan. She shook her head and leaned against the now closed door. "All right, what's wrong? If you're this angry, there must be something serious going on."

"Do you know where the guard was?"

"Not at the desk, that's for sure."

"Watching TV in the ER waiting room. He figured all the nurses were gone. He should have been there."

"You're right. What about Julie? Do you think she'll remember who attacked her?"

Marge shrugged. "She was unconscious for a couple of hours. She doesn't remember anything about last night after giving report."

Susan frowned. Had Julie forgotten De Witt's storm trooper tactics or was she protecting him? "She sounds like a rusty hinge."

"From pressure applied to the throat during the attack. For a while, they thought they'd have to do a trach. I'd like to get my hands on the bastard who did this."

"I wish I had arrived a few minutes earlier."

"And caught him." Marge's grin was fierce. "We could have had a lynch party. Three of us, Susan. It's not right."

Susan stared at the floor. And all three knew something about De Witt. Why can't Julie remember? "You're right. It's a nasty situation and everyone's wondering who'll be next." For a moment, she thought about the gifts. Fear swamped her. She inhaled and gained control.

"Damn guard."

Susan nodded. "When I yelled about the attack, he came strolling down the hall. It took him an eternity to follow me."

"If they don't fire him, let's take him into the alley and show him how it feels."

"Good idea." Susan reached for the doorknob. "What's in store for Julie?"

"When she's stable, they'll cast her leg. I think they should keep her here until the killer's caught."

"Maybe she'll be sent to Five Ortho."

"Maybe you're dreaming."

"You're right. Our nurse manager has some strange ideas about the presence of friends and relatives as patients on the unit. She's afraid they'll get special attention."

"Who deserves it more than one of our own?" Marge emptied the remains of her coffee in the sink. "Meg has funny ideas about a lot of things. When is she due back from vacation?"

"Monday."

"Did you get a good look at the mugger?"

"I was too far away and I made enough noise to scare a battalion." She stepped into the hall. "I'll try to get down later. Who's on?"

"No one you know." Marge followed Susan past the desk. "I'll let whoever has Julie know you're coming. Are you sure you didn't get a good look at him?"

"I was more concerned with stopping the attack."

As she rode the elevator to the fourth floor, Marge's question echoed in Susan's thoughts. She hadn't seen his face, but she believed she knew who he was. What if she was wrong? She shook her head. Who else needed these deaths? It had to be him.

Without proof would anyone believe her? Though Julie's amnesia had prevented a confirmation of the attacker's identity, Susan hoped Trish's answer would give her the proof she needed.

Susan entered the cul de sac on Four Med/Surg and walked to the private room beside the patient's lounge. When she knocked, Trish called out. Susan opened the door.

Trish stood at the window. "A colleague. What an unexpected pleasure." Bitterness tinged her voice.

"I wanted to get down last evening, but we were short."

"As usual. Bet you don't get a break tonight either."

"I guess you've heard about Julie."

"Is she all right?"

"Post concussion. Amnesia for the period of the attack. Fractured tib/fib. We're down two RN's until you get back."

"Don't hold your breath." Trish turned her head but not before Susan saw tears in the other nurse's eyes. "I'm out of here on medical leave. On Monday, I enter a drug rehab program. Mandated."

Susan touched the thin nurse's arm. "You'll make it."

"Will I? What do you know about me?" Trish walked to the bed. "Damn him."

"Who?"

"De Witt, who else?"

Susan nodded. "I saw the two of you at the Pub. Is he your supplier?"

"Not anymore."

"How long?"

"Four years. You don't think I followed him out of love. He introduced me to the benefits of amphetamines and then wrote me scrips for a price. Tuesday's were the last. He's gone legit." While Trish talked, she prowled the room. "This isn't the first time he's cut me off. He tried when Barbara found my stash and tried to blackmail him."

Susan leaned against the wall. "Why did he change his mind?"

"She died."

"Why should he stop now?"

Trish laughed. "His uncle died and now he has a large and lucrative practice. He can't afford shady dealings. Tell Julie what he's about. Maybe my story will open her eyes."

"She broke off with him Tuesday. She's stopped trusting him. Maybe she knows."

"I wish everyone did. He's slime."

"Do you think he's the one who killed Barbara?"

"De Witt?" Trish laughed. "Wrong. He's too much the coward. He'd never do anything where he couldn't push the blame on someone. If anyone had learned how he was supplying me with drugs, he would tell everyone how he pitied me and he thought he was helping."

Susan pursed her lips. As angry as Trish was, she sounded as though she believed the things she said.

"That's not what I wanted to hear."

"It's all I can say. You'd better go up or you'll be late. Days will panic if they think one of them has to pull a double."

Susan paused at the door. "Keep in touch. I mean it."

Instead of waiting for the elevator, Susan ran up the stairs and pushed open the door on five. She waved to the physical therapist helping a patient master crutch walking.

What if De Witt wasn't the mugger? Then why had he wanted Julie to alibi him? She pushed these questions aside.

After hanging her coat in the locker room and changing into white oxfords, she headed to the lounge. Kit strode toward her.

"Bet you went to see Julie," Kit said. "How is she?"

"Improving." Susan edged past the secretary, opened the refrigerator and put her sandwich on the shelf.

"So who did it?"

"She doesn't remember the attack."

"I bet she never dashes out of here alone again." Kit held the door open. "So tell me what happened."

"She was mugged. That's all I'm going to say."

"Aren't you tired of witnessing all this violence?"

Susan poured coffee and walked to the door. "Yes."

Kit pushed her hair from her face. "Aren't you scared? You found Barbara, stopped at Mendoza's accident, Leila was your best friend and you rescued Julie. You could be next."

"Of course I'm scared and so are most of the nurses who work evenings. Aren't you scared, too?"

"Petrified. Who do you think it could be?"

"I don't know." Once again doubts arose. What if it wasn't De Witt?

"I bet he recognized you last night. Who was it?"

Susan bit her lip to keep remarks about De Witt from escaping. "Some coward."

Kit smiled. "So you do know who he is."

Susan shook her head. "What else could he be but a coward. He could have stayed and attacked me, too."

"Come on. Is it someone we know?"

Without answering, Susan walked to the station. When she saw the pair of part-time nurses at the desk, she smiled.

"How's Julie?" the blonde asked.

"Awake and alert but doesn't remember anything."

Susan became the center of a gathering of nurses. "How does it feel to be a heroine?" Rhonda asked.

"Did you really interrupt the attack?" the dark-haired evening nurse asked. "Did you recognize him?"

"I was too far away." Susan reached for the care plan book. "How about report?"

During report, the many interruptions with questions about Julie and the attacker made Susan want to scream. She was glad to see the day nurses leave and to begin her work. When she left to eat her dinner in the lounge, Kit followed her.

"Aren't you going to the cafeteria?" Susan asked.

"Not when I haven't heard the whole story about last night. I called the police and told them about De Witt storming in here and demanding Julie go with him."

Susan groaned. "Why did you do that?"

"They needed to know. Now tell me what really happened."

"You've heard everything I have to say." Susan opened the sandwich.

"You didn't describe him," Kit said. "Even if you didn't see his face, you must have seen more than you're saying."

"If I knew who it was, I'd tell the police, not you."

The lounge door opened and the volunteer entered. "Hi, Mr. Martin," Susan said.

Kit turned. "Did you know Susan's a heroine? Someone attacked Julie in the parking lot and Susan chased him away."

"That was very brave." He stood near the bulletin board. "Weren't you afraid of being attacked, too?"

"I didn't think, I acted."

"Will Julie be all right?" he asked.

"Of course."

Kit walked to the door. "See you later."

Mr. Martin sat across from Susan. "Does Julie remember anything about her attacker?"

"Very little, but she will. It wouldn't be fair for him to get away without paying."

He gasped. One hand felt to his chest and he fumbled in his pocket with the other.

"Mr. Martin," Susan said.

Something flew from his hand and rolled across the floor. Susan scrambled after the object. She returned to the table, opened the vial and offered one of the tiny tablets to him. His face contorted with pain. With shaking fingers, he placed the tablet under his tongue. Seconds later, the signs of pain vanished from his face.

"Let me take you to the ER."

He shook his head. "The pain's gone. I'll rest a bit and then be out to help you."

"Are you sure you should work tonight? Maybe you should go home and call your doctor."

"You might be right. I'll go home." He sighed. "I feel like I'm letting you down."

She shook her head. "Never. I'll be back to check you in a few minutes. If you don't look better, I'll take you downstairs."

"Thank you."

AT QUARTER after ten, Susan hurried to the elevator. Med rounds were finished, charts written. There was time to talk to Julie and demand answers. Though Trish had confirmed De Witt's involvement in her addiction, that only proved he was unethical. Susan hoped the information about Trish would force Julie to name the leonine doctor as her attacker.

As she walked past the ICU desk, one of the nurses looked up. "You must be Susan. Marge said you'd be down. She's been sleeping since I came on duty."

"I won't wake her." Though the thought of a delay didn't suit her plans, she couldn't force the issue.

Susan entered the glass-walled cubicle. Before she reached the bed, she knew something was wrong. Julie rolled her head from side to side. The rumpled covers added to the picture of restlessness. Susan turned back to call the nurse but no one was at the desk. In two steps, Susan reached the bed.

"Julie," she called.

The younger nurse's eyes were wide and staring. Susan began a neurological assessment. The left pupil reacted sluggishly. Julie moaned. The random movements of her head and body increased. A stream of vomitus shot across the room. Susan turned Julie on her side and stabbed the call bell.

"What's wrong?" The nurse who had spoken to Susan on her arrival appeared in the doorway.

"I'm not sure. She's restless. No reaction from her right pupil. Projectile vomiting."

"Can you stay while I call the house doctor and the neurologist?"

"Yes." Susan wrapped a blood pressure cuff around Julie's arm. With her stethoscope in place, she inflated the cuff and then listened carefully. The results alarmed her. The wide pulse pressure indicated an increased intercranial pressure.

Within minutes, Susan was no longer alone with Julie. Someone pulled the curtains to screen the cubicle from the ones on either side. Susan stepped back from the bed. Two nurses and the house doctor assessed Julie. The neurologist arrived, listened to the report and snapped orders.

"Call Boyleston. I want him ten minutes ago. Hang a bottle of Manitol. Call CAT scan stat. I want an enhanced head. Get a trach set. Insert a CVP line and alert respiratory. I want a therapist to go to CAT Scan with her."

Susan stood with her back against the pale green curtains. Her fear for Julie held her frozen. She inhaled deeply several times and then edged out of the room. At the desk, she slumped on a chair.

Julie's nurse rushed from the cubicle and reached for the phone. "Glad you were here. She'll be fine."

How glib those words sounded and how often she had used them. The words brought memories of the previous night. Her thoughts filled with the knowledge of all that could go wrong. She looked at the clock and knew she had to return to Five Ortho.

She paused beside Julie's nurse. "Here's my phone number. If she goes to surgery, call me."

The young nurse nodded. "I will and thanks."

CRITICAL, HER condition was critical. At least that was what the operator had said. Mommy had been critical, too. Then Mommy had left him.

He stood in Mommy's room surrounded by the scent of roses. "Susan knows. Mommy, I know she does. Are you ready for her to come to you?"

He cocked his head. A scowl appeared on his face. "She didn't tell, but she will. I know she will."

With slow steps, he approached the bed. He crawled beneath the satin comforter. The soft fabric caressed his skin. Just like Mommy had when he was a child. He closed his eyes and fell asleep.

AN EXHAUSTED Patrick questioned his sanity. He dropped four present-filled shopping bags on the couch. His jacket landed between them. This year, he'd decided to do his Christmas shopping early rather than wait until Christmas Eve. He wondered if everyone in the county had made the same decision. The long lines at the mall had allowed him too much time to think about the deaths at Bradley Memorial Hospital and Susan.

No matter what arguments to the contrary he found, he remained convinced she was on the killer's list. Her refusal to accept her danger frustrated him. Four deaths and Julie's aborted one. Though he admired Susan's desire to remain strong and in control of her life, couldn't she see she needed his help?

He walked to the kitchen and started a pot of coffee. The mantle clock struck eleven times. While he waited for the coffee to brew, he sat at the counter and doodled.

What was the connection between the deaths? Unlike the police, he wasn't convinced the doctors had died in accidents. Though Susan suspected De Witt had attacked Julie, had the man killed the others? He printed De Witt's name in the center of a circle and added the other names around the perimeter.

The Denton woman had been a gossip and a blackmailer. How did Mendoza fit the picture? The rhythmic beat of the pencil stopped. Dr. Barclay had been De Witt's uncle and employer. Leila Vernon had been Barclay's mistress and confidant.

Susan Randall. Patrick's hand slipped and the pencil slashed a line across the paper. She knew too much and not enough.

He picked up the pencil. Would De Witt jeopardize the chance to take over his uncle's practice? What would Julie say about her attacker?

Would she remember? He recalled the time he'd been beaned by a baseball. Several hours had permanently vanished from his memories. The pencil snapped in two. If she never remembered, Susan's suspicions would remain unreported. Wrong! He reached for the phone.

"Davies residence."

"Laura, it's Pat Macleith. Is Greg around?"

"He is... While I have you on the phone, we're having a party next Saturday. Please come. I have several friends I think you'd like."

He laughed. "I hope to be taken by then."

"Bring her. It's been ages since I've seen you."

"I'll see if she's off. She's a nurse and works evenings." He poured a cup of coffee.

"If she works at Bradley Memorial, tell her to be careful. Here's Greg."

"What's up?" Greg's deep voice boomed in Patrick's ear.

"The muggings."

Greg groaned. "Not you, too."

"Have you considered De Witt? He's Barclay's nephew."

"He's clear."

"Do you know about his involvement with the latest victim?"

"We know about De Witt and the Gilbert girl. She's his alibi for his uncle's death. As I told you, we have a line on the mugger."

"Who?"

"He worked at Bradley Memorial five years ago. He and the Denton woman had a burglary ring going. Ms. Vernon testified against him, but there was no proof of the Denton woman's involvement. He vowed he'd teach her a lesson. Vernon, too. A week before the first attempt, he was released from prison."

"What about Julie Gilbert? Five years ago, she was a teenager."

"I think your friend overreacted. Some nurse called the station this morning and reported a quarrel between De Witt and Gilbert. What we figure is she ran and he chased her. When she fell and hit her head, he panicked. Once the girl's able to talk, that's how it will turn out. Why the heavy concern?"

"Susan."

"Aha! Tell her to follow the rules. Our suspect was an orderly on her unit." Greg chuckled. "You could always play chauffeur."

"If she'll let me."

"I want to meet her outside of official business. Bring her to the party so Laura and I can warn her about your overactive imagination.

Have you set the date?"

"Don't rush me. See you." Patrick hung up. Greg's news should have erased his fears but the uneasiness remained strong.

The doorbell rang. He answered. The look on Susan's face warned him of a new tragedy. "All right, what's wrong?"

She buried her face against his chest. "Julie."

"Is she..."

"When I was on break, she went sour. The doctors are considering surgery as soon as they get the results of the CAT Scan." She ran her hands over his sweater. "Do I smell coffee? Is it hot? I don't think I'll ever get warm."

Patrick guided her to the counter and handed her the cup he'd poured for himself. "What went wrong?"

"I'm not sure. A bleed. A fatty emboli. A missed skull fracture." She put the cup on the counter. "I have to go home. If she goes to surgery, they'll call me."

"I'll come with you." He reached for his jacket.

She shook her head. "I'm sorry. It's always some tragedy. That's not fair to you."

He opened the door. "I love you for better or worse." As they crossed the porch, he kept his hand at her waist.

A FRUSTRATED dream woke Susan. In the dream, Julie screamed a name that Susan couldn't hear. For several minutes, she stared at the window. The dream had reflected her feelings. She turned on her side and snuggled against Patrick. The steady rise and fall of his chest lulled her into a dreamy state.

With an abrupt jerk of her body, her descent into sleep ended. Julie. Was the younger nurse all right? Susan rolled onto her side and looked at the clock. Three A.M. Why hadn't the ICU nurse called? In hopes of slipping from the bed without waking Patrick, she eased from the covers.

The instant her feet hit the carpet, the phone rang. She pulled a blanket around her shoulders and reached for the receiver.

"Mrs. Randall, this is Gail, Julie's nurse. Sorry I didn't call before. She went to surgery at two fifteen. Things were hectic and I got rattled."

"What happened?"

"Dr. Boylestone saw the CAT and decided to operate. There was a bleed."

"Where? How bad?"

"I don't know."

"Are her parents there?"

"I think so. Dr. Boylestone called them for a phone consent."

"Let them know I'm on the way." For several seconds, she stared at the wall while the dial tone wailed in her ear. A hand touched her arm. She jumped.

"Is everything all right?" Patrick asked.

"Julie went to surgery." Her voice trembled.

He embraced her. "She'll be fine."

The tremor spread from her lips through her body. Patrick didn't know how serious the surgery was. If the bleed had affected a vital area of the brain, Julie could suffer permanent damage. "She could die."

"She'll be all right. Get dressed. I'll make coffee."

Susan kissed his cheek. "Julie was a good nurse. I saw that when I was her preceptor. What if—"

His mouth cut off her speculations. She clung to him. "She'll be a good nurse again."

She stood at the side of the bed. "I hate him. How could he have *done* this to her, to Leila and even to Barbara?"

"Who?"

"De Witt."

"He's clear. The police have a suspect under investigation."

She shook her head. "I can't believe that."

"Greg told me about him last night. Shower. Dress." He pushed her toward the bathroom. "Meet you in the kitchen."

Ten minutes later, Susan took a steaming cup from him. She inhaled and sighed. "Thanks."

"Should hold you 'til you get to the cafeteria and grab a cup."

She looked up. "I'd sooner die of coffee underdose than drink a cup from there."

"That bad?" He leaned against the counter. "How long will the surgery take?"

"Hours."

He caressed her with his eyes. "Call if you need me and I'll be there. Do you want me to drive you?"

She kissed his cheek. "I should be home before seven."

SUSAN PAUSED in the doorway of the surgical waiting room. Julie's parents sat on the dark green couch facing the door. She went to them.

Mrs. Gilbert half-rose. "Susan, we should have called but I didn't think. When Dr. Boylestone reached us, we dressed and flew over. We didn't even wake her sisters." Hysteria hemmed her voice. "She looked awful, almost like she was...was—"

"I know," Susan said. "I was there when she got worse. I'm frightened for her, too." She sat beside the woman who looked like she could be Julie's older sister.

Mrs. Gilbert grasped Susan's hand. "She admires you so much. Last year, for months, all we heard was Susan says this and Susan thinks that."

Susan smiled. "And it was boring. Julie tends to have enthusiasms."

Mr. Gilbert nodded. "I think you're an excellent role model. I feel more optimistic now and I can see why Julie wants to be your kind of nurse. The young woman in ICU told us how you helped her last evening."

Susan didn't know how to respond. She had done very little.

"How long does this kind of surgery last?" Mrs. Gilbert asked. "She's been there for nearly two hours."

"I'm not sure. Part of the time was spent prepping her for the operation. They may have shaved her head."

"Why?"

"So they'd have a clean surgical field. If they did, one day next week, we'll go wig shopping."

"What happens—" Mrs. Gilbert pressed her hand to her mouth. "I can't think that way...I wonder where Larry is? It would mean so much to her if he came."

Susan studied her hands. Didn't they know Julie had broken off with him? How could she tell the Gilberts that De Witt could be the one who attacked Julie? "Does he know?"

"I left a message with his answering service." Mr. Gilbert scowled. "We're not pleased by what she was doing, but she's old enough to make her own decisions."

Mrs. Gilbert walked to the door. She stared into the hall. "I thought I heard his voice." She returned to the couch. "It's hard being a parent these days. There are so many temptations for kids."

"Julie's a good person and she's an excellent nurse."

Mrs. Gilbert held the remnants of a shredded tissue. "We were so pleased about her decision to go to grad school. Do you think she'll ever work again?"

"She'll be fine." Susan remembered what little comfort those words had for her. She searched for others. "It may take months for her recovery, but we have to think that way." She rose. "I'll be back with coffee."

"I'll pass," said Mr. Gilbert.

"Even if I can find fresh brewed? There's always a pot on Five Ortho." She took their smiles for acceptance.

When she returned to the waiting room with three cups of coffee, milk and sugar, she halted just inside the door. De Witt stood in front of the couch. The sight of his blond hair and black jacket sparked her anger.

As she listened to the words of concern she knew he didn't mean, chills walked her spine. How did he have the nerve to come and act this way? Was he convinced Julie would protect him? When she handed the tray to the Gilberts, De Witt met her glance with a dismissive glare.

AT FOUR FORTY-FIVE, Dr. Boylestone arrived. In an attempt to guess the results of the surgery, Susan studied his face,

As a unit, the Gilberts rose. "How is she?"

"So far it's good news. We found the bleed. Small and not affecting a vital area of the brain. She tolerated the procedure well."

"Thank God," said Mr. Gilbert. "When can we take her home?"

"Don't rush things. She'll be in ICU for about seventy-two hours. Then she'll be transferred to a regular unit. She'll need physical therapy." He turned to leave.

The Gilberts embraced.

Susan felt like laughing and crying. She followed Dr. Boylestone and De Witt into the hall. "Is the news as favorable as you told her parents?" she asked.

Dr. Boylestone turned. "Mrs. Randall, what are you doing here?"

"Julie's my friend."

"Just what did you do?" De Witt asked.

Dr. Boylestone gave a detailed description of the surgery. "Since she was under anesthesia, Dr. Phillips set the fracture. I'm pleased with her response." He opened the Recovery Room door.

De Witt attempted to push past Susan. "Excuse me."

Susan moved to block him. "Just a minute. I'd like to talk to you." The anger she had contained earlier rang in her voice.

"Make it quick. I want to get home and grab some sleep before office hours."

His attitude and her exhaustion made her snap. "Leave Julie alone.

She doesn't need you hanging around. You've done enough already."

"Just what do you mean?"

"Why did you attack her?"

"You're crazy. I'd never hurt Julie."

Susan put her hands on her hips. "Even if she refused to supply you with an alibi?"

His eyes narrowed. "I remember you. You're the nurse who was spouting off about my shooting ability. Last night, you overheard Julie and me having a disagreement. She ran off. I didn't chase her."

"So you say."

"I went to see a patient on Four. Check it out."

"Don't worry. I will."

Chapter 12

PATRICK STOOD beside the bed and looked at Susan. Her lips curved in a smile that matched his and he wondered if she dreamed of him. He nearly laughed at the touch of egotism. More likely her dreams were of Julie's surgery and the happy results. He reached out to touch her and stopped. She had returned from the hospital around five thirty, mumbled a few words about Julie and nestled against him. He couldn't wake her. She needed her sleep as much as he wanted her.

As he backed away from the bed, he thought about the day he'd met Julie. She'd been bouncy and quite concerned about Susan's spirits. Would she wake, remember the attack and name her assailant? When that happened, Susan would be safe. In the meantime, how could he keep her out of danger?

"You could always play chauffeur." Though Greg's suggestion had been a joke, Patrick decided the idea had merit. Convincing Susan was the problem. She resented any attempt to curb her independence. While he understood her fear of returning to old habits, couldn't she relax her hold just this once? He gripped the banister. Nothing would happen to her. He wouldn't let anyone hurt her. He had to try and persuade her to accept his help, at least until the killer was caught. He crossed the living room and opened the front door.

At home, he showered and changed clothes. Then he did some cleaning.

The phone rang and he caught it on the second ring. His ex-wife's hysterical voice shrilled in his ear. Once he realized the twins were fine, he let her continue the excited stream of chatter while he made toast and poured a glass of juice.

"What do you want me to do?" he asked when Lisa, paused to take a breath. His question evoked another rain of complaints and exclamations. "Lisa, calm down. So you have to leave for Europe on Wednesday instead of next Sunday night. I'm sure you have a lot to do. No, I can't take them today. I'm covering a concert... She's working. Let Rob watch them while you finish shopping...Why not...Tomorrow morning. That's the best I can do."

After he hung up, Patrick stared at the phone. How dare she call him selfish and uncaring? He shook his head. Perhaps life would be less complicated if the twins lived with him. During the time they were here, he would ask them how they felt about that.

He gulped the glass of juice and ate the toast. His plans for a leisurely morning and brunch with Susan had to be changed. Another thought occurred. How was he going to entertain the twins tomorrow? Maybe Susan would have a suggestion.

As soon as he finished the Saturday chores, he returned to her side of the house. He let himself in. She stood at the head of the stairs. "Hi," he said.

"Good morning." She started down the steps. "Did I tell you about Julie's surgery when I came in? I barely remember undressing and getting into bed."

He walked to the foot of the stairs. "Through a yawn. I'm glad things went well for her. How long before she's awake?"

"The doctor said today."

"Will she remember the attack?"

"She may never remember." Susan stopped on the second step.

"What would you like me to make for breakfast?" he asked.

She laughed. "Shouldn't that be my line? You didn't have to wait for me."

"I had toast and juice at home. How about a ham and cheese omelet?"

"Sounds delicious."

Patrick lifted her from the step and held her close. As he lowered her to the floor, his lips captured hers.

She caught his hands. "Breakfast first. For the first time in weeks, I'm hungry."

"That's good." She brought her hand to his lips. "We've been invited to a party next Saturday."

"By whom?"

"Greg Davies and his wife."

Susan moved ahead of him. "I'm not sure I want to go."

Patrick turned her to face him. "Why not?"

"When I call him about the things I've been sitting on, he might want to arrest me."

"What?"

"Nothing. I thought I'd seen the bracelet before but I never got a close look."

"It's not like you're a suspect. You'll like Greg and Jane. He's not your typical cop. She's a photographer. The best thing is they're not friends we shared with Jim and Lisa."

"I am off."

He smiled. "If you switch to days, life would be less complex for us."

"With the holes in the evening staff, a change could take months." She walked to the counter and poured the remains of yesterday's coffee down the drain. "Did I tell you Trish is entering a drug rehab program? That leaves her spot open."

He shook his head. "How long will Julie be out?" He opened the refrigerator and took out the omelet ingredients.

"If all goes well, at least eight weeks. Could be longer."

While Patrick shredded cheese and diced ham, he noticed Susan writing on a list she had taken from the bulletin board. "What are you up to? Shopping for a month?"

"Christmas baking. I plan to go to the store after we eat and pray I get back in time to get ready for work."

"That's it." Patrick laughed. "The perfect way to entertain Robin and Adam tomorrow."

"I didn't know they were coming."

"Neither did I until this morning. The European trip has been moved up. They leave Wednesday and Lisa has so much to do. Apparently so does Rob." Patrick whisked the eggs.

"Are you sure you want to bake cookies with the twins?"

"I've run out of ideas. The mall will be mobbed. All day at the movies—ugh."

Susan moved to his side. "We'll make it a group project. I can help until two."

"I was hoping you'd volunteer." He grinned. "Can you handle the energy level?"

She nodded. "They'll help me forget. Besides, what we don't finish before I leave for work, the three of you can do." She looked at the clock. "Let's eat. I want to leave for the hospital in time to see Julie."

He poured the omelet mixture into the skillet. "I'll do the shopping."

"Bless you."

"I'll be back in time to drive you to work."

"Back up a step. I can drive myself."

He dropped the ham and cheese into the omelet. "When I talked to

Greg, he suggested I play chauffeur until the mugger is caught."

Susan frowned. "I'm not into taking chances. I'll be fine."

"The suspect once worked on your unit. Leila testified against him and the Denton woman was somehow involved." He divided the omelet in half.

She shook her head. "I don't remember—Oh, the orderly. He barely knew me." She dug into the omelet. "How many dozen cookies do you want?"

"Enough to stuff the kids for six weeks or so."

The discussion about the kinds of cookies carried them through lunch. While Susan added the last item to the list, she pushed her chair back. "Let me get the money for my share."

"And let me get my own list." His fingers massaged her shoulders. "See you in a few."

AS SUSAN came downstairs with her purse slung over her shoulder, Patrick opened the front door. They met in the middle of the living room. When she handed him the money, he caught her hand and tugged her toward him. Their lips met. He caressed her back. Susan raised her head. "Thought you were going shopping."

"I am." His hands moved along her spine creating delicious sensations.

"And still be back in time to drive me to work? Good luck."

"Call in sick."

"On a weekend, are you crazy?" Susan stiffened. Hadn't Leila said those words the day Joe Barclay had died?

"What's wrong?"

"Just a thought about Leila. I offered to call in sick when she came to me after Joe's death and she reminded me of the rule. If I don't go in today, I'll have to work next Saturday." She chuckled. "Now that's an idea. Where's the phone?"

He kissed her check. "I'm on my way. Promise you'll be here when I get back."

"I'll stay until quarter to two. I want to check Julie."

"Can't you call her?"

Susan laughed. "I can see your experience with hospitals is limited. There are no patient phones in ICU." She ran a finger along his jaw line.

"Keep doing things like that and you'll be making up a week." He kissed her again. "See you soon."

Susan watched him bound down the steps. She closed the door and leaned against it. His reluctance to leave her was sweet, but she wished he would control his tendency to smother. Even though his friend had suggested Patrick drive her to work, there was no reason for his escort. Her danger of being mugged was less than that of most of the evening nurses. Since Barbara's death, the night of Julie's attack was the first time she'd gone to the parking lot alone.

The police had a suspect. She frowned. Though she could see their reasoning, she knew they were wrong. If the mugger wasn't De Witt, he had to be someone familiar with the nurses' routine. How could a man just released from prison know that?

She hugged herself. Slowly, she moved from the door. How easily she could fall into the dependency trap again. Would it be so bad this time? She thought of her married years. There had been comfort, ease and—boredom. She wanted Patrick in her life but until she felt sure of her strength, she couldn't commit herself.

The phone rang and she answered. "Mrs. Gilbert, how are you? Has something gone wrong with Julie?"

"She's wonderful. Even her hoarseness is gone." Joy filled the other woman's voice.

Susan laughed. "I'm glad."

"How can we ever thank you? This makes twice you've saved her life."

"Don't try. Both times I was on automatic pilot. Ask Julie about running on instincts and adrenaline during an emergency. Does she remember anything about the attack?"

"Not yet. The police are pushing for an interview. They have pictures they want her to see."

"Are you going to let them in?"

"We'll have to, but not yet. Dr. Boylestone said to wait until she's out of ICU. He said she might never regain those memories. That didn't please the police. They insist they need a statement."

Susan straightened. Police. Statement. She needed to read and amend the one she had given after Barbara's death. "Let me go. I have a dozen things to do and I want to leave in time to see Julie."

After Susan loaded the dishwasher, she went to the basement for the laundry she had done the day before. Since she had to stop at the police station, she needed to leave by one thirty. Patrick might not make it home in time to take her. She imagined his reaction and shrugged. Got to do my duty, she thought.

At one fifteen, she taped a note to the door and ran to her car. Fifteen minutes later, she parked in front of a rambling Victorian house that bore little resemblance to a police station. She hurried past the first floor town offices, dashed up the stairs to the second floor and opened the door marked "Police."

A plump woman with blonde hair teased into a pouf rose from the chair behind the counter that blocked entrance to the main area of the room. "Can I help you?"

"I was told to come in and read my statement."

"Which case?" The woman cracked her gum.

"Actually, it's two."

"Busy, aren't you? Which cases?"

"Julie Gilbert and Barbara Denton."

The blonde searched through a stack of folders. "Do you make a habit of finding bodies?" She giggled. When she handed a folder across the desk, a gold bracelet glittered on her arm.

Susan thought of the one that Barbara had worn the evening she had been killed. The bracelet had been missing from the practical's arm. Something about the bracelet seemed familiar. She read the typed statement regarding the attack on Julie.

"Can't find the Denton file."

Susan looked up. "There's something I need to add. Is there a chance I could talk to Detective Davies?"

"Is it important?"

"I'm not sure."

"Why don't you write a note and if he stops in, I'll see he gets it."

Susan felt reluctant to commit her information to paper. The blonde reminded her of Barbara and she feared the story might reach the News before Greg Davies. Tonight, she'd ask Patrick for his friend's number. "I'll call him. Is there a good time?"

"Monday between eight and nine. What do you think this is all about?" The woman licked her lips in a manner that made Susan think of a gourmand contemplating a feast. "Three nurses. Two dead. Aren't you afraid you'll be next?"

Fear walked Susan's spine. She laughed and the sound rang false. "I'm the cautious one. I don't go to the parking lot alone." Or to the storage room either. She walked to the door and hurried downstairs.

The only place she went alone was to work and home. Fear solved nothing, so why was there a giant lump in her stomach?

As she stepped into the cold air, she glanced at the sky. During the short time she'd been inside, the color had changed from blue to pewter. Snow had been predicted for early morning, but the dullness made her hope the storm would wait until she finished work and returned home. Being stuck at the hospital for a double shift after the trauma of the past two nights would be more than she could handle.

SUSAN PAUSED at the desk in ICU. The petite black nurse looked up. "I know. You're not a float. You're here to see Julie. Congratulations on your quick actions last night. Are you sure you don't want to work here?"

"I don't think so. Thirteen hour shifts are too long. How's Julie?"

"Terrific. PT was in this morning and got her out of bed. Your nurse manager stopped by. On her vacation yet. She's holding a bed on your unit."

"That's good news." Susan hurried across the hall to Julie's cubicle.

Julie waved. "Susan I really owe you. Mom told me you saved me again."

"I'm glad I was here."

"Me, too. The box on the stand is yours. I was saving it for Christmas, but I want you to have it now."

Susan opened the box and found one of the teapots that had eased her sorrow for a short time on the day of Leila's funeral. "I thought you bought this for your mother."

"I bought two and you never guessed. This is the first installment. When I get back to work, I'll bring you a present every day."

Her comments triggered a shrouded memory and reminded Susan of the presents she had received. She grasped the side rail. "No need."

"Then how can I thank you?"

"By coming back to work as soon as possible. We're working with a patchwork crew."

"Meg told me. She wasn't too happy that I'm here." Julie stared at her hands. "She told me about Trish going into rehab. Do you think she'll make it?"

"The choice is hers. I told her to keep in touch."

Julie touched her turban. "Mom said you're going wig shopping with her. A complete selection, please. How about auburn or ebony?"

"With luck, we'll find one the shade of your hair."

"No way. Maybe platinum. How can I miss a chance to be glamorous?" Julie sighed. "Speaking of glamour, Larry was in this morning. Why is he so darned attractive?"

"He practices."

Julie giggled. "I'll remember that. He wants to start again when I'm out of here. What am I going to do? He's more tempting that a hot fudge sundae."

Susan sat on the chair beside the bed and stared at the box on her lap. Didn't Julie realize De Witt was responsible for her injuries? "I can't decide for you."

"I know." Julie made a face. "When he's not around, I can dust my hands and say no more. Then he arrives and smiles and my resistance vanishes."

"What did you tell him?"

"Who tells him anything? He was so full of plans for us. What I want doesn't matter. I mentioned grad school and he pouted. After awhile, I closed my eyes and pretended to be asleep. He left."

Susan shifted the box. She had been part of a similar duo, but she had little knowledge of how to escape. "Keep telling yourself you don't need him in your life until you believe." If Patrick turned into another Jim, could she follow her own advice?

"Maybe by the time the doctor springs me, he'll have found someone new." Julie touched her cast. "It's going to be forever. When PT got me up today, I lasted ten minutes. I don't like being a patient. You have no control."

"Who wants to be sick?" Susan smiled. "Think of this as a learning experience."

Julie laughed. "It's a lesson I'd rather not have, but I'll try to remember how I feel about being helpless when I get back to work."

Susan leaned forward. "Do you remember anything about your attacker?"

"He...he..." Julie closed her eyes. "I can see him. I can hear his voice. He...he.... Why can't I say his name?" Frustration made her voice shrill.

Susan grasped Julie's hand. "Try to think around him. Maybe the name will slip out."

"Maybe I don't want to remember."

Susan glanced away. Was the younger nurse's amnesia selective? Was she protecting De Witt? Susan looked at her watch. "I'd better get upstairs and see what's in store. I'll see you tomorrow."

"And Monday on Five Ortho."

"Nice of Meg to arrange that."

Julie chuckled. "Self-protection. She'd never see her staff if I was on another unit. I think everyone on days has been down. And of course, Dr. Boylestone demanded I be transferred there."

"That explains her generosity." Susan waved from the doorway. "Thanks for the teapot."

WITH A sigh, Trish packed the last of her white uniforms and sealed the box. She looked around the bedroom, now bare of the touches that made it a home. Eight boxes waited in the living room to be taken to the basement storage room. She stood with her hands on her hips.

Since her discharge from the hospital this morning, she'd been too busy and too wired to think. Though one of the nosy hens from the Nursing Office had discovered most of the stashes of amphetamines, she had missed several. Trish sat on the couch and popped another pill.

When she thought about her interview with the President for Nursing, anger arose. Someone had been found to sublet her apartment. She would be paid for her sick and vacation time. Her job would be waiting when she completed the program. She should have felt relief but the woman's promises had burned like drops of acid. By now, everyone at the hospital knew about her addiction. How could she come back and face petty and condescending sneers?

She leaned back and waited for the familiar rush. What would they do if she didn't enter the treatment program?

De Witt. He owed her. Anger and the amphetamine rush rose like twin geysers. This was his fault. He had introduced her to speed as a way of releasing her inhibitions. Had he ever shown Julie the joy of drug-induced sex?

As the memory of what Susan had said about the pair surfaced, Trish laughed. "How does it feel to be discarded?" Had any woman broken off with him before? His pride must have been battered.

She reached for the phone and dialed his service. "This is Miss Fallon, Five Ortho. I need to speak to Dr. De Witt."

"Page him. He should still be there."

"Thanks." Page him. She laughed. Better than a call, she would intercept him. She grabbed a jacket.

When she reached the street, she realized her car keys were in her coat pocket. She shrugged. Walking was good exercise.

Six blocks later, she stood in the doctor's parking lot beside De Witt's black Jaguar. Unfortunately, the doors were locked. As she headed for the hospital, a few snowflakes landed on her jacked. She entered the ER waiting room, walked to the hall and stationed herself near the doors to wait for De Witt.

HE STOOD outside the Emergency Room entrance and shoved his hands in his black jacket pockets. Earlier, he had tried to enter ICU through the stairwell door only to find it locked. Critical. That had been the report. Critical meant near death. Mommy had been critical. Had she died? Had she remembered?

The door opened. De Witt strode outside. A thin nurse followed him. She grabbed the doctor's arm. De Witt wheeled. "I said no."

She stabbed a finger at his face. "You owe me." She swung her fist.

The blonde man caught her hand. "The past is done...gone... ended."

"Bastard. I'm not asking for much. A job in your office."

"Reserved for Julie."

"She doesn't want it and she doesn't want you." She laughed. "How does it feel to be rejected?"

"Aren't you scheduled to enter a treatment center?"

"You can't afford to turn me down. I know too much."

"Don't threaten me," De Witt said. "You sound like the Denton woman and look what happened to her."

"You don't scare me." Trish stood with her hands on her hips. "You gave Barbara money but you're too much of a coward to kill anyone."

He laughed. "Don't be so sure."

"Larry, please. I don't want to go to that place." She reached for him.

De Witt pushed her hard enough to knock her down. He strode away.

The watcher emerged from the shadows and helped her to her feet. "Thanks," she said. "What are you doing here?"

He shrugged. "Dr. De Witt isn't a very nice man."

"You are so right." She brushed snow from her jacket.

"Is there anything I can do for you?"

"Drive me to his apartment. I'm not finished with him."

He smiled. "I can do that." He walked with her to his car. Excitement made him fumble with the lock.

Trish settled in the passenger seat and rattled off directions. She spoke at high speed, detailing how De Witt had supplied her with drugs. "I never thought I'd become addicted, but nothing beats the rush that comes from speed."

Nothing? He could show her something better but he didn't want so share the feelings of power with anyone.

She gulped a breath. "Barbara found me out. She was going to report me to the Nursing Office unless I told her the name of my supplier." She rubbed her hands together. "I told her but they found out any way. Make a right."

He turned the car into a street where tall apartment buildings edged the river.

"Let me out here," she said. "I have to use the terrace entrance. He doesn't like his guests to sign in. Besides, he'd have the guard send me away."

He stopped at the curb. "Do you want me to wait?"

"I'll call a cab."

He watched her walk down the path beside the building. Mommy, what should I do? She wasn't one of the ones who was there on that dreadful night but the doctor was.

He left the car and scanned the street. After removing his rifle from the trunk, he stood beneath a street light and loaded the gun. His hands stroked the smooth wood stock and his fingers caressed the cold metal barrel. Guns had been good to him. They never let him down the way people did.

The falling snow made the flagstones slick. He grasped the rifle in one hand and the railing with the other. When he reached the end of the walk, he climbed the steps to the walled terrace. The sound of raised voices reached him.

The sliding doors stood open. De Witt stood with his back to the terrace. Trish waved her arms and shouted obscenities.

He raised the rifle, aimed and fired. De Witt pitched forward. Trish screamed. Why? She should be happy. He fired again. Her scream died. He ran down the steps, slipped and nearly fell. The rifle clattered on the flagstones. A scream pierced the air. He reached his car and dove behind the wheel.

Tonight would see his mission ended. He looked at the dashboard clock. Too early to meet Susan. His wheels spun on the snow-dusted street.

He tapped the steering wheel with an impatient rhythm. "Are you angry, Mommy? Barbara Denton, Dr. Mendoza, Leila Vernon, Julie Gilbert, Dr. De Witt. Dr. Barclay, did I kill him? I must have pulled the *trigger. Who else would want him dead?*

Cautiously, he drove through the snow to the house he shared with Mommy. He found the presents for Susan. Then he headed for the diner and a hot meal.

At the diner, he bought a newspaper. Julie's picture stared at him.

"Weird events," the waitress said. "If I was one of those nurses, I wouldn't go to work."

He looked up. "Sorry."

"Guess you're not safe anywhere these days. A lot of nurses come in here after work." She pointed to Julie's picture. "She was here not long ago." She flipped open her order book. "What will you have tonight?"

"The turkey dinner with mashed potatoes, French dressing on the salad and coffee." He stared out the window at the snow. The weather was perfect for his plans. His meal arrived and he began to eat.

Sometime later, the waitress returned to refill his coffee cup. "Dessert?"

"Hot apple pie and ice cream."

THERE WAS nothing wrong with the orchestra or the music, but Patrick shifted restlessly in his seat. At ten o'clock, he slipped out of his seat in the last row of the community college auditorium. Ever since coming home from the grocery store to find Susan's note, he had felt uneasy—and angry—and disappointed. The many facets of his emotions surprised him. Did she realize he wouldn't smother her the way Jim had? Why didn't she see how much he approved of her growing independence? Most of the time, he thought.

As he unlocked his car, his imagination ran wild. He visualized a dozen scenes with Susan as the victim of some madman. With an effort, he forced his thoughts back to reality. Susan was safe. She wouldn't finish work and leave the hospital for an hour and a half.

He turned the key in the ignition. The CB radio tuned to the police band, a habit from the days when he'd chased stories, crackled. "Riverbank Apartments. We need the detectives and a supervisor on the scene."

Another murder, Patrick thought after translating the message. He shook his head. There hadn't been this much violent crime when he had worked the police beat.

As he pulled into the driveway, a familiar voice spoke. "Davies here. Is the ME on the way? Tell him to use the terrace entrance."

"He wants her to use the terrace entrance." Once again, Patrick heard Susan's indignant statement. His hand froze on the key. De Witt lived in one of those luxury apartments on the river. Had the man killed himself?

Patrick shifted gears and backed out of the driveway. Ten minutes later, he reached a barricade that blocked the street in front of the apartment building. Clusters of spectators lined the sidewalks. He flashed his press card at the uniformed policeman. "What gives?"

"Some doctor and a woman."

"Was she another Bradley Memorial nurse?" Patrick asked. The officer shrugged. Greg's booming voice issued orders. Patrick strode to his friend. "De Witt and who?"

Greg turned. "Thought you weren't doing crime."

"Who was the woman?"

"Not your friend. A Trish Fallon. What are you doing here?"

"I heard your report and knew De Witt lived here. Was it a murder/suicide?"

Greg shrugged. "The ME just got here."

"I need to know."

A young officer hurried over. "I interviewed the neighbor who found them. She heard a quarrel and then two shots. The Fallon woman was still alive when the neighbor arrived. She said something like bola or vola." The young man looked from Greg to Patrick. "Sorry, sir."

"No harm done," Greg said. "Mr. Macleith was just leaving." Greg grasped Patrick's arm and led him to the barrier. "Go home."

"I'm not after a story. Did De Witt kill Fallon? I need to know. Susan thought he was the mugger."

Greg shook his head. "Get out of here and take your imagination with you. I have a case to investigate."

Patrick stopped at the barrier. "Then there's only one person who knows the truth."

"What are you talking about?"

"The muggings." Patrick grabbed Greg's arm. "Hear me out. These deaths are connected. There's a madman out there. Someone with a grudge against these people."

"I don't have time for theories now. Call me in the morning. I'll know more then."

Patrick strode to his car. Though De Witt was dead, his gut feeling told him Susan was in danger. But from whom?

Julie knows. He had to talk to her. He headed toward the hospital.

Several blocks later while waiting for a light to change, he spotted a flaw in his plans. Visitors in ICU were restricted to immediate family and close friends. The nurses would never let him in, but Julie's parents might. They owed Susan a lot.

He drove home at a speed that risked a ticket. At Susan's, he searched her address book for Julie's number. When he found it under J, he shook his head. While waiting for an answer, he beat his fingers in an impatient rhythm on the kitchen table.

"Gilbert resident."

"Mr. Gilbert, I'm Patrick Macleith, a friend of Susan Randall." He gulped a breath. "I believe Susan is in danger from the man who attacked Julie."

"I thought the police have a suspect."

Patrick inhaled. "Trish Fallon, a nurse who worked with Julie and Susan, was shot tonight. So was Dr. De Witt. The killer has to be the man who attacked Julie." As he waited for Mr. Gilbert's response, Patrick mulled over what the young officer had said.

"Larry shot? When? Is he still alive?"

"Not long ago and I don't know if he's alive. Mr. Gilbert, Susan needs Julie's help."

"She doesn't remember anything about the attack."

"So Susan said. I might find the right question to trigger her memory." His voice tightened with the tension that gripped his body. "Please. Would you meet me at the hospital and convince the nurses to let me see your daughter?"

The pause continued until Patrick wondered if they had been disconnected. "All right, Mr. Macleith. I'll let you see Julie. Are you sure this will help Mrs. Randall?"

"Absolutely. Thanks. I'll meet you at the hospital in fifteen minutes."

GUSTS OF WIND scooped snow from the sides of the road and created a curtain through which he drove. To keep the windshield clear, the wipers worked at high speed. Entranced by the rapid, hypnotic rhythm, his head swayed until the scraping sound became a toll of the recent dead. Though no cars followed him, he flipped the turn signal and slowed the car before he turned into Susan's street.

Seconds after he passed her driveway, a car backed into the street. Where was Susan's tenant going? How long would the man be gone? The tenant represented a potential spoiler of his plan.

He parked across the street from her house and stared through the wind-blown snow that shrouded the house. Only the porch light created a pale island of brightness.

It had to be tonight. An ache filled his chest. He chewed the inside of his lower lip and visualized the expression on Susan's face when she realized the truth. Her mouth gaped. Her eyes shone with awe. He savored the moment.

Barbara, Leila and Julie. Then there was Trish—a mistake. They had all seen him for an instant, but not for long enough for him to taste their terror. The encounter with Susan would be a feast. His shoulders straightened. Dreams of power electrified his body.

With furtive movements, he reached for the white silk nightgown. He kneaded the cloth, then raised the soft fabric to his face and inhaled the scent of roses.

Mommy had worn this gown the night she died. Beneath the fading aroma of the familiar perfume, he inhaled the odor of her fear. Tonight, Susan's fear would be delicious. Though he envisioned her clad in white silk, he couldn't think of a way to entice her to change her clothes. He closed his eyes. In kaleidoscope fashion, the face in his vision shifted from Mommy's to Susan's, again and again.

The gown was a gift to celebrate Julie's gift. Surely she was dead. He slammed the car door hard enough to cause snow to slide down the windshield. Wind gusted and showered him with snow. He crept down the driveway and walked onto the porch. There, he hung the nightgown from a pair of hooks that must have held plants in the summer. He left the porch and watched the gown dance. He could almost see Mommy and he yearned to touch her in ways that weren't permitted.

He reached into his jacket pocket. He had another gift for Susan. Perhaps there should be two but Trish Fallon was a mistake. He retreated to the clump of rhododendrons and gripped the tri-colored bracelet. He rubbed his fingers back and forth along the thick links. Faster and faster, the chain moved. He stared at the swirling snow and retreated into the past.

He stood in the doorway. A liquid sound rose from the figure in the bed. "Mommy, don't leave me. You promised you would never go."

Over and over again, he repeated his litany. "I'll never leave you. They'll have to kill me first."

The nurse, the kind one, raised the head of the bed. She reached for a plastic tube connected to an apparatus on the wall. He inched toward the bed. Mommy's eyes were dark pools reflecting fear. Her *fingers clawed the sheets. Susan slid the tube into Mommy's nostril. He reached to stop her. She pressed the call button. "You'll have to leave so we can help your mother," she said.*

He backed into the hall and stood where he could see into the room. The loudspeaker above his head crackled. "Code Blue, room 514. Code Blue, room 514."

The fat practical dragged a blood pressure machine down the hall. The wheels left a trail on the dark green carpet. A young nurse pushed a red cart past him. The house doctor followed at her heels.

The door closed and cut his view of the action. He strode across the hall and pressed his head against the painted surface. What were they doing? For an instant, he imagined a coven performing an arcane ritual. His hands tightened into fists.

"I'll never leave you. They'll have to kill me first." He clung to the promise.

"Is there anything I can do for you?" the supervisor asked. He shook his head. She opened the door and slipped into the room.

He paced to the end of the hall and back again. A blond doctor strode toward him. What was that man doing here? Mommy didn't like her doctor's young partner. He moved to block the door.

"Get out of my way," the doctor snapped. "There's an emergency here."

He turned and strode to the patients' lounge. There he stood at the window that filled most of one wall. Drops of rain like the tears he couldn't shed ran down the window.

"Mommy, please." His cry echoed from the past to the present. He looked at his watch. Susan would be home soon.

Chapter 13

WHEN PATRICK opened the ER door and started down the hall, a guard rose from behind the desk. "No visitors at this time of night."

"I'm meeting Mr. Gilbert, the father of the nurse who was attacked Thursday night. I need to see the girl."

"I can't let you in."

"Has Mr. Gilbert arrived?"

"No one's been past this desk since nine thirty."

"Then I'll wait." Patrick leaned against the wall and stared at the glass doors. Snow fell faster. A man entered and stamped his feet against the floor.

"Mr. Gilbert?" Patrick asked.

"Yes, and you must be Mr. Macleith."

Patrick held out his hand. "Thanks for coming."

Mr. Gilbert clasped Patrick's hand. "Let me call ICU." He reached for the phone on the security desk. A short time later, he turned to Patrick. "They'll let us in. Just before I left home, I heard Larry is dead. When you talk to Julie, be careful. My wife and I don't want her to learn until tomorrow when we're both with her."

"I agree. Things have been rough enough for her."

They strode down the hall. Mr. Gilbert paused at the door to ICU. "Are you sure Susan's in danger? Julie's frustrated because she can't remember. I don't want to put her through more stress."

Patrick let out his breath. "Susan's in danger and Julie will be too. What's to stop the killer from reaching her when she's transferred? She's the only one who can name him."

Mr. Gilbert reached for the door. "I'll go in and talk to her first."

Patrick paced from the closed door to the entrance to the ICU corridor. He wanted a phone to call Susan's unit to ask her to wait for him. The only phone he'd seen was at the security desk and he didn't want to go that far.

The door opened. Mr. Gilbert motioned to Patrick. "I tried, but she blocks on the name. She wants to see you."

Patrick moved past Mr. Gilbert. How could he help Julie find the name? He paused outside her cubicle and prayed for a way to trigger her memories.

SUSAN CLOSED the care plan book and looked at the clock on the wall across from the Desk. Impossible, she thought. I'm finished. The oddity of the situation stunned her. She turned to the night nurses. "Are you sure I've told you everything? I've never finished this early before."

"You've never had nine patients instead of twelve and a full staff. Why is Meg being sweet?"

"More like Grace Greene. Meg's not due back until Monday. I'm not sure there's a reason. The census for the entire house is down."

"Let's enjoy the lull while it lasts, especially with the way the snow's coming down. Go home. Weren't you here last night waiting with Julie's parents?"

"I was and I learned a lot about patience."

"Spare me the lecture. You were born patient, kind and thoughtful." She handed Susan the phone. "Call. Heroines deserve a reward."

"I'm hardly that." As Susan tapped the numbers, the two part-time nurses finished report. "Grace, it's Susan Randall... Hardly, just a favor. We're done and I'm beat. All of us...Thanks." She hung up. "We can go."

"Even me?" Kit asked.

"She said the entire evening staff."

"How did you manage that?"

"I asked." Susan walked to the lounge and pushed the door open. "We're free," she called to the practicals. "Someone grab my teapot."

"Hey, this is cute," Tina said. "Where'd you get it?"

"Julie bought it at the Potter's Wheel."

In the rush and confusion with seven people banging lockers and acting like prisoners freed from captivity, Susan reached the elevator carrying the teapot, her oxfords and the heavy stethoscope. Oh well, she thought. If she returned the shoes to the locker, she would hold the others back.

At the ER exit, the guard waved them on. "Take care, ladies. Don't anyone leave before everyone's in their cars."

"And check the back seats for strangers," Kit said.

Snow swirled through the air. Flakes melted on Susan's face. "I'm glad we're on our way home."

"It's too soon for snow," Kit said. "Should have waited until closer to Christmas."

"There's plenty of time for several storms before then," Tina said.

"I hope it doesn't snow all night." Susan juggled the shoes as she stepped from the curb. "Since I live so close, they'll call and ask me to work. They'll even come for me."

"I'm glad I live upstate," one of the part-time nurses said. She pushed Susan's shoes into a better position. "The trip home will be bad enough. No one's about to ask me to come in tomorrow morning."

"Take your phone off the hook," Kit said. "That's what I do."

"I have an answering machine that broadcasts the caller's message so I can decide if I want to talk," Tina said. "Get one like that."

Susan shook her head. "I don't need an answering machine." She stopped beside her car while searching for her keys, juggled shoes, stethoscope and teapot.

Once she settled behind the wheel, she started the wipers and waited for the others to reach their cars before she backed out. A train of cars followed her to the gate. In hopes of finding a weather report, she turned on the radio.

"...another bizarre death involving a nurse from Bradley Memorial Hospital." Susan's hands tightened on the wheel. "Police report the bodies of Trish Fallon and Lawrence De Witt were found earlier this evening in the doctor's riverfront apartment. Further details are expected as the investigation continues."

The voice droned on. Susan felt sick. When Trish had talked about De Witt's involvement in her addiction, she had barely controlled her anger.

What about Julie? How would the younger nurse handle this news? Though Julie had broken with De Witt, she said she still loved him.

Susan sighed. With De Witt dead, the truth about the attacks would never be learned.

PATRICK ENTERED Julie's cubicle. No miraculous method of memory recovery had occurred. If she couldn't tell her parents or Susan, why did he think he would succeed? He clenched his fists. He had to find the answer. Susan was in danger.

After drawing a deep breath, he walked to the bed where Julie sat propped by pillows. Only the luminous eyes in the pale face beneath the white turban seemed familiar. "How are you? Thanks for agreeing to see me." He stared at the monitor on the wall above her bed without understanding the meaning of the moving lines.

"I'm fine. Dad said you think Susan's in danger from the man who attacked me." She shifted her position. "I know you're right, but I can't remember why."

She looked away but not before he saw sadness creep into her expression. "Do you remember who attacked you?"

"He...he..." She crushed the sheet. "I'm sorry. This happens every time I try to say his name."

Patrick stepped closer to the bed. "Are you protecting someone? Susan thinks De Witt attacked you."

"Larry? No way." She licked her lips. "It was him...he...why can't I say his name? I can hear his voice, deep and threatening. He brought her presents."

"Susan?"

"No...Maybe...I mean his mother. She was here. A patient. Why can't I say his name?"

Patrick stared at the monitor. Susan had received presents but he had thought they were part of a practical joke or something equally nonthreatening. Was there a sinister connection? He shifted from foot to foot. Should he tell Julie that someone had killed Trish Fallon. Something had to shake the name loose.

"Could your attacker have been a former patient? Someone whose name sounds like Bola or Vola?"

"Volunteer." Julie threw the covers back and reached for the side rail. "That's who it was. The volunteer."

"Are you sure?"

"He came out of the fog and grabbed me. I fought and nearly got away but he caught me. I'll never forget the look on his face."

"One hundred percent sure?"

"A thousand. You've got to warn Susan. 'You hurt Mommy.' That's what he said. Susan likes him. She thinks he's nice." Tears rolled down her face.

Patrick felt torn between learning more and dashing to the phone. He should have called Susan before he left the house. "What happened to his mother?"

"She died. During a code. About a year ago." Her eyes widened. "Barbara, Ms. Vernon, Mendoza and Larry were there, too." She grabbed Patrick's hand. "You've got to warn Larry and Susan. You've got to stop Mr. Martin before he hurts them."

Patrick stepped back from the bed. "I'll try." He backed to the door. When Julie heard about Trish Fallon and De Witt, would she blame herself? He pushed past Mr. Gilbert. Susan would help the girl understand she wasn't at fault, but only if he reached her in time to prevent another tragedy.

Several strides took him to the desk. "What's the extension for Five Orthopedics?" As the nurse replied, he tapped the three-digit code. The phone rang once and was answered. "Susan Randall, please."

"She's not here."

Patrick gripped the receiver. "It's not eleven-thirty."

"I know but sometimes miracles happen. She finished early."

"How long ago did she leave?"

"Ten minutes or so."

Patrick hung up. How long would it take her to get home? Could he catch her? He had to try.

"Are you all right?" Mr. Gilbert asked.

"Susan's left the hospital. I have to go after her."

"Do you want me to come?"

"No. Call the police. Ask for Greg Davies. Tell him Julie named her attacker as a Mr. Martin, a volunteer on her unit." Patrick gulped a breath. "Tell him to send a man to 1447 Broadway to warn Susan."

"Will do."

"Thanks." Patrick hit the door at a run, barreled down the hall past the security desk. He dashed across the snow-covered parking lot to his car. In almost a single movement, he started the car, fastened his seatbelt and pulled away. The wheels spun on the slick pavement.

A short time later, the CB crackled with an alert for Fred Martin, five-foot-ten, one-hundred-and-ninety-pounds, gray hair. A description of his car and license plate followed. "Be alert. He may be armed."

Patrick erased everything from his thoughts except the road and his fear for Susan. Would he be in time?

AS SUSAN pulled into the driveway, a series of yawns caused her eyes to water. She set the handbrake and slumped in the seat. Exhaustion made her body limp. As she gathered shoes, stethoscope, teapot and purse, she was tempted to leave all but her purse in the car.

She reached for the door and realized Patrick's car wasn't there. A cascade of relief rushed through her thoughts. There would be no need for lengthy explanations about her failure to wait for him to drive her to work. By the time he returned she hoped to be asleep. In the next instant, a perverse need to see and touch him demanded her attention.

She shook her head, slung her purse over her shoulder and left the car. She grabbed the other things.

Where was Patrick? Hadn't he said the concert was over before eleven? But that had been when he had planned to pick her up at the hospital. Had he gone to meet her? There was no way he would think she could leave early.

Anticipation of a scene like those Jim had staged when she had failed to follow his instructions tightened her shoulder muscles. She locked the car. Patrick wasn't like Jim. Patrick listened. She tucked her shoes in the crook of her arm and held the teapot against her chest. Snow blew against her face. She looked toward the porch and held in a gasp. Something white gyrated in the wind. She took several steps away from the car.

"Susan." She looked around. Had someone called her name or had it been the wind. "Susan." She turned a half-circle and peered through the falling snow. "Over here." She whirled and nearly dropped the teapot. A dark figure emerged from behind the clump of rhododendrons. He moved across the lawn. Light from the porch illuminated his face.

"Mr. Martin, what are you doing here?"

"I came to see you. I brought you some presents."

His voice held an odd stilted quality with none of the warmth she usually heard when he spoke. A gust of wind whipped snow from the ground and veiled the volunteer. Susan swallowed a gulp of cold air. A tinge of fear crept along her nerves. His gray hair and black jacket blurred. Julie's attacker. Susan pressed against the car. How could she have mistaken him for De Witt? As she sought an escape route, she tried to calm her racing thoughts. He blocked the path to the house.

"What's wrong?" His deep voice held a sinister tone.

"Nothing." With her right hand, she stabbed the keys against the car in hopes of making contact with the lock. She lost her grip on the teapot. It shattered on the ground at her feet. He continued to walk toward her. A scream throbbed against her vocal cords. She couldn't let him know how frightened she was.

"Why did you attack Julie?" She barely recognized the voice as her own.

"She killed Mommy. You were supposed to protect her. She protected you."

A pulse throbbed in her throat. He was insane. Barbara, Mendoza, De Witt. Even Leila had been present at the Code.

"No one killed your mother. We did everything we could." The key flew from her shaking hand.

"She promised she would never leave me. She said they would have to kill her first."

Susan slid along the side of the car. His advance marched with her retreat.

"She was going to tell everyone how bad I was. We made a bargain. I would be good and she would never leave me. She did. They killed her. They're dead and you have to be like Mommy."

"You're not making any sense." Susan hated the way her voice cracked. Keep him talking until Patrick comes, she thought. "Would you like to come in for coffee so we can talk about your mother's death?"

"Not tonight. I have two presents for you. One is on the porch." He edged closer. "Did you like the gifts? Mommy always did."

"So you were the one who left them."

"Did you know what they were for?"

Susan couldn't force an answer past her trembling lips. On the porch, the nightgown danced like a ghost. She stepped back. The gown continued its macabre gyrations.

"Mommy wore that gown the night she died. Would you put it on for me?"

Susan's hand flew to her mouth. Though she felt she had endured an eternity of terror, she knew only minutes had passed.

He reached into his pocket. "I brought Mommy's bracelet for you."

She saw the glitter of gold in his hand. She moved back and stumbled. Of course. The bracelet Barbara had worn had belonged to Mrs. Martin.

She reached the end of the car. He grabbed her purse. A scream built in her chest until it exploded in a single word. "No!"

To wait for his attack was foolish. He wouldn't listen to anything she said. A memory of his angina arose. Exercise and stress could trigger chest pain. She turned and ran up the driveway.

"Stop!"

She stretched her legs in giant strides and was aided by slides along the snowy sidewalk. Her purse banged against her side. Snowflakes fluttered in the air. Christmas lights on houses cast multi-colored patterns on the snow. She clutched the shoes and pressed the bell of the stethoscope against her chest.

"Don't run away. You're just like Mommy. She promised she would never leave me."

His voice sounded loud. In anticipation of being caught, her body tensed. How long could she outrun him? She sped past dark houses and some that were brightly lit. She dashed past lines of cars parked at the curb. She scurried across two side streets that promised no escape because they led up steep hills.

The houses on the fourth block abutted the sidewalk. Lights in the far house on the corner revealed a group of people inside. Though her breath should have been saved for flight, she screamed. Chill air burned her lungs. Pain shot down her shins. A sharp ache stabbed her side. Why didn't one of the people standing near the windows turn and see her? She had to gain someone's attention.

She glanced over her shoulder and saw she had gained ground. She slid to a halt and banged on the door of the corner house. Another glance showed the volunteer had nearly reached her. She hurled one of her shoes at the multi-paned window and then smashed the bell of her stethoscope against the glass. "Help!" she screamed.

"Now I have you." His voice boomed in her ears.

She turned. Mr. Martin stretched his arms to grab her. She ran. He caught the sleeve of her coat. With a twisting movement, she pulled free. His labored breathing sounded in sync with hers. Tears stung her eyes and lay like crystals on her cheeks. She inhaled and swung her purse. The contact nearly overbalanced her. She swung again. The purse strap slid from her chilled fingers.

PATRICK'S CAR skidded around the corner and barely missed the snow-covered car parked across the street from the house. He steered into the driveway and slid to a halt several yards from Susan's car. His relief was momentary. The house was as dark as it had been when he had left. He jumped from his car and strode to hers.

The shattered teapot caught his attention. Another gift? He picked the card from the snow and saw Julie's name. When he looked up and saw the white garment hanging on the porch, his heart stuttered. "Susan," he cried.

The snow around her car was trampled but he saw no signs of a struggle. Then he fished her keys from the snow. The CB radio in his car crackled. He turned and listened to the message.

"Car 27 proceed to 52 Broadway. EDP breaking windows with white shoes and other objects."

Automatically, Patrick translated the code. "Susan." He dove into his car and closed the door. Pride in Susan's resourcefulness brought a smile. He shifted into reverse and shot out of the driveway. A car loomed in the rearview mirror. He tapped the brakes and blew the horn. The other car swerved and skidded into the snow-covered car that stood across from the driveway.

Damn, Patrick thought. There was no time to argue about the blame. Susan needed him. As he shifted into drive, a man jumped from the other car and ran toward Patrick's. He rolled down the window. "Catch you later. Greg, what are you doing here?"

"Warning Susan Randall."

"She isn't here. Her car is but she's gone."

"Shit, that's Martin's car. Did you check the house? He might have her in there." Greg slid into the passenger's seat.

"I found her keys on the driveway. She's the EDP." He shifted gears and sped down the street.

"I should have listened to you."

A sense of righteousness filled Patrick's thoughts. "Fine time to decide that."

"Look, we had a suspect and the Gilberts wouldn't let us see their daughter."

"You could have insisted. Got a court order."

"When we found Martin's rifle at De Witt's that was the next step. His name was etched on the stock. Can you believe that?" Greg shook his head. "This has been a bizarre case. I even gave Martin the derringer to check out. I bet it was his."

Patrick ran a red light. Susan had been in danger since the first death. "If it makes you feel better, I didn't have the slightest idea who until Julie told me. Susan liked the man."

The flashing dome light of the patrol car caused Patrick to brake. A crowd milled on the sidewalk. Greg touched Patrick's arm. "Sit tight. I'll extract her from the mob and you can take her home."

HE LUMBERED after Susan. His gloved fingers touched the bleeding spot at the corner of his mouth where her purse had struck him, twice. The dull, yet ever present ache in his chest threatened to bloom into agony. He couldn't quit the chase. As long as he could see her, there was hope. He chuckled. She was headed in the right direction. The dark cliff of the Overlook loomed at the end of the street.

Each breath of cold air, each step, compounded the pain in his chest. An exquisite thrill leaped from his heart and sped down his left arm to jolt his fingertips. After exhaling slowly several times, he reached into his jacket pocket for the nitro bottle. He flipped the lid. One tablet, two and finally a third dissolved beneath his tongue. A wave of near euphoria followed the diminished agony.

The vial tumbled to the snow. While stooping to retrieve it, he remembered the monument situated near the foot of the trail to the Overlook. The circle offered Susan a chance to escape that he couldn't permit her to seize. He forgot the vial and pushed his body forward.

"Susan," he shouted.

She stumbled and fell. Before she scrambled to her feet, he grasped her wrist and pulled her struggling body erect.

"Please," she said.

He smiled and ran his tongue across his lips. Her ruddy cheeks and the audible wheeze in her breathing reminded him of Mommy during one of her attacks. Fear darkened Susan's hazel eyes. He savored the feelings of strength and power that rose in response to her fear.

"You're just like Mommy." He drank the dread mirrored in her staring eyes. Hazel eyes, Susan's eyes, Mommy's eyes. Dark eyes reflecting fear.

SIT TIGHT, Patrick thought. He tapped an impatient beat on the steering wheel. How could he pretend calmness when Susan was in danger? He scanned the group gathered around the patrol car and failed to find her. He had to move, to act. He jumped from the car.

A dozen voices shouted comments. People pointed in every direction. Patrick stared at the snow-covered walk and saw tracks leading away. He trotted across the side street and nearly fell when he stumbled over a black purse. He picked it up and opened the clasp. Susan's ID from the hospital was the first thing he saw. If Susan's purse was here, where was she?

The trail continued as far as he could see. The Overlook. From this point, there were no side streets and no escape. Patrick wheeled and ran back to his car.

"The Overlook. She's headed there. He must be on her heels." He got in his car and started forward.

In the rearview mirror, he watched Greg and the uniformed officer dive for the patrol car. A siren sounded. Patrick gripped the wheel. Susan would hear and know help was on the way, but so would her pursuer.

AS MR. MARTIN pulled her up the path to the Overlook, Susan struggled to free herself from his bruising grip. He grasped her wrist so tightly, she feared the bones would break.

In summer, trees and bushes grew along the path. The winter skeletons seemed too thin and too distant to grab. For several seconds, she wondered why she continued to fight. Once they reached the picnic area at the top of the trail, there would be no escape. She felt too tired to run. Her attempt to push him into an angina attack had failed. Had he been lying about his heart condition to gain her sympathy?

"Did you kill Dr. Barclay?" she asked.

"I must have. Who else would want him dead?" He stopped so abruptly she nearly fell. "No, he did. I watched him follow the doctor into the woods."

"Who?"

"The doctor Mommy didn't like. He's dead. They're all dead. Even Julie."

For a moment, Susan believed him. But news that dreadful would have spread through the hospital like a flu epidemic. "She's not dead."

"She has to be. Mommy told me wishing makes things come true. I've been wishing hard. You shouldn't have saved her when you didn't save Mommy."

The singsong rhythm of his voice chilled her more than the bitter December wind. He yanked her several feet closer to the top of the hill. Susan saw the branches of a bush dangling over the edge of the wall. She grasped them in an attempt to keep from being dragged further.

He jerked her hard enough to break the thin branches. Her arms felt as though he had pulled the bones from the sockets. She screamed. He pushed her so hard she fell on the snow-covered ground. Though she was free, she couldn't move. He pulled her upright and held her in a tight embrace. His chest heaved. A whistling wheeze sounded each time he gulped a breath. Susan felt her grasp on reality slip.

"I killed them. Years and years ago. Daddy yelled at me and he died. Mommy brought me here. It was the best day of my life. They ruined our special place and I made them dead. The boarder came. Mommy didn't need another man 'cause she had me. He left and never came back. Mommy made me promise to be good. She said she would never leave me but she did."

His babble continued until it lost sense and form. Inch by inch, he forced Susan across the picnic area. In an attempt to resist the pressure of his body against hers, she locked her knees.

The wail of a siren halted him. Susan's body sagged. Somewhere, there was an emergency and help was on the way. Not here. For her, there would be no rescue. Unless she found an escape, she would die.

Patrick, she cried silently. When he came home and found her car, he'd be frantic. Though she wanted to shout and plead, she didn't want to feed the pleasure on his face or the hunger in his eyes.

"Will Mommy be proud of you?" she asked. "Won't she think you're a naughty boy?"

PATRICK PUMPED his brakes in an attempt to slow the car. The monument circle was too close. Several seconds of fancy steering kept the car from slamming into the concrete and metal statue. He left the engine running and leaped out. Long strides carried him to the path leading to the Overlook. The scuffled snow bore witness to Susan's struggles.

"Susan," he shouted. The wind flung the words against his face. He used the stone wall beside the path to propel himself up the trail. Evidence of her fight grew with each step he took. At the midpoint, he paused and gasped for breath.

A siren blared and ended in a gurgle. "Pat, wait," Greg shouted.

"I can't. Susan's alone with a madman."

"Be careful. He may be armed."

Instead of growing cautious, Greg's warning spurred Patrick along the path. Was Martin armed? Wouldn't he have shot Susan at the house? Patrick's breathing became labored. On Monday he intended to start working out. He gathered a handful of snow and lunged the final few feet to the level area.

The struggling couple teetered at the edge of the Overlook. "Fight, Susan, fight." As he ran toward the couple, he aimed and hurled the snowball. His foot hit an icy patch and he fell to the ground.

"FIGHT, SUSAN fight."

He flinched. The commanding voice startled him. Who had come here and why? This was his special place. "No!" he screamed in defiance.

Not fair. Not fair. Why would anyone want to save Susan? He had trusted her. She had let Mommy die.

A lightning storm of pain, exquisite and awesome built in his chest. Numbness crept down his arm.

"Mommy, help me," he cried. "Not yet. Not yet. It's much too soon. Help me, please help me." Tears ran down his face. He braced for a final attempt to push Susan over the railing. "Help me, please help me."

"FIGHT SUSAN, fight." She heard Patrick's voice, but he wasn't here. The words rose from her unconscious mind. There was only the cold, the snow and the man who wanted to kill her. The encouragement acted as a goad. She had to save herself.

"Mommy, help me. Not yet, not yet. It's much too soon. Help me, please help me."

The volunteer's desperate and strained cry brought the realization that his exhaustion was as deep as hers. She shook her head. Why had he asked her for help? Why did he want her to contribute to her own death?

She gulped a breath of frigid air and braced herself. The pressure of his hands against her shoulders slackened an infinitesimal degree. She tightened her muscles and lunged against him. He staggered back. She pushed again, then twisted her body and smacked him with her hip. He toppled. She landed on his chest and rolled across him. She stared at the snow. Exhaustion kept her from accepting the chance to escape.

Like a crab, he moved across the ground. Hypnotized by his steady progress, she stared until some niggling thought told her she was the quarry. She slid away.

"No," he screamed. "Mommy!"

His cry extended into infinity. Susan collapsed with her cheek against the snow. She felt so cold. She had to move. Finally, she lifted her head and watched the man lying on the snow.

There was something she had to do. She pushed to her knees and got to her feet. Her hands brushed her snow-clotted coat. The world narrowed to focus on the man who stared at the dark sky.

She knew him. His hands clawed the snow the way his mother's had clawed the sheets.

"Mr. Martin, are you all right?" The familiar words formed a path through the chaos of her thoughts. She knelt beside him. His hands stilled. His eyes lost their terror.

Dead, he was dead. She smiled, then shook her head. How could she rejoice over a death? She was a nurse. Nurses helped people. A response, carefully honed and nurtured, guided her actions. Her fingers touched his neck and searched for a carotid pulse.

PATRICK GASPED for breath and rose to his knees. The belly whopper on the snow-covered grass had winded him. Slowly, he got to his feet and stared at the scene on the other side of the picnic area. What was Susan doing?

"Mr. Martin, are you all right?" she shouted.

Her question startled Patrick. He strode past the picnic tables. Was she crazy? CPR for the man who had murdered her friends and tried to kill her?

"No pulse. Check respirations."

Her toneless voice frightened him. Her hazel eyes, devoid of expression, stared into the distance. "He's dying. Call a code."

"You're not at the hospital."

"He killed Leila, Trish, Barbara, Mendoza and De Witt. He hurt Julie. He has to live so he can pay."

"Did he kill Dr. Barclay?" From the corner of his eye, Patrick saw Greg and the uniformed officer top the rise.

"He must have. Who else wanted him dead? No. De Witt did. He saw it happen." Tears flowed down her cheeks. "I have to help him."

"Someone else will." Patrick drew her away from the body. He touched her hair and wiped her tears with his fingers. "You're safe." He pulled her into an embrace. The instant his arms tightened around him, she began to struggle.

THOUGH SHE felt too exhausted to fight the arms that held her too tight, too close, she tried. She didn't want to die. Patrick waited for her and she wanted to live and be with him.

Why was Mr. Martin so strong when she was so weak? She put her hands on his chest and pushed. She kicked at his legs. Tears born of her frustration fell freely.

Lips touched hers. She twisted her head away from the kiss. Hands caught her head and held it fast. She stared into blue eyes, not dark ones glittering with madness.

"I love you."

The whispered words removed the last vestiges of her fear-edged insanity. "Patrick." She clung to his name and to him.

"Why didn't you wait for me this afternoon? Why did you leave work early? Why didn't you stop to see Julie before you left the hospital? You could have been killed and left me to endure a long and lonely life. I want you in my arms forever, but if not, for as long as you'll have me."

His words battered her. His confession soothed. She waited until he sputtered to a halt.

"I love you," she said.

His lips brushed her cheek. "I'm glad."

While still held in the circle of his arms, she looked back at the volunteer. "Did I actually try to revive him or was that part of the nightmare?"

"You tried. I thought you'd gone crazy."

"I had. Thank you."

"For what? You saved yourself."

"For being here. For being you." She smiled. "Do you think we can learn to be partners?"

"We're going to try." His kiss was tender yet filled with desire and love.

She felt as though she had come home. Patrick wasn't Jim. Silence would have been her husband's punishment for her failure to step to his tune. She leaned against Patrick. "Let's go home."

"Shouldn't you go to the hospital to be checked out?"

"Home. Everything I need will be there."

Patrick squeezed her hand. Tomorrow there would be questions and answers. Tonight, she wanted to be held and loved by him and no words.

~ the end ~

Printed in the United States
6148